PRAISE FOR *RESET*

"A vivid, evocative journey through a postapocalyptic world...
Told with an assured, graceful touch, this compelling debut is
a story for our current world, where our beliefs and
memories are the new battlegrounds."

—KIMIKO GUTHRIE,
author of *Block Seventeen*

"*Reset* is a thought-provoking journey into the human psyche
that will instantly have you pondering deep questions about the
nature of memory, dreams, and reality itself. This bittersweet
love story is as cerebral as it is emotional."

—BOBBY AZARIAN,
cognitive neuroscientist, *Psychology Today* blogger,
and author of the forthcoming book *The Romance of Reality*

RE
SET

RE
SET

A NOVEL

SARINA DAHLAN

BLACK
STONE
PUBLISHING

Printed in the United States of America

First edition: 2021
ISBN 978-1-0940-8630-9
Fiction / Science Fiction / General

1 3 5 7 9 10 8 6 4 2

Blackstone Publishing
31 Mistletoe Rd.
Ashland, OR 97520

www.BlackstonePublishing.com

To my family
&
my editor, Peggy Hageman

Human intellect at birth resembles a tabula rasa, a pure potentiality that is actualized through education and comes to know.

—Avicenna, tenth-century polymath

The best way to rid society of the evils of human nature is to periodically wipe each person's mind of their prejudices learned through life experiences. With the mind a blank slate, everyone has the freedom to author their own soul. Tabula Rasa. It is the future. It is what will save humanity.

—The Planner

CHAPTER ONE

In a mahogany-paneled room in a Victorian house on a hill, inevitability creeps in like a thief, but no one stirs. A man sits in a velvet chair the color of sapphire. A woman curls against his chest, her lashes wet like blades of grass covered in morning dew. They have been in the same position for hours. Neither intends to move.

He is afraid she will disappear. Like dandelion seeds, one gust of wind: gone.

His hand weaves through her hair, playing absentmindedly with the silky strands. He stares at the books on the table next to them, some with pages so brittle they could fall apart at the slightest touch. Fear overcomes him. His heart drops into the cavity of his stomach, making him nauseated.

He gathers her in his arms, and she tightens her grip around his neck. Her eyes are fixed on a spot on the far wall.

"It's the first day of spring," she says.

"It is."

"When do you think it will happen?"

"I don't know." He buries his face in her hair.

"If we don't go to sleep, maybe it won't happen."

"Sooner or later, the Sandman will come." He chuckles but there is despair in his voice.

Outside the window, dawn approaches. And with it, bird songs, the first music of the day.

The man takes her hand and brings it to his lips. He brushes it lightly, tracing the green veins of her arm, memorizing it.

He has been imprinting her into his memory all night, on all the nights that passed between them. If he does it enough, he hopes he will be able to remember her. Like a piece of music.

He feels it. The haze of sleep. Only it is stronger than any he has ever experienced. It comes from deep inside him—a black hole that draws in all surrounding light.

He struggles to keep his heavy eyelids from closing. But how does one prevent a landslide from covering the entrance of a cave? Eventually it will consume it, taking away light until only a sliver is left. Then complete darkness.

"Good night, sweetheart. I love you," he whispers and kisses her hand.

In a slow and deliberate move, he eases a ring off her finger. Warmth emanates from the silver metal. He puts it on his little finger, next to his own ring. She reaches up and kisses him. He tastes like the ocean. Salt and earth.

"Good night, love," she says.

He is losing his grip. His body begins to slip into the warm embrace a rest promises. He presses his lips on her forehead. She lays her head against his chest and closes her eyes.

"Tomorrow, we will be strangers."

CHAPTER TWO

The light is unnaturally bright, glaring and white on her eyelids. Water laps against sand from outside the window, lulling her. A lazy wind eases in as if it has a lifetime to flow east. She feels sweat seep from her pores, dripping down her back.

A finger, warmer than her skin, runs along her spine, painting images of rivers and hills with her sweat, chasing goosebumps down the landscape of her body.

Aris bolts upright.

"Lucy, turn off alarm," she says, wiping sleep from her eyes.

The cry of her wake-up call ceases. Jazz music replaces it.

"Thanks, Lucy. That's a better way to wake up."

"You are welcome. I am glad. Based on your proclivity tests, there was a fifteen point six percent chance you would not like this music," Lucy speaks, her bodiless voice emanating from concealed speakers in the apartment.

"Well, I'm eighty-four point four percent liking it this morning."

"It is 7:02 a.m. on Monday, September twenty-second. You have a meeting at nine o'clock with Thane. After that, you have docent duty at eleven."

Aris sighs. She despises that part of her job. Not that it matters. It is impermanent, like everything else.

"Coffee?" she asks in a small voice.

"It will be ready for you by the time you get out of the shower. Your bagel is toasting."

"Lucy, you're so good to me," she says and gets up.

"It is my job."

With "Lucy in the Sky with Diamonds" on her lips, Aris steps into the shower. She pushes a button, and a stream of water rains down her body, washing the night's stale air off her skin. The timer ticks. Five minutes. 1,825 minutes per year. 7,300 per cycle. She will have spent five full days showering this cycle. So much time, yet never enough.

The dream lingers. The only thing she remembers is the feeling. Warm skin. A breath at her ear. The echo of a whisper. *What did it say?* She feels her core heating. The water stops.

She steps out and dries herself off. A glimpse of her reflection in the foggy mirror catches her attention. She wipes her hand across it. She stares at her face and tugs at the skin on her cheeks. She wonders how old she is. Twenty-eight? Thirty? She does not know. No one knows.

"Your coffee is ready," Lucy says.

"Thank you."

She follows its rich, nutty aroma. The curtains lift as she passes. Sunlight streams in, brightening the white apartment. In the kitchen, in the same spot it's always been in, a cup of coffee awaits. Next to it is a plate with a toasted bagel, just as Lucy said it would be. She picks them up and walks to the wall-to-wall window. She places the bagel on the side table she put there for this specific purpose. With both hands on the cup, she takes her first sip of the day. The hot liquid travels down her throat and warms her stomach.

Outside, skyscrapers carpet the terrain as far as the eye can see—an image of silver and glass glinting in the sun. Below, kaleidoscopes of walkways with emerald trees and plants weave all the buildings together, making them look like silver flies caught in a lush spider web. Dots of people cross the pathways like insects from one tree branch to another. Up here, she is an eagle in its aerie, surveying the world. The apartment has been her home this cycle. Then it will be erased from her memory.

Beyond the spikes of skyscrapers, she sees the sky—pale blue with a wispy layer of clouds. Above the tallest building, streams of drones travel in organized lines before breaking off into their respective directions, delivering the weekly supplies to all homes.

She wonders what would be in her shipment. Probably more corn and summer squash. Maybe some lettuces. Whatever is in season. The system gives everyone the same things. It's the most efficient way. *No excess, no waste.*

"Lucy, when will it rain today?"

"It is scheduled for two o'clock."

If Aris wants to be alone in the city, all she has to do is go outside when it rains. Or snows. The usually bustling streets are abandoned like a ghost town. After the sky clears, people slink back from wherever they hid, painting the street with shades of rainbow. The weather is planned with precision. It must be. Water is precious. Regardless of what this place may have been disguised to look like, it cannot escape what it truly is. A desert.

The music changes. The sweet melody of a tinkling piano catches her attention.

"What's this song?" Aris asks.

"*Luce*, by Metis."

Her eyes follow a group of the delivery drones as they fly toward the horizon. They could be heading to Lysithea. Or Europa. Or maybe Elara. All of them miles away, beyond the expanse of the arid, rain-shadow desert. Together with Callisto, where she lives, they are the only populated cities left after the Last War. The drones appear smaller and smaller, until they are only dots.

Sadness trickles down like spring rain, inexplicable and sudden. It happens periodically. She has come to know it like her own shadow. She even has a name for it—"the emptiness." It lives in the middle of her chest. There's a shape to it. She feels along its edges, trying to understand what it is she had lost. But it's a word forgotten before it leaves her lips.

Luce ends.

"Is Metis a living musician?" Aris asks.

Most of her favorites died before the Last War, the rest during. She only learned of them through the Metabank.

"Yes."

"Tell me about him." She places the coffee cup on the table, picks up the bagel, and bites.

An image of a man cloaked in partial shadow appears in front of her. Sharp and vivid, as if he were there in person.

"Metis was discovered by the acclaimed AI music aficionado, Salvadore Patronico, at the auditorium of the music school where he worked as a teacher at the beginning of this cycle," Lucy says. "Metis said he had been composing music for as long as he remembered. He claimed he had been doing that through all his lives, and that music had always been inside him."

"A natural," Aris murmurs.

She finds these "naturals" fascinating. They can do extraordinary things they do not remember learning to do. The gifts are usually with art and music. She wonders in which areas of the brain artistic ability resides and why it is safe from Tabula Rasa.

"When's his next concert?" Aris asks.

"Friday, October third. At Carnegie Hall."

"I'd like a ticket," she says.

"It is mostly sold out."

"Just get whatever's still available," she says and swallows the last of her bagel.

"Do you want to know how many entertainment points that costs before I get one?"

"No," she says. *Who cares. Only six months left.*

The thought of the next cycle makes her heart flutter with both excitement and dread. A new home. A new life. Who will she be then? She hopes she will like her new name, whatever it may be.

The light from the rising sun hits the dune of salt at the edge of the city, making it shimmer like snow. The byproduct of ocean desalinization. She wonders if one day the mounds will grow tall enough to puncture through the atmosphere. Would she still be here to witness it?

Her watch beeps, tugging her out of melancholy, reminding her of the time.

《

The cottage smells musty, like fungus and moss—the scent of waterlogged forest floor. Moisture-soaked wallpaper separates from the walls like dirty bandages. The dilapidated roof is held up by vines and ivy. Despite all its faults, it is his sanctuary. Because it's hers.

She is cloaked in a silvery gown that billows in a nonexistent wind. It looks like a combination of water and air. Her hair is pure white, and her face a landscape of cracked, parched earth. Four well-defined lines are etched like deep scars between her pale eyebrows.

"Hello," he says, with the familiarity of an old friend.

"Hello, Metis," the Crone greets, her voice high and whispery like the winter breeze. "How many days?"

It is the same question she asks him every time.

"It's September twenty-second. One hundred and seventy-nine days before the next Tabula Rasa."

In half a year, a new cycle will start. Metis feels like a fish in a glass with just enough water to not suffocate. Three and a half years gone. Squandered.

He reminds himself that he did not completely waste the past few years. He has spent them being the Sandman. A purpose that saved him.

"Are you ready for another Release?" the Crone asks.

"Yes," he says. "But isn't it cruel with so little time left?"

"There will never be enough time," the Crone says. "Anyone who wants to remember should."

"But what's the point?"

"It's not up to you to decide whether their memories are worth having."

Metis knows. His responsibility, the same for all the Sandmen throughout the cycles, is to help those who want to free their dreams. To help them find their way to the Crone. To Absinthe. It is the only tool to take back what has been stolen from them. He can't help but wonder what his life would have been like had he not been able to remember. The knowledge that somewhere out there the woman he loves is lost in the sea of forgetfulness has brought him nothing but pain.

He feels her stare.

"Something weighs on you," she says.

He sighs. "It's just—sometimes I—"

"Wish you didn't remember?" she asks, taking him by surprise.

She glides to the window, her eyes staring through the grimy glass into the overgrown garden, now covered with a thin layer of fog. He follows her gaze. Shaded by the trees' dense canopy, the cottage appears to be in perpetual twilight. The setting makes it look otherworldly, as if it were in its own plane of existence.

"I've been on this earth a very long time. Longer than I should," she says. "Would you believe me if I told you I've seen more than I wish to remember?"

She turns to him. Her eyes make him feel vulnerable, as if his mind is a house she has full access to. "Life can break your heart. But living it the way you're forced to—with no memories, no past, no purpose—you're ghosts of who you're meant to be. This is no life."

"But what's the point of remembering the past if you can't have it back?"

"You mean have *her* back?" she asks.

His heart skips a beat. *Her.* The woman in his dreams. The one he tried and failed to find. The one he sometimes wonders if is simply a figment of his imagination.

The Crone's wispy figure—a consciousness without body—shifts and changes, struggling between states of existence like evaporating water. For a moment, he thinks she will vanish back into her book. Her mood is unpredictable. But she stays.

"Remember the first time we met?" she asks.

"Of course."

The day he found her in this crumbling place, his life changed. Before that, she was just a myth among unhappy souls, and he was just a man grappling for light in darkness.

"And do you remember what we talked about then?" she asks.

He nods. Her words have been haunting him.

"In this world—this prison—where the past and the present converge, there's pain," she says. "You haven't experienced agony until you stare into the eyes of someone you love and see no trace of recognition. I've witnessed what it can do to a person."

Her face is a calm pond where sadness swims like fish underneath. She has seen and experienced more loss than Metis can imagine, and he knows he can never truly understand the depth of her suffering.

"I do not wish you that level of pain," she says. "But more than that, you know confusing the past and the present will lead to our exposure. I've seen it happen too many times to count. Absinthe must be protected."

She walks to him and places her hand on his cheek. Although he cannot physically feel her touch, the gesture makes him feel thin and brittle, like the paper he uses to write music on.

"Absinthe is the boat that carries people back to their past," she says. "A Sandman, its captain, cannot point it in two directions at the same time. There's no place for him in the present. That's the burden you must bear."

CHAPTER THREE

Aris crosses a walkway that connects her building to another. The lush paths are old train tracks, repurposed after the need for them disappeared. In the spring, they explode with the bright colors of wildflowers. Now, greens and blues dominate.

Clusters of free-flowing grass sway next to the rigid rosemary shrubs and leggy lavender. The silvery blue of pygmy eucalyptus trees erupts from the green bushes below. Black-eyed Susans—bright yellow with dark centers—repeat every twenty meters.

Along both sides of the walkway are plants of various textures and shapes. Tall and skinny. Short and round. Petite and fragile. Some are feathery. Some are broad and rigid. Some wear their leaves like fur, their limbs laden with thick foliage that cast green light over the path.

She breaks off a sprig of lavender and crushes the head between her fingers. She brings it to her nose and breathes the scent in before dropping it in her coffee. The purple bud floats in the java sea.

A breeze sends the leaves swaying, surrounding Aris with a rushing sound like running water. There is a slight chill in the air. She looks up and notices a speck of orange on a leaf in one of the trees. It is almost imperceptible, but a beginning nonetheless. She looks at her watch.

Right on time.

Everything here runs on a tight schedule. The seasons and all they affect—the weather, the plants, the animals—follow the designed rhythm of the constructed ecosystem. Just as the Planner had intended. Callisto was modeled after the city of his childhood. It was the first to be created. The seat of all the councils. The most populous. The center of the Four Cities.

A young couple passes her, their black clothes crumpled from last night's dalliance. Their hands are like tentacles around each other.

"A week," she mumbles to herself as she sips her coffee.

A striking old woman with platinum hair catches her eye. She is sitting on a bench under a fan of lacy-leafed Japanese maples. In her cupped hands, a bird pecks at seeds. Mesmerized, Aris approaches her.

"Hello," Aris says.

"Hello, dear," the old lady says.

"It trusts you," she says, staring at the bird in the old woman's hands.

"He likes my seeds. They all do. Here, take some from the bag." The old lady gives her an encouraging smile.

Aris finds a spot next to her and pours some seeds onto her open palm. A bird hops into her hand and begins pecking. Her face breaks into a wide smile.

"See, he trusts you too," says the old lady.

Another couple walks by. One woman is dressed in a suit, the other in jeans and a T-shirt. They kiss and separate. The woman in jeans stops, turns, and runs back for another kiss. Aris raises her eyebrows.

"Three months if she tries really hard," she says under her breath.

"What did you say, dear?" asks the old woman.

"Oh nothing," she says, smiling. "Just a thing I do. I guess how long a couple will stay together. It's fascinating how pairing seems a compulsion in some."

The old lady laughs. "A compulsion is right."

"It's so outdated and irrelevant, don't you think?"

Aris doesn't understand why a person would waste an entire cycle on another. Coupling had once been useful to provide a stable environment to raise offspring. But bearing and raising the young is no longer a burden on the populace. Children are medically conceived and born at the Center of Discovery and Learning. Quality and quantity control. It's vital to managing resources. Just enough. *No excess, no waste.*

"Oh, it's not so irrelevant," the old lady says. "Being in love is a wondrous thing."

"But isn't it a waste?"

"Why would you say that?"

"What's the point when everything will be wiped away?" Aris says.

"One day when you find yourself in love, you will know exactly the point to it, dear."

The old woman gestures for her to look across the way. On a bench under the shade of another maple tree sit a man and a woman. The woman leans her head against the man's shoulder. Their hands intertwine like a pattern on a woven basket. He kisses her hair, inhaling her scent.

"That's love," says the old woman.

Aris looks at them. Sadness washes over her. It is like watching a drawing in sand. The tide will soon roll in, wiping it from existence. Her hand automatically goes to her watch. She does not look at it. She already knows.

Half a year.

All that's left.

The elevator to the subway is packed, usual for a workday. The glass elevator, built into a corner of the building, gives her a clear view of the city block. Through the transparent floor she sees passersby moving along the crowded streets like dry leaves floating on streams.

One minute she sees them from a bird's-eye view, the next their faces, then their feet before she disappears below ground. Her stomach sinks. Her ears pop. She shakes one ear with her fingers. She never gets used to the feeling of falling from a great height.

The elevator stops at the subway level, deep underground. The door opens to a busy intersection. Signs mark the directions to Europa, Lysithea, and Elara. All paths but to Elara are filled with people. No one ever goes there except for the Ceremony of the Dead. It was the last city the Planner erected and was still under construction when the bombs lit up the world.

Its weather system is not regulated like the other three, making it the closest to the natural habitat of the Mojave Desert. Aris does not know how many people live there, but she can't imagine the number to be high.

She heads toward the local train that travels within her city. On the platform, she finds her favorite circle. The sign "To Center Square" glows above her head. There are other circles like it, but she is partial to this one. It is assigned to a seat by the window toward the front of the train. She prefers sitting next to the window even if the scenery is just a long stretch of gray wall. On those mornings she finds it occupied, her mood is ruined for the rest of the day. She doesn't know why.

A heavyset man bumps into her, pushing her slightly off her circle.

"Oh, pardon me," he says.

She looks at him. His khaki shirt has a small purple dot on it. His gray hair needs combing. She has the urge to smooth it down with her hand. Silver-rimmed glasses decorate his round face, unnecessary when sight correction is done at each doctor's visit.

He carries a briefcase, the type with multiple compartments. The weathered leather bag has a soft patina from regular use and the passage of time. It is an archaic item, like his glasses—earthly unlike most things of this time, which live in the clouds. They belong more in a museum than on an elderly gentleman.

"Are you going to the Natural History Museum?" she asks.

"How did you—?"

"Just a guess. I work there."

"What a coincidence. I have a meeting there this morning."

"With Thane?"

"Yes! You're quite a guesser," the old man says.

"He's the director."

The train approaches. The commuters file onto it like ants entering the cavity of a dead snake. Aris goes to her seat by the window. The old man sits next to her and places his large briefcase in front of him.

"Hope you don't mind. That way I won't forget it when I get off," he says. "My memory is not so good in old age."

"Not at all. I'm Aris." She gives him her hand.

He takes it. "Professor Jacob."

"Professor Jacob? The one who wrote *Manual of the Four Cities*?"

"You know me?"

"Yes! Of course. I've been reading your book every night."

"Everybody keeps telling me it's my book."

"It's the best interpretation of the Planner's ideology I've ever read."

"It's just rewriting his words, my dear. I don't really think of it as mine."

"I found the section about dreams thoroughly fascinating," she says.

Professor Jacob smiles. "It's a favorite subject. A never-ending search, you see. There are so many schools of thought on dreams."

"So, which do you subscribe to?"

"Oh. Well, let's see. One thought is that dreams are meaningless, random firings of neurons that happen when the body rests. Excess energy working its way out of the system."

He notices the purple dot on his shirt. He pulls out a handkerchief and wipes it to no effect.

"Another is that the brain uses dreams to work out problems the person encountered during the day, connecting them with solutions that the person may have overlooked. Or strengthening the knowledge they gained while awake."

He licks the end of his handkerchief and rubs at the spot. It smears the dot, making it look worse. He gives up and puts away the handkerchief.

An odd expression crosses his face, and he leans in, his eyes hard and penetrating.

"There's another, and this is a dangerous one. Some people believe that memories seep back through dreams. Some go as far as attempting to get back to their old lives using their dreams as guides, not caring about the consequences of their reckless pursuit."

"Why is it dangerous?" she asks.

"Unearthing the past—even just believing it is possible—undermines Tabula Rasa, the system that holds us together. It could tear the fabric of our society apart."

Professor Jacob's eyes soften.

"Today is a gift. That's why they call it the present," he says in a lighter tone. "You must pardon me. I have a weakness for old, funny sayings. I can't help myself."

He doesn't have to convince her that Tabula Rasa is necessary. She likes the idea of a blank slate. You can be whomever you want to be, four years at a time. Still, it's hard to fathom how people chasing their dreams could be detrimental to the Four Cities. Dreams are not reality.

"Was there a question you asked? I'm sorry I don't remember," the professor says. He points a finger to his head. "Old age."

She gives him a gentle smile. "I was just wondering what your belief on dreams is."

"Ah. Well, I'm partial to thinking that dreams are a combination of synapses making connections and your brain trying to make sense of them. We humans have a need to find meaning in even the most random, insignificant thing," he says. "Like our existence."

The train slows. A flash of an image on the side of the subway wall catches her attention. Red. A flower maybe? She has seen it every day for as long as she can remember. Graffiti done by a brave and idiotic artist. She wonders about the probability of the artist being hit by a train as it passes. Brain splatter would make impactful art.

She looks down and sees a thin cut on her hand. It's new and an angry pink. She doesn't remember when she got it. She touches it gently.

"You have a wound," Professor Jacob says.

"Just a scratch."

"Here. Let me help." He pulls out a small bandage from his wallet and places it on the cut.

"You keep that in your wallet?"

"I always do."

"Why?" Aris asks.

He thinks about it. "I'm not sure. But it's useful today."

She stands up. "Here's our stop, professor."

"Thank you, my dear."

She looks at her watch.

"I can take you to Thane's office, if you'd like."

"Are you sure that's not too much of a bother?"

"Not at all. You would actually give me an excuse for being late."

They get off the elevator at the street level. The sidewalk is busy with pedestrians. Just as Aris turns toward the Natural History Museum a block away, she hears shouting. It comes from across the street. She and everyone near her stop to look, transfixed by the unusual sight.

On the corner adjacent to them is a man. Sun-bleached blond and muscular. He's shouting at the top of his lungs, his voice crazed and desperate—teetering between begging and threatening. His skin marks him as someone from Elara. Brown, with a thickness to it from time living under the harsh desert sun.

"How can you walk around like everything's fine?" the man yells at a woman in a red coat, his hand reaching out toward her.

The woman startles. Her face flushes pink. She grips the front of her coat and rushes past.

"They took everything from us," he hollers after her. "Our lives, our past, the people we love. All we have left are our dreams!"

A man in a suit, eyes fixed on his watch, ears plugged with headphones, walks toward the Elaran man, unaware of the trouble ahead. The angry man steps in front of him and grabs him by the collar.

"Stop looking at your stupid watch!" he screams. "It's how they track your every move. Don't wear it!"

The suited man cries out in surprise, as if confronted by a rabid animal. He struggles out of the man's grip and runs off. People begin crossing over to Aris's side of the street to avoid him.

"They stole our memories and left us with nothing!" he shouts at all of them. "They can't keep doing this to us. They can't take away everyone we care about. It must be stopped. We must fight back!"

Aris has never seen anyone behaving this out of control in public before. He reminds her of the angry bear in the museum. She looks down and sees her arm has looped around Professor Jacob's. When she did that, she does not know.

A white car with flashing lights whooshes past them. It must belong to someone in the councils. Only officials are allowed personal transports. The car comes to a stop in front of the angry man. Its door opens, and a man steps out. He wears a brown fedora, reminding Aris of the old black-and-white movies she saw during the Old World's cinema festival.

The next scene unfolds as if it is from one of the films. The fedora man approaches the angry man slowly and deliberately. The angry man steps back until his body hits a column of the building. For a moment, Aris wonders if he is going to hurt the newcomer.

In a quick move, the man in the fedora grabs his hand as if wanting to shake it. Instead, he puts a silver bangle on the angry man's wrist. Instantly, the angry man becomes as silent and still as the column behind him. His rage dissipates into the air like smoke.

Aris feels a tug at her arm.

"Wait." She tries to pull away. But she is too late. Professor Jacob is crossing the street, taking her with him.

"Officer Scylla," the professor calls.

The officer stops in mid step and turns slowly. His face is stern.

"Professor Jacob." His voice sounds stilted, as if the professor is the last person he had wished to see.

"This man is under the care of the Interpreter Center," says Professor Jacob. There's no trace of the jovial man she had met earlier.

Officer Scylla looks from the professor to the Elaran man who is staring ahead with glazed, sleepy eyes. "Is he now?"

"His name is Bodie. He needs to be taken to the Center so he may finish his treatment."

The muscles in Officer Scylla's face twitch. "Thank you for informing me. I will contact the Interpreter."

"Very well," the professor says.

Officer Scylla walks off. The Elaran man follows obediently, his footsteps sluggish, as if he is in a trance. Aris watches them go with an uneasy feeling.

"Was that the police?" she asks Professor Jacob.

"Have you never seen one before?"

She shakes her head. "I know they exist. Just never met one."

"That's Officer Scylla of Station Eighteen."

"He doesn't seem to like you."

Professor Jacob laughs. The amiable man is back. "We at the Interpreter

Center make life a little harder for him. He'd be happy if he could just keep the troublemakers locked up for a night. But we believe you must get rid of the root cause."

"What's that?"

"Dreams," the professor says. "Remember I told you about the people who believe dreams are memories? That man is one of them. It's a form of mental illness. But don't worry. With the help of an interpreter who's trained to interpret dreams, we can target and erase the harmful ones. He'll be fine again. It's like a partial Tabula Rasa—but for dreams."

She had seen the Interpreter Center near her favorite picnic spot—a gleaming white building surrounded by a sweeping green lawn and forest. A solitary inorganic object in the middle of life. But she had never heard of the procedure until now. Up until Professor Jacob told her, she did not even know that dreams could be dangerous. How could they be? They're not real.

CHAPTER FOUR

"All right, follow me, children," Aris says to the restless group of eight-year-olds in white-and-blue uniforms.

They are surrounded by a 3D image of mountains and plains so realistic it makes Aris feel as if she were in the middle of the nature preserve she loves.

"Billions of years ago, the land you're standing on was not here. Do you know how Southern California came to be?"

She looks around from face to face.

"Anyone?"

The children stare at her blankly.

"It slowly assembled from the earth's crust, dust and ash from the air, and other materials accumulated from the rain and the oceans," she says.

The image changes to that of a volcanic eruption. Angry geysers of red and orange lava shoot up from blistering melted earth. The gas-filled bubbles burst, sending explosions into the pitch-black sky like fireworks.

"Then volcanoes and earthquakes built up the landscape. Sediments eroded and were deposited along the coasts of the North American continent."

Half the class yawns. One kid plays with a loose string on her skirt. Aris sighs but continues.

"Much of the continental crust that's now California came from the crust that formed beneath the Pacific Ocean region. Over time it moved onto the margins of the continents. Land is built in many stages through Earth's history. An endless series of materials being uplifted and recycled over and over again."

A hand shoots up.

"Yes?"

"I'm hungry. When's lunch?"

"We're almost done. Okay?"

The image surrounding them turns into a wasteland of broken buildings, collapsed bridges, and upturned roads. Columns of smoke rise from the rubble. Orange flames flutter out of the broken windows of cars, making them look as if they had sprouted wings of fire. The children sit up straight, straining their necks to take in the entire landscape.

"Fast forward years later, after a prolonged drought that devastated the world's crops, tornadoes and storms ravaged the lands. Famine led people to turn against each other. Governments became cruel and controlling. Neighboring countries fought each other for resources. Conflicts escalated and grew until the Last War. Half of California was destroyed in it. It wiped out most of the planet's population. Major cities and the people in them perished."

Aris looks around at the little faces stricken by fear.

"What happened?" a girl with skin the color of milk chocolate asks. Her eyebrows scrunch together in worry.

"There are historical records of people who reported seeing the sky light up and feeling tremors under their feet. And the world burned," Aris says.

The image around them changes to a panorama of gleaming skyscrapers and lush green vistas.

"But there was a man. We call him the Planner. Before the Last War, he had created four cities in the desert, far away from civilization. These self-sustaining cities harnessed the energy of the sun and represented his ideal of what model cities should be. They're connected to the coast and to each other by tunnels with high-speed trains. In his time, he was ridiculed. But they are what survived. One such city, Callisto, is where we stand today. Without him, the survivors of the Last War would have died from starvation. And without them, whose genetics were randomly mixed to create us, we would not exist."

"How did the Planner escape the war?" a small voice asks. Its owner has hair that reminds Aris of cotton candy.

"History states he was in a space station," Aris says. "And it was a good thing for us that he survived, because he was a peace-loving man. After seeing the horrific results of the war, he dreamed of a civilization where the same atrocities would never repeat, where people could learn to live alongside each other in peace. From that dream, he created Tabula Rasa. Can anybody tell me what that means?"

"It's Latin and means 'blank slate,'" a boy says in a proud voice.

"Very good. It's also a philosophical idea. At birth, the human mind is a blank slate, without rules for processing data. Data is added and rules are formed solely by one's sensory experiences. It is in these experiences that we're exposed to prejudices that breed hatred, which leads to fighting, resulting in wars."

She looks around. She has all their attention now.

"The event we call Tabula Rasa is like pushing the reset button. A rebirth. Every four years, we are born again into another life. We shed our prejudices and simply share the world."

"When's the next cycle?" a boy with a round face asks.

"About half a year from now. March twentieth. The first day of Spring. A new cycle always starts on that date."

"How many cycles have we had?"

Aris shakes her head. "I don't know. That information is not shared. But it doesn't matter, does it?"

"How come *we* don't change our lives?" a child in pigtails asks. Aris can almost count the number of freckles on her pink nose.

"Well, children must grow up first. Once you're eighteen, you'll graduate into a life outside the Center. Then on to higher education. After that, depending on where you are in the cycle, you'll get your first Tabula Rasa."

"Will we forget everything?" a girl asks. Her hand reaches that of her friend's and holds it.

"Only the things the Planner believed would affect our ability to keep peace. So, learned knowledge, languages, and other innate abilities stay."

A hand shoots up.

"Yes?"

"Are there others outside the Four Cities?" a girl with a solemn face asks.

"The Planner brought as many survivors as he could to the Four Cities. It's a destroyed world outside our borders. I don't imagine there are others. At least not close by. The Planner would have found them. Or they would have found us."

The girl's face falls.

"I'm sure everyone who could be saved was. We're fortunate to be here. The Planner has given us all the gift of life," Aris tells the class.

"If we want to, can we leave the Four Cities?" a boy with a mischievous smile asks.

"Nothing is stopping you. But why would you do that?" asks Aris.

The boy shrugs.

"We're in an oasis in the middle of a vast desert," Aris says. "Here, you have everything. Out there, you have nothing. As long as we live here, we'll never go hungry. Speaking of which, you may now go have lunch."

The children rush to form one line and walk toward the cafeteria.

At least they're obedient.

Her job would be astronomically more difficult if she had to wrangle them into order. The Matres are doing a fine job raising them.

"Oh, remember, children, in each life, we all have the freedom to author our own souls," she yells at their backs.

Aris makes her way up the circular stairs to another part of the museum. It's a dark and quiet section where there are rarely visitors. It is her hiding place, a sanctuary after every docent duty.

She never gets used to the children. They do not venture outside the Center of Discovery and Learning except for occasional field trips. They ask too many questions, sometimes the most random ones. They always stare at her like they expect her to give them something or say something or do something for them. On their faces is always a mysterious smudge. And they are so . . . little.

But the worst thing about being with them is having to show them the most horrific part of the past. Especially to the littlest ones. The terror in their eyes. The look of panic and anxiety. She wants to comfort them, but there is nothing she can say. She knows they question whether humanity needs to be regretted. She has done it many times over.

It's hard to believe she was once one of these children. She cannot remember her time at the Center of Discovery and Learning or the Matres who raised her. Her life began at the Waking.

She doesn't like to think of it—her first memory—the moment she opened her eyes after Tabula Rasa. Inside a bright room filled with hospital beds lined up like the keys on a piano, she startled awake to the sound of screaming and crying. She was drifting. Alone. Terrified. Around her was a sea of white-clad men and women in various states of confusion, trying to grasp for logic with their frail, muddled minds. She thought it was death, but it was worse. It was a birth into blankness.

She remembers feeling herself drowning inside the chaos, her legs and arms tied down by fear. Until a calm voice spoke, soothing her. *Everything will be okay.*

The voice told her stories. Through it, Aris learned about the Last War and how the Four Cities came to be. It taught her the way things worked in their world, gave her a name, told her where home was, and assigned her a place of work. It was her access to every book and all the knowledge contained inside the Four Cities. Without it, she would be lost. *Lucy.*

Aris lets out a big sigh, and the sound echoes in the dark space, making it seem as if she is surrounded by others hiding from the weight of the world. In the cool room, dead animals of the Americas gaze out with their marble eyes. Stuffed bison, bears, and deer perch on their constructed habitat behind their glass confines. They are frozen in postures that resemble their living states—or someone's perception of them.

A black bear stands on its hind legs, startled by a rattlesnake at its feet about to strike. She thinks of the angry man from earlier, wondering where he is now. Professor Jacob said the man's dreams were the culprits behind his outburst. She thinks of her own recurring dream. It leaves her with many conflicting feelings, but never anger.

She swipes across her watch absentmindedly. She sees something she likes on the screen and taps on it.

"That was quite a lecture," a familiar voice says.

"Oh hey, Thane," she says without looking up.

Aris has given up being surprised by his presence. He shows up in the most random corners of the museum, as if he can materialize anywhere inside its walls at will. Maybe Thane is a part of the museum, like its walls and its exhibits. She has never seen him outside it. He is always here before her and never leaves until after. Does he even go home? Does he have a life of his own? She rarely hears him talk about dates.

She cannot understand why. Although plain by her standards, Thane is not unattractive. He has nice periwinkle eyes. He wears his brown hair cropped short. Though his pale skin could use some sun.

"If that's to butter me up to do more docent duty, you're in for a world of disappointment," she says. "I was horrible. Kids yawned. One asked to go to lunch. I almost forgot to close with the slogan. If I were you, I'd reexamine whether I'm equipped to do docent duty."

He laughs. "I'm not here to butter you up. Just wanted to say thanks."

"For what?"

"For getting Professor Jacob here."

Aris waves her hand. "Oh, it was just a happy coincidence."

"He's quite taken with you."

"The professor?"

"Said you're charming. For a young lady."

"There's a disclaimer?"

Thane laughs.

"So why was the superstar of academia here?" Aris asks.

"There's a project he wants my help with."

"Really? What's it about?"

"Oh, nothing fun," Thane says. His eyes are on the mountain lion stalking a rabbit behind glass.

She narrows her eyes. "A secret mission?"

Thane scoffs. "Why do you always think everyone has a secret?"

"Because they do."

"Most of the time it's just boring."

"So why aren't you telling me?"

"Because I can't."

"Aha! It is a secret. Come on, you can tell me. We've known each other long enough. I'm trustworthy."

He sighs.

"Thane?" she says, advancing toward him. Her lips curl up on one side as if he has already given in.

He takes a step back. "All right, all right," he says, "But you have to promise."

She nods vigorously.

"Professor Jacob is getting on in age. He wants someone—me—to help him."

"On what?"

"Research, mostly. He's writing another book. On the Planner's personal life."

"You're right. It's boring."

Thane looks at her as if she has an arm growing out of her head.

Aris laughs. "I'm kidding. It sounds fascinating. I'd like to learn more about the Planner. I can't imagine it being easy to find personal information about him. But why can't you tell anyone about it? It doesn't sound like a secret to me."

He shrugs. "I don't know. I'm not going to ask. I'm just happy he chose me."

"I forgot he's your hero." Thane had often spoken of his admiration for Professor Jacob over the three and a half years he and Aris had worked together.

"He's an amazing man. I don't know how he did it. His book is a marvel."

Professor Jacob's book on the Planner's ideology was published near the beginning of this cycle. The behemoth tome is so complete and thorough that some refused to accept he had worked on it for only a few months after the Waking. Rumors flew that he had composed the book over multiple cycles. But that's not possible. All minds are wiped every four years. Aris suspects the gossipers are jealous, latching on to an absurd idea to discount the professor's brilliance.

"We saw someone being arrested today," she says. "He looked like he was from Elara. Not sure what he was doing here."

"What happened?"

"He was yelling at people mostly. He was so angry. At the world. At Tabula Rasa."

"Why?"

"For taking his past away."

Thane looks confused. "But that's its purpose. Why would anyone want the past back?"

Aris shrugs. Like Thane, she doesn't see the point. Tabula Rasa is the reason they have peace.

"Although you should have seen the expression on the guy he grabbed. He was looking at his watch and wasn't paying attention." She couldn't help but laugh.

"That's not funny. Disturbing the peace in the Four Cities is an offense." Aris scrunches her nose.

"Listen," Thane says, "I have something I've been meaning to ask you." Her watch beeps.

"Sorry." She glances at it and smiles at the message.

"Something good?"

"Looks like I have a date tomorrow night," she says.

"Another first date?"

"Are there others worth having?" She remembers. "You have something to ask me?"

"Uh, when can you do docent duty again?"

She rolls her eyes and walks off, leaving Thane to the collection of dead animals.

Metis's practiced hands move in quick, successive motions. His fingers are like waves as they travel across the ocean of azure paper, changing its shape in a choreographed dance he has made countless times this cycle. He finds the task meditative—a meandering journey from one thought to another, to different places and times.

Always, the path leads him to the same face. Her face. It rises like a phoenix from the ashes of dreams.

"You see that over there? That's called the Summer Triangle," she said, holding his finger and drawing with it an imaginary triangle.

In the nature preserve on the outskirts of the Four Cities, they can see the night sky in all its magnificence.

"What are the stars?" he asked.

"Altair, Deneb, and Vega, the brightest stars in their constellations." Silence followed before she continued, "You should really get to know Vega. It's the next most important star in the sky after the Sun."

"Oh yeah?"

"It's the second brightest star in the northern hemisphere. It was the northern pole star around 12,000 BC and will be again around the year 13,700."

"Do you think we'll still be around?" he asked.

"No, we'll be long dead."

"I meant humanity."

She laughed. "I know that's what you meant. It's such a human-centric question. But whatever I say would just be a guess."

He touched the tip of her chin and turned it to face him.

"I'll still be around," he whispered.

She made a sound in her throat that implied her skepticism.

"My soul will fly to Vega. I'll be watching over you for eternity." He pressed his lips on hers. Her skin was warm from the summer heat, making her scent all the more intoxicating. She smelled like lavender, sweet and grassy.

She pulled away. One side of her lips curled into a smile. Without another word, she climbed on top of him, her hands on his chest. Her body overwhelmed the sky, just as she did his heart. His hands traveled to her waist, encircling it. The thinness of her body felt fragile in his hands.

"Sweet husband," she said, "If anyone's going to be doing the looking

down, it'll be me. You're staying here with me until we become stardust when the earth collapses."

Metis folds one side of the paper down, making a triangle shape. He runs the top of his nail along the edge to form a sharp crease. He picks the folded form up with one hand and pulls at the tail with another. A crane, the bird of happiness, appears. He places it on the wooden table, joining it with the rest of the flock as blue and freeing as the sky.

CHAPTER FIVE

Aris plays with a corner of the tablecloth. The feel of the crisp material against her index finger relaxes her. Linens in expensive restaurants have the best texture. Her date chose the place.

Golden light shines through a perforated metal ceiling, creating geometric patterns on the floor below. The walls are a combination of rough-hewn granite and dark taupe paint. Thick mahogany tables paired with tailored chairs in soft mohair are strategically placed in the intimate space to give each table privacy.

She takes a sip of red wine and looks around. The restaurant is popular with couples. Aris loves first dates. There are few things more enjoyable than the thrill of discovering a new person. It's like unwrapping a present—before discovering the flaws, the nasty habits, the trite dramas. For that reason, she doesn't do second dates.

A serial first dater, Thane once called her. Why not, when the food is always better? She looks at the dinner menu and gasps at the entertainment points for each item. She thinks she will forego dessert this time.

A black-and-white-clad server droid assigned to her table comes by with a pitcher of water and refills her half-empty glass.

"May I take your order?" he asks.

"I'm still waiting for my date."

He's fifteen minutes late.

The droid stares at her blankly, his eyes unblinking.

"Come back when he's here, please," she says.

The droid nods and walks off. Even though their eyes and smiles lack the warmth of humans, Aris likes them. They do not judge. The Planner created them to serve the functions no humans wanted to—waiting on other humans and cleaning up after them. Together with the AIs, they run the infrastructure and maintain consistencies in the Four Cities. They are what allow the four-year cycle to work.

The energy in the room changes. She looks up and sees a tall man entering the room. Heads turn as he passes. The light from the ceiling catches his golden-brown hair, and Aris catches her breath. He sees her and smiles.

He makes his way toward her, strolling with the calmness of someone walking through an art museum. Her heart skips a beat, and she thanks the accuracy of her proclivity tests.

One of the pretty ones.

She wonders if he's an artist. The best of them live in the city of Lysithea, in a section with beautiful and grand Victorian "Painted Ladies." The painters, the sculptors, the poets, the actors, the musicians. In the Four Cities, where creativity is celebrated, the good ones are discovered quickly. The great ones become stars.

He stops at her table. "Hello."

Aris clears her throat. "Hi."

"You look just like your picture," he says, obviously pleased. He takes the seat across from her. "I'm Benja."

"I'm Aris. It's nice to meet you." *And your cheekbones.*

"So, you're a scientist," he says.

"Something like that. And you?"

"I write."

"Anything I know?" she asks.

"Not yet. I still have half a year left."

"What story are you working on now?"

"It's a quest of a sort. The main character is on a long journey home, and he meets all kinds of monsters that delay him."

"Like the *Odyssey*?"

"It's an influence." He smiles and leans back in his chair. "'We come too late to say anything which has not been said already.' If La Bruyère felt this at the end of the seventeenth century, what hope do I have?"

"Everyone has a unique perspective," she says.

"You're sweet."

"Tell me more about it."

"You don't really want to know, do you?"

"I do."

He gazes at his interlaced fingers on the table. "It's about a man searching for his way home. He wakes up in the middle of the desert, not remembering his name or where home is. He only has this urgent feeling that if he doesn't get back, something bad will happen. So he treks across the desert. On his way he encounters strange visions—hallucinations from thirst and hunger. But he realizes they are clues and learns to use them as a map."

"You thought up all that?"

He shrugs.

"Why did you decide to be a writer?" she asks and sips her wine.

"There are words inside me trying to break out. My job as a writer is to birth them and raise them into responsible adults," he says.

She looks blankly at him, and he guffaws.

"Too melodramatic?" he asks.

"Yeah. I was deciding whether to walk out."

"A more honest answer to your question is 'Hell if I know.' Aren't we all clueless most of the time? I mean—how can we not be?"

She decides she likes him. She leans in. "Now that we're being honest, I think we should skip the boring first-date conversation. Let's just cut the crap and talk. We only have four years at each life, and this one's almost gone."

"Aris." He gazes at her with glinting eyes. "That's the best idea I've heard from a date this cycle."

An empty bottle of wine sits between plates scraped clean.

"Would you like another bottle?" the server droid asks as he clears their plates.

"No, thank you. We're good here," Aris says.

After he leaves, she says to Benja, "Any more, and I might get in trouble."

"Trouble is a good place to be in," he says and winks.

She rests her chin on one hand and studies his face. Candlelight reflects off the gold flecks in his hazel eyes.

"You want to know a secret?" he asks.

A corner of her lips curls up. She tugs a lock of stray hair behind her ear and leans in. There is a light scent from him—something familiar that she can't put a finger on. The back of her neck begins to feel damp. She gathers her long hair and moves it over one shoulder.

"Sometimes I dream about places I've never been to. Faces I've never met," he whispers, "Do you know of the Dreamers?"

She shakes her head.

"They're a group of people who believe their dreams are manifestations of their past lives, and they use them as clues to lead them back."

She thinks of the angry man. The one taken away by the policeman. "Are you one of them?"

He laughs. "No. But I'm looking for them."

"How?"

"They meet occasionally."

"Where?"

"Places with books. Bookstores. Libraries. I've never been in so many libraries. Or maybe I have; I just don't remember." He sighs.

Books. That's what he smells like.

"How you do know all this?" she asks.

"I hear things. I find if you sit somewhere long enough, you become a part of the room. No one sees you anymore."

Aris doubts anybody would fail to notice him.

"Yesterday I saw a man being arrested," she says. "He was assaulting people. Yelling for everyone to fight against Tabula Rasa. He seemed . . . dangerous."

"You're wondering if he's a Dreamer?"

"He wanted the past."

"Maybe he is and maybe he isn't a Dreamer. Or maybe he's just mad as hell he can't remember his past."

Benja draws circles on the rim of his wineglass. She finds it difficult to keep her eyes off his long finger. She wonders how it would feel circling her—

She clears her throat. "Why do you want to meet them?"

"Maybe they can help me, you know, understand myself better. Don't you ever wonder what your other lives were like? What you were like? Were you different?"

"That's what personality and proclivity tests are for. They help determine your propensity for liking or hating something."

"You mean like there is a forty-six point seven percent chance you will like sushi. And a sixty-eight point nine percent chance you will want to see this play." He mimics the monotone voice of an AI.

He moves his wineglass to the side and leans forward. "What if the person I was when I took the last tests is not the person I am now?"

"We're always who we are," she says.

"Are we?" He leans in closer. "What if I only sleep with women because I'm fifty-seven point three percent curious?"

"What about the other forty-two point seven percent? Is he curious too?" Benja reaches over and kisses her.

"All strangers are sexy. *You* more than most," he says.

Metis navigates the darkness of his house with one purpose: to resist. The claws of sleep will not get him tonight. He has nothing against sleep. It's the dreaming he dreads.

Dreams were once a destination he looked forward to visiting each night. Now, they serve to remind him that he is not with her when he wakes. In reality, his wife is as far away from him as if she were on Jupiter's moons.

Years of searching—an obsession that almost destroyed him—have unearthed nothing. He doesn't even know her name. Only her face. Her smell. Her laugh. The way her skin feels against his. This cycle she could be anyone, anywhere.

There were times he thought of turning his back on his vow. To find someone else to love. A warm body in his bed. A person to connect with. But he could never bring himself to get there. Each time weakness threatened to overtake him, his wife's face would invade his mind. He would never be able to forgive himself. That's the problem with memory.

He snickers. If only the Dreamers could see him—the Sandman afraid of his dreams. The Crone told him the past is what he must bear and the present is not a place for him. But he feels he is in neither place. He lives suspended somewhere in the in-between.

He walks the solitude of his house, trying to evade the sticky grasp of fatigue, flitting between states of consciousness. There are no other sounds but his steps on the creaky wooden floor. The smell of centuries past is in everything: the walls, the ceiling, all the furnishings. Even the shadows.

This house features prominently in his dreams. How many times has he been here? Sometimes he wonders about others who came before him. He does not like the idea of a stranger living in his house, sleeping on his bed, cooking in his kitchen. A home is an intimate place. He has never believed the idea that the Dwelling Council randomly assigns them. A person is always meant to be somewhere, he thinks. There are no coincidences in life. He is meant to be here. Alone.

In a moment of carelessness and exhaustion, his sleepless feet take him to the arboretum. It is a large room at the back of his house filled with giant ferns so tall their tops almost reach the vaulted ceiling. Windows the height of the wall overlook the backyard, now gray from the light of the moon. Ahead stands his piano, black like a crouching panther against its surroundings. He feels its pull, calling him to descend into the bottom of its well.

He settles on a spot where the habit of his body has made an impression on the bench. He stares ahead, fighting against the urge. But he is weak. His fingers find the keys, attracted to each one with the familiarity of an old lover.

Music flows out, and he is helpless to stop it. It is her song—inspired by a dreamed past that stretches back for a length as pliable and changeable as memory.

How many cycles were they together? One? Two? Three? He could never be sure. She is younger than he. Maybe her malleable mind was wiped clean by Tabula Rasa. He, on the other hand . . .

He lets his fingers continue their torment as his mind travels back.

It was the time of the Jinn, the moment before dawn when the sky had not yet prepared itself for the arrival of the sun. They sat on the same piano bench, so close he felt heat rising off her. She wore nothing but her skin, as she did every night they were together. Her long hair gathered to one side. An arm wrapped around his shoulder like a shawl.

"What's this song?" she asked. The point of her chin rested on his shoulder.

"I'm not sure yet. Do you like it?"

"Very much. It's beautiful. For a change."

He stopped playing and looked at her. "For a change?"

She laughed. Her laughter had the crispness of morning dew.

"Your music is usually very . . . intense. It grabs you by the throat and forces you to see its truth. This one is different. Lovely. Private. Like the secret of first love."

"Perceptive," he said and pulled her close. He brushed her hair back, exposing her throat. He nuzzled it and inhaled her scent. "Only love."

"Do you think you'll remember this song in the next cycle?" she asked as she played with a curl at the base of his neck.

"I don't know. If not, then hopefully something close to it."

She sighed. Her eyes far away.

"What's wrong?" he asked.

"Time."

"There's still some left."

"Not enough," she said.

"It's never enough."

"Doesn't it make you sad?" she asked.

"I try not to think about it."

"I wish I didn't think about it all the time. But I can't help it," she said.

He placed his lips on her jaw, tracing its line. His hand found the curve of her breast. He pressed on it, feeling its fullness in his palm.

She pulled back. "That's your answer to everything."
He stopped and looked at her. She seemed sad.
"I'm sorry, I'm just . . . tired. I'm going back to sleep," she said and walked off.
He watched her body meld into the shadows of the house like a ghost.

A creak stirs him. He looks up. There is nothing there but darkness. The old house is restless, like him.

Aris takes in the chaos of her room. Articles of clothing drape over various pieces of furniture. Her dress lies rumpled on the floor. One of her favorite stilettos is on her nightstand. She hopes the other one is nearby. She looks up. Her silk panties dangle like an errant kite on the chandelier.

She feels blood rushing to her face. Last night was exhilarating. She looks at the sleeping beauty next to her, tracing the contours of Benja's face with her eyes. Dark, well-shaped eyebrows. Enviably long lashes. Nose the perfect shape of a Greek statue's. Lips—those lips. She fights the urge to kiss them.

The dreamer stirs. She pulls the bedsheet over her bosom. Benja lifts his eyes at her and smiles.

"We're past modesty, don't you think?" he says and buries his face back in the pillow.

She remembers last night and feels heat blooming on her cheeks, but she lets go of the sheet.

"You want breakfast?" Aris asks.

"Nah. I'd have to enter my biodata and all that."

"Or you can just tell Lucy what you like," she says.

"Lucy?"

"My AI," She says. "I know it's a little old fashioned." *But poetic.* The Beatles knew how to name their songs.

"That's a thought. I forget I can just tell people what I like. I expect them to just know," he says. He feigns incredulity. "How dare you people not have my data? Don't you know who I am?"

Aris laughs at the absurd truth in the statement.

"Sometimes I wonder if I've always liked asparagus," she says. "The palate changes over time."

"I hate asparagus. But maybe I used to like it. Who knows." Benja turns to face her. "Don't you think it's wrong to not be able to know your own history? To have your past zapped out of your brain?"

"But it's for the good of society."

"That's what we were taught, but is it really? I once read about a person with multiple personality disorder who would wake up with a different identity, forgetting they were someone else the day before. That's essentially what Tabula Rasa does."

"So we're a society of the mentally ill?" she asks.

"Maybe. But I'm not sure what's worse—the acceptance of it, or ignorance."

"Of what?"

"Our fate."

"I'm not following," she says.

"We walk through our lives like it's normal, knowing all the while that it's not. So our brains ignore it, making light of our past, shrugging it off like last season's outfits. What if there's something there we can't live without?"

She rolls her eyes and plops onto her soft pillow. "There's nothing in the past we can't live without. We're living now. And quite comfortably."

Benja turns over and looks up at the ceiling. She reaches for his hair and plays with a curl on his forehead.

"I had fun last night," she says, feeling warmth between her legs. Perhaps once more before they part ways.

She likes him. But not enough for a second date. No one is worth that. Maybe they would meet again in the next cycle for another first.

"Me too," he says and looks at her with a serious expression on his face. "I should have been more honest with you last night. I wasn't kidding about being fifty-seven point three percent curious. At least in this cycle. I can't vouch for my past."

She shrugs. "Okay."

"You don't care?" Benja asks.

"I don't see what that has to do with anything. Attraction is attraction. Good sex comes from all places."

Benja laughs. "Ambivalence doesn't sit well with some."

"I'm not one of them," Aris says.

She feels his index finger running along her thigh under the sheet.

He sighs. "Have you ever been in love?"

She drops the curl. *What a way to kill the mood.*

"I don't do relationships," she says. The heat of anger rises. She does not know why. It's just a question.

"I'm not asking about relationships. I'm asking whether you've been in love."

She sits up and wraps the cover around her, holding it like a shield. "I'm a scientist."

"Don't scientists fall in love?"

"Why, when I won't even remember?" she says, a little more harshly than intended.

"Because we're not butterflies in a specimen box," he says to the ceiling. "Despite this existence saying otherwise."

He turns to look at her, his eyes digging. "What are you afraid of?"

She feels a jab inside. Something gapes open, like a scab picked raw.

"Nothing. It's just a waste of time," she says. But she knows it's a lie.

CHAPTER SIX

"Hello Thane," says Professor Jacob, "This is Apollina."

Thane reaches out his hand only to be met with thin air. The pale woman with platinum hair appears not to see him—or does not care he is there. Her eyes are transfixed by the figure on a bed in the room next door. The figure is a man with bright yellow hair and skin painted brown by the sun. The man appears to be unconscious—so motionless that Thane wonders whether he is dead.

Thane walks closer to the glass wall that separates the two rooms. From this spot, he can see the rising and falling of the man's abdomen. *Still alive.*

On the man's head is a helmet attached to colorful wires that rain down from above. Thane's eyes trace the wires up to a giant machine made of shiny metal the color of sunset.

"What's that?" Thane asks.

"A Dreamcatcher," says Professor Jacob from behind him.

"What does it do?"

"Erases disturbing dreams so the patient won't remember the reason for his troubles," Apollina says, eyes still fixed on the man on the bed.

"He's troubled by his dreams?"

"Why else would he be here?" she says in an irritated tone that makes Thane feel stupid for having asked the question.

He glances at Professor Jacob. The old man gives him an encouraging smile, making him feel slightly better.

After a long moment of silence, Apollina turns to him. Thane immediately notices her icy blue eyes—cold as a winter morning and hard as a frozen pond. Her face is just as empty. He would have mistaken her for a droid were it not for the pale pink face indicating the suffusion of blood beneath her skin. Her light hair is pulled taut into a bun at the nape of her neck, accentuating her sharp cheekbones. She's pretty. If only she would wear it with less severity and a little more warmth.

Thane cannot decipher her expression, or rather lack of it. He begins to feel nervous until he notices there are no smile lines on either side of her mouth. Her frigid manner has nothing to do with him.

"You came highly recommended," Apollina says.

"I'm honored to have been selected."

"I see you have the briefcase. You've studied the contents?"

Thane nods. Over the last five days, he has studied the profiles of those the Interpreter Center calls "suspects." Names, addresses, pictures. Young and old. Men and women. They all look like harmless, ordinary citizens—people he would cross paths with on the street or at the coffee shop.

"That list represents years of hard work by me and Professor Jacob. But we suspect there are many more of them," says Apollina.

There are about two dozen names on the list. If three and a half years had yielded so few, Thane wonders how difficult the job will be.

"They operate under secrecy. Like vermin," she says as if she knows his thought.

Thane suddenly recognizes the man on the bed from the list of suspects. *Bodie.*

"He's one of them?" Thane asks.

"Yes. By chance, Professor Jacob witnessed his psychotic episode in public. Because we've been building a case against him, the professor knew exactly what needed to be done."

This must be the same person Aris told him about, Thane thought.

"If we didn't know about him, he would have been taken into police custody for one night then released, like all public disturbance cases. It would have been useless. This way, he can be treated. He'll no longer be a threat."

"That's why we need you," says Professor Jacob.

"We need more information. Who they all are. Where they meet. We don't know enough," Apollina says.

"But why wouldn't you just use video surveillance and drones? Wouldn't those be more effective?" Thane asks.

"Only the police have access to those," Professor Jacob says.

"Oh, I was under the impression that you work together," Thane says.

"Reluctantly," says the professor. "We don't always agree."

"In order to treat them, the law says we need consent," Apollina says. "As you can imagine, people in love with their dreams aren't exactly lining up to erase them."

"Unfortunately, the police would rather follow an archaic law written hundreds of years ago instead of doing what needs to be done," Professor Jacob says. "So it falls on us. We're the guardians of the Planner's ideology—of Tabula Rasa."

Apollina steps forward, so close Thane can feel warmth emanating from her skin. At the same height, he is looking right into her cold, fierce eyes.

"After running tests, we've been able to determine one commonality among them—those we were able to treat," she says. "A drug. We found a trace of it in his system. It makes people believe they can remember their past. Based on our database, it's been around for as long as Tabula Rasa—invented to create unrest. The Interpreter Center's goal is to destroy it each time it reappears. But it keeps returning every cycle."

Thane feels as if the ground is shaking underfoot. "But how? How can it keep returning when everyone's memories are wiped after Tabula Rasa?"

"We don't know. We can only assume the source was never destroyed. We believe that once it's eradicated, we should be rid of it for good," Apollina says.

"The Planner's hope for a peaceful existence for mankind rests on Tabula Rasa," says Professor Jacob. "There's nothing in the past but the Last War. That past has no place in the present."

Thane imagines a world of chaos. Of people fighting against one another. A world where distrust grows like cancer of the mind. The image is too easy to conjure.

"That drug is a direct assault on peace. We need you to follow the suspects and find the source," the professor says.

Thane looks at the man on the bed and begins to see him as dangerous. The Four Cities need to be protected. It is the only home he has—that everyone has. He must find the source that threatens to unravel this place and their way of life. He needs to destroy it before it destroys everything.

A breeze blows through curtains. The tinkling of wind chimes comes from somewhere nearby over the constant sound of waves rolling on sand. The air smells as if it is about to rain.

"Wake up sleepyhead," a voice says. But instead of making her want to get up, the voice sinks her farther into the soft bed. She feels the hard tip of a finger running along her skin, outlining her. It moves down toward the supple part of her, rousing something primal.

"Aris, you have a reach," says Lucy, waking her. "It's Benja."

"Put it through."

She pulls the cover over her body and turns on her side. Benja's image appears in the middle of her bedroom. He has a pencil behind one ear and his hair is tousled as if he had just wrestled with a bear. It only adds to his allure.

"We should go to the main library today," he says.

He is not looking at her. Instead, his eyes are focused on something offscreen. She hears a crinkling sound like static.

They have been spending a lot of time together this week. It started by accident. They ran into each other at a library the day after their first date and got into a discussion about a book, one of the classics. When the library closed, she realized she did not want the conversation to end. She told him all she wanted was friendship. He was of the same mind. They've been together every day since.

They bonded quickly as if they'd always known each other. The more time she spent with him, the less his good looks distracted her. She learned there was quite a brain behind his gorgeous face. *But he is . . .* She struggles to come up with a word to describe him.

Benja doesn't appear to fit or want to fit into any box. His edges are all blurry. But he is interesting. And life could be worse than having an interesting, blurry friend. If only he was not a romantic. It's a useless state of being.

Aris narrows her eyes. "Another library?"

"I just have to do some research," Benja says.

"Research or stalking?"

He laughs and looks up at her. "Wait. Are you still in bed? What time is it?"

"It's Saturday. I was out late last night."

"Another first date?" he asks.

"Maybe."

"Did he spend the night?"

"None of your business."

"Anyway, if we happen to see the Dreamers, I'm not going to walk out."

She rolls her eyes. The Dreamers are the focus of many conversations with Benja. In an attempt to talk sense into him, she had told him about the angry man from Elara and what Professor Jacob had shared with her about the Interpreter Center. But Benja had laughed it off, telling her to stop worrying about his mental health.

"You're obsessed," she says.

"I prefer *tenacious*," he says. "It's a quest for knowledge."

He has dragged her to more libraries and bookstores than she cares to remember. Not once did they find anything or anyone resembling a Dreamer—not that she knows what they're supposed to look like. She's afraid he will soon run out of places with books to search for them. What will he do then? She has begun to think the Dreamers are an urban myth, created by those preying on romantic minds.

"Come on. Please," he says.

"You don't need me."

"Yes, I do. Come on, I'll buy you dinner."

"Just go by yourself," she says.

"I don't want to. I already spend too much time by myself. We're humans, Aris. We need social interaction—to see the faces of others, to have meaningful conversations. Without all that, we're denying our nature. Do you want to deny the essence that makes us human?" he says in one breath.

She realizes that if she does not agree to his request, she will be spending the rest of the day listening to the reasons she should. He is a writer.

"Fine," she says and sighs. "Meet me at the park."

Aris leans back on her elbows. The green lawn is strewn with bodies on blankets like hers. Their shiny skin reflects light like solar panels. It is an unusually warm day—a good day to soak up the sun, to memorize its feel before the gray clouds return. The Planner was a true genius for having designed variety into the weather. Unpredictability makes life more interesting—feigned or not.

Dampness seeps through the square blanket. Under her is grass, squishy from the last sprinkle of rain. It smells sweet and earthy. Did grass from before the Last War have the same scent? It's been engineered to require minimal water. All the plants and trees in Callisto are that way.

In her view is a glistening white building. The Interpreter Center sits alone, the only structure within the vast park. Professor Jacob told her they erase dangerous dreams. During the time she's been waiting for Benja, no one has gone inside.

The dream from this morning stalks her like a slinky feline. She still cannot remember the precise image—only the feelings. They haunt her and follow her, scratching at the edges of her mind, unraveling the threads that bind it together. She wonders whether she should seek the Interpreter's service.

Maybe if it gets bad enough. She's more of the suffer-in-silence type. She raises her face to the sun, letting it warm her skin and chase away the troublesome dream.

A familiar voice rouses her. "Aris?"

She lifts her head and sees a face she does not expect. The bright sun bounces off his skin, making her squint.

"Thane?"

It's the first time she has seen him in the real world. In a city as vast and populated as Callisto, chance meetings are rare.

"I thought it was you," he says.

"Walking the park?"

"I just came from a meeting with Professor Jacob." He gestures toward the white building. "Now I'm off to Griselda."

"At the Interpreter Center? That place is a mausoleum. I haven't seen anyone go in. What's it like in there?"

"It's not much different than going to the doctor's office. Everything is white—white walls, white floors, white furniture. It's a big place, with lots of rooms. But the doors to them were closed, so I couldn't see what's behind them."

"Did you meet an interpreter?"

"Yeah. Her name is Apollina."

"What's she like?"

Thane cocks his head to one side. "She doesn't smile."

"Is she a droid?"

"No, human. She's just . . . serious."

"So her job is to erase dreams?"

"Yeah. She's like a psychologist for dreams. She interprets them and helps eliminate the harmful ones."

"I wonder what happens afterward," she says, thinking of her pesky dreams. "Do you forget your erased dreams entirely? Or do you remember them, but you just don't get them anymore?"

"I imagine it would be like how Tabula Rasa works. What you don't remember can no longer affect you."

"So why did you meet Professor Jacob there? He works for the Interpreter Center?"

"He consults with them for his research. What else can it be?" he says, "You know, you're nosy."

"I'm a scientist. I have a curious mind."

"Your questioning is going to get me in trouble one of these days."

She laughs. "Fine. We don't need to talk about your secret mission." She pauses. "So, what's at Griselda? A date?"

Griselda is a popular music venue with gray glass walls and a ceiling that projects images of the galaxy. It's normally filled with young black-clad artist types. She does not see it as a place that would naturally attract Thane. Thirteen point eight percent chance, if she had to guess. That's for the color of the walls.

He shrugs. "Something like that."

One side of her lips curls up. She finds Thane's evasiveness funny.

"Are you waiting for someone?" he asks.

"Yeah. He's late."

"I'm not that late," says the man who has kept her waiting. Aris whips around, sees him, and brightens.

Thane straightens.

Benja offers him his hand. "I'm Benja."

Thane shifts the briefcase to his left hand. "Hello. I'm Thane. Aris and I work together at the Natural History Museum."

"You should stop making her do docent duty. She hates it."

Thane's eyes widen. Aris kicks Benja's foot. He shrugs and settles on a spot next to her.

"Hi, beautiful. Sorry I'm late," Benja says and pecks her on the cheek. Without another word, he roots through her basket, ignoring Thane who is still standing next to Aris.

He makes a face. "I'm starving, and you only have fruit?"

"You said you'd bring cheese from that fancy shop near your place," Aris says.

"I did? Sorry I was writing and completely forgot."

She rolls her eyes. "Figures."

"I brought you something even better." Benja hands her a package.

"What's this?" Aris weighs it with her hand.

"Something I found at the gift market. I thought of you when I saw it."

Aris unwraps it and reveals a small desertscape painting. Her face breaks into a wide smile.

"You told me you like hiking in the nature preserve," he says.

"I love it! You're officially forgiven for being late." A perk of being Benja's friend, aside from constantly being treated to costly meals at restaurants, is his random thoughtful gestures.

Thane clears his throat, and they both look at him. Aris had momentarily forgotten he was still there. Benja has a way of consuming all her attention.

"So, you're a writer?" asks Thane.

"On most days," Benja says.

"Anything I know?"

"Not yet. It's a work in progress."

"It's an epic journey, in the vein of the *Odyssey*," Aris says.

"Really? Is it almost done?" Thane asks.

"Getting there."

"There's only six months left. Sure you can get it done in time?" A small smirk frames the corners of Thane's lips.

Aris feels Benja's body tighten. She doesn't look at him, afraid she would burst out in a fit of giggles from this awkward situation.

Thane looks at his watch. "I must go. Aris, I'll see you Monday."

Benja watches Thane's back as he walks away. "I don't like him."

Aris arranges her face in an expression of mock surprise.

"What a jerk," he says. "Six months left—like I don't already know that. Who asked you, asshole?"

Aris laughs. "Well, I think the feelings may be mutual. He didn't seem to like you either."

"That's because he's in love with you, and he thinks I'm competition. You're not dating him, are you?" He gives her a critical look.

"No! He's never even shown interest. In any case, I don't think of him that way." She is not interested in the complication that comes with dating someone she works with.

"Why was he here?" Benja asks.

"He was on his way from a meeting at the Interpreter Center."

Benja throws a blackberry into his mouth and looks over his shoulder in the direction of the gleaming white building. "The place gives me the creeps. Doesn't it give you this weird feeling?"

"It's just lonely," she says.

He looks back to her. "Or haunted. You can't get me in there."

"No one's going to make you." She smirks. "Unless you misbehave."

Benja laughs. "I'd like to see them try."

"Yeah, you're very vicious."

"I can be. I could have ripped Thane's face off. But I didn't want to ruin that beautiful dress you're wearing with the spray of blood."

Aris laughs.

"How was your date last night?" he asks.

"Disastrous. He was as interesting as the sidewalk."

Benja makes a face. "So was mine. What's wrong with men? Why can't the good-looking ones be as fascinating as me?"

Aris guffaws. "It's because you're so exceptional."

"That's why I've decided to save myself for something more existential."

"Like the Dreamers? That'll be the day."

"You'll eat your words when I find them."

"If they actually exist. You have a better chance of finding a mountain lion than finding them."

"Mountain lions did exist," he says, "Seriously. Don't you ever wonder about your past cycles?" he asks.

"Even if I did, what's the point? An experience is only valid if you can verify it. And if there isn't a way to authenticate, did it really happen?" she says.

"Ah, the old tree-falling-in-the-forest argument."

"Is it any different?"

"The tree knows it fell. Just because no one was around to hear it doesn't mean it didn't happen," says Benja.

"But what if the tree doesn't even remember itself falling?"

"The act of falling happened."

"But did it? If the tree can't remember and no one else was there?" she asks.

"There would be a mark on that tree, the physical consequence of its fall. A gouge on its bark. Or a broken branch. A trace," he says.

Aris lifts her arm, turning it side to side, studying it. "Nope, no marks."

"Just because you don't see it, doesn't mean it's not there."

"An invisible trace. Now we're talking."

"I think we're going to be here a while," Benja says and drops his head onto her lap. It surprises her, but she does not move. She leans back and follows his gaze to the fluffy clouds above.

He sighs. "There has to be more to this life than the four years allotted."

"There is. Just because you can't remember the past cycles doesn't mean you didn't live them."

"Oh, so she changes her argument. So fickle," he says.

Aris rolls her eyes. "I'm not. I didn't say the past cycles didn't happen. It's just pointless to try to remember your old life, because you can't prove it. There's evidence of the past cycles, just not yours specifically."

"People do try. When I moved into my apartment, I found a couple of ink drawings hidden in a cabinet," he says.

"Was there a name?"

"Yeah. But that's useless, isn't it?"

"You finally get what I mean," she says.

Benja scoffs.

Creativity is celebrated in the present, but since everyone gets a new name after Tabula Rasa, authorship is futile. Works of art, books, music, technological and scientific advancements are collected after each cycle and become the property of the system. Innovations are shared for the benefit of all.

She bites into a strawberry. Somewhere nearby is Strawberry Field, where there are no strawberries—only the memory of a musician and black and white mosaic tiles encircling one simple word.

Imagine.

It fascinates her how a song can birth an ideology that governs lives. Without it, there would be no Four Cities or their way of life. She wonders if the musician who wrote it thought his lyrics would ever become reality.

Aris hums its melody and watches the clouds make patterns against the bright blue desert sky. A big cloud that resembles a sheep runs into a smaller one, absorbing it in the slow way a carnivorous plant would a fly.

"I wonder what it'd be like to not have Tabula Rasa's curse," Benja says, disturbing Aris out of her reverie.

"It's not a curse. It did what nothing else could. It brought us peace."

No memories. No attachment. No possession. No one has a need to fight because nobody owns anything. The things they acquire in a cycle become meaningless in the next because they will not remember owning them.

"It takes away all reasons to fight," Aris says, "All grudges. All prejudices. Each cycle we're assigned a place to live. Our basic needs are taken care of by the system. The Distribution Council is responsible for equal distribution of goods, Dwelling Council for housing, Police Stations for peace management, Center for Disease Control for hospitals. Everyone gets equal access to education. The same amount of entertainment points. The service industry is entirely managed by AIs and droids. We are free to explore. To create, to invent. Yet we are each a productive part of a whole."

Benja scoffs. "Sounds like heaven."

She scrunches her face. "Hardly."

"Oh? Does someone have an opinion on this matter?"

"I don't like the term *heaven*. It implies we can't make this earth, this present, into a wonderful place. That humans only deserve it after death— and only if we follow some predetermined set of rules. I think the act of striving for an idea instead of living it is ridiculous."

"Well, that's harsh," he says with a laugh.

"I mean, you've read history. How many wars were waged because one group wanted to save the souls of another in the hope of attaining paradise?"

"The human paradox," he says.

"You end up killing those you want to save. That's genius."

"But human nature is what it is. We want to own and expand. We want to compete to be on top. We want to be right."

"It's lucky we have Tabula Rasa then," she says and stretches languidly.

Maybe Benja's use of the word *heaven* isn't wrong, she thinks. How is this place different from the Old World concept of a paradise where no one goes hungry and peace exists among men? Yes, the price of admission is your memory. But isn't there a cost to everything?

"I want to remember," Benja says. His voice is wistful.

"I know. I just don't understand why."

"Don't you ever get the feeling that you're stuck in a loop? Like sometimes in the middle of doing something new, you find yourself feeling as if you've already done it," he says.

"You mean like déjà vu?"

"Yeah. How can you know a new experience isn't an old one? For all I know I could be writing the same story over and over again and never finishing."

"So you want to know the past so you don't keep doing the same thing?"

"Yeah—but not just that," he says, "I think there's something I'm supposed to find out about the past."

"Like?"

"I don't know. But I keep getting these dreams."

"Dreams aren't real, Benja. They're just your mind firing synapses, making connections, cleaning out junk."

"They feel real to me," he says.

She thinks of her own nonsensical dreams and how they, too, feel real to her. But they are just dreams. They're not links to the past nor premonitions of the future. And even if one could visit the past, why do it?

To her, Tabula Rasa is a gift the Planner had bestowed on humanity. Every four years minds are erased of all the reasons to hate so everyone can coexist in harmony. Every time she gives the children a tour at the museum, she is reminded of how fragile peace is. Scattered human skeletons. Scorched sky. Collapsed buildings. She will gladly take this version of reality over the alternative.

Yet Benja's foolish words on dreams and memories burrow into her brain like firefly larvae. She fears what they will do come the night.

Dreams are not real.

Metis gazes through the gray haze of the window to the backyard. Blackberry brambles cover the land in its entirety, burying it under their sharp thorns. He almost did not come inside the first time he was here. How different his life would have been had he not set foot in this forsaken place.

"The Interpreter Center erased Bodie's dreams," Metis says. "The police arrested him for public disturbance, and somehow he ended up at the Interpreter Center."

By some means that Metis doubts was Bodie's will, he underwent the Dreamcatcher treatment. All Dreamers know the consequence of dream erasure. Once erased, the memories attached to those dreams are gone. They will no longer resurface. Not even with Absinthe.

The Crone's aura brightens, casting white light on his arms, making them look ghostly. He turns to her. The Crone's ancient face distorts in anger.

"Their answer to every human weakness is to wipe it from existence. No choice. No learning. How do we move forward if we keep repeating the past?" she says.

He knows her anger. It is the same one he has toward Tabula Rasa. They are stuck in the web of perpetual forgetfulness—bound to make the same mistakes over and over again.

"I failed Bodie," says Metis.

The Crone turns to him. Her glow dims. "All Sandmen face this at one point. Don't blame yourself."

"Will he be okay?" he asks.

"There are side effects to Dreamcatcher. Just as all brains are different, they'll vary from person to person. We can't know its full impact on Bodie. Until we do."

Aris places the now empty picnic basket and the blanket under a tree, in a bin labeled "Take Me Home." It sits with a collection of things in perfect condition. She pulled this wicker basket out of a similar bin on her way home from work last week. She wonders who its next user will be.

Sometimes she ponders the same about her apartment. Who will live in it next? Where will she be?

She looks up at the blue sky above. It's an Indian summer day—sunny with a light breeze. Lucy told her there is no rain planned.

"Let's go through the forest," she says to Benja.

They enter under the shade of giant trees presiding over a primordial forest. Aris's feet sink into a layer of decomposed leaves, branches, bark, and needles that have fallen from above. The scientist in her knows that underneath are invertebrates, fungi, algae, bacteria, archaea—an ecosystem of decomposers working to repurpose the organic materials to support life. The creative in her feels as if she is cradled by the collective nature. One day her body will join it, recycling into the earth and breeding more life.

She is not the only one attracted to this area. Here and there hang hammocks of woven rope. Aris hears singing coming from one. She is reminded of old folklore about fairies, monsters, and witches. In the green haze of the forest, it's easy to imagine magic seeping out of the crevices of the old trees.

"How long do you think we've been living here?" Benja asks.

"Between two to three hundred thousand years."

"No, in the Four Cities."

She shrugs. "I don't know."

"You're a scientist. Give me a hypothesis."

She looks up at the giant trees. "Well, if, let's say, these trees were planted when the Planner created the Four Cities. Judging by size, these must be hundreds of years old. We can't tell of course unless we cut them and count the rings. There are quite a few factors that could accelerate or decelerate growth. Water, temperature, light, even technology can play a part. So really, there isn't a way to truly know," she says.

"Ugh, just give me a number," Benja says.

"No."

"Come on!"

"I'm not going to."

"Why not?"

"Because there's no point," she says. "Except one."

"What's that?"

"To shut you up."

Benja mumbles something unflattering about her profession.

Aris finds his question amusing—not in itself, but in its human-centeredness. However long the tenure of humans has been, it is dwarfed by the amount of time prior to them. In the history of the earth, they are but a blip.

Under the canopy of needles and leaves, she pictures a world where trees are the only permanent structure. Years from now, humans will cease to exist, and nature will take over—just like millions of years ago. Cycle. And recycle. These are the only states of being as true as time.

"What if I don't go to the hospital?" Benja asks.

"When you're sick? Why not?"

Benja sometimes speaks to her as if she were a part of his internal conversation. More than once she has been left to hypothesize about the missing words like an archeologist.

"No, silly. You know, how at the end of each cycle we're supposed to check ourselves in at a hospital to await Tabula Rasa?"

"I'm sure there's a way to collect the stragglers somehow. I don't think you're the first person to wonder this, or even want to try it," Aris says. "Besides, where are you going to go?"

Her friend does not look capable of surviving in the wild. She doubts he has even set foot outside Callisto. Ahead she sees the steps to the main library. Benja quickens his pace. She trots to keep up with his long legs.

The temperature is cooler inside the majestic Rose Room, a great hall of marble walls and wooden shelves filled with books. It's one of Aris's favorite rooms in the library. And this library is her favorite place in the world. Here, time eases like a raft drifting on a slow-moving river, making her feel like she is suspended inside a mahogany-paneled lockbox instead of racing toward inevitability.

Sometimes she comes here to just sit and inhale the scent of old books. Woody and earthy, with a hint of smokiness. It is a unique smell. Since paper is rare and books are rarer, Aris equates it to the scent of history.

"I'm going to walk around," Benja says. His footsteps echo toward other parts of the library.

She is not the only one partial to this place. Every table is occupied. Where else can one touch the memories of time? She settles on an oak chair. At the table are two others: a woman and a man. The woman is young, and Aris wonders if this is her first cycle. Not that she would know.

Natural light shines in through the grand arched windows, supplementing the orange globe lights of the enormous chandeliers overhead. On the ceiling are mural paintings of fluffy clouds and a brilliant blue sky framed by an ornate baroque frieze.

Aris leans back on her chair, her neck resting on its back. She studies the orange-and-pink-tinged clouds on the ceiling. They look like cotton. Their edges gray, pregnant with rain. She wonders if the mural was painted to capture the moment of rivalry between a storm and a sunset. Perhaps it's meant to represent the struggle between the beginning and end of one's lifespan.

It's an empty pursuit, she thinks. The beginning and end of a life are not two separate states but one continuous state of being. Everything that lives must die—is that not a law of biology? And does not the principle of mass conservation state that mass can neither be created nor destroyed? Things die, but they do not disappear. Life leads to death, and death to life again. An unbroken circle.

When she lifts her head back, the man who was there had left. On the table in his place sits a blue origami crane. She reaches over and picks up the folded bird. It's light in her hand. *Paper*—an uncommon material no longer used for general purposes as it was prior to the Last War. Only a few specific trades have a need for it. She runs her finger along its lines, feeling its coarseness.

"Nothing," Benja says from behind her, his voice laced with frustration. "I walked through the whole place, and nothing."

His eyes zero in on the crane in her hand. "What the hell is that?"

"A crane."

"I know. But why . . . what . . . I mean how did you get it?"

"A man who was sitting here left it."

Benja snatches it from her.

Before she can protest, he whispers, "O flock of heavenly cranes, cover my child with your wings."

He looks at her, his eyes glinting with excitement.

"Do you know what this is?" he asks and gazes at the crane in his hand as if it were a precious baby bird.

"Other than it's a folded paper fowl? Genus *Grus*. Species *japonensis*."

"The ancient Japanese called the crane 'bird of happiness.' They believed its wings carry souls up to paradise," he says.

"And?"

"The Dreamers use it to communicate," he whispers.

"What!" she says in a high voice.

She remembers where she is and looks around to see if anyone is watching. No one is.

"How do you know?" she whispers.

"I hear things."

"I can't believe they really exist."

"And you thought I was insane," says Benja.

"Wait, so if they use it to communicate, and it was left for me . . . But why?"

He shrugs. "How would I know what they use as criteria? Maybe it's your face."

"What's wrong with my face?" Aris bristles.

"It's that innocent, lost look you wear."

"I do not!"

He laughs. "I'm just kidding. You're cute when you're mad."

He begins to unfold it.

"What are you doing?" She jumps up, trying to grab it back.

He lifts it above his head, taking it out of her reach. People stare in their direction, but Benja does not seem to care. Aris stops trying to take the bird back. The curious eyes make her feel uneasy.

"Let's get out of here," she says and leads Benja out of the room.

They find a quiet corner behind a column.

"We have to get to the message," Benja says and begins to unfold it.

"I hope you know how to put it back together," says Aris.

"Do you know that the Japanese believed if one folded a thousand origami cranes, one's wish would come true?"

"I just want the one back," she says, "Do you know how insane this is? Getting a message in a folded bird from a mysterious group?"

"You have no idea. I've been looking for them forever."

He continues to unfold the crane. His hands tremble as he reveals each fold as if undressing a new lover.

"There. I think that's it." Benja lowers the blue paper so Aris can see.

The inside is blank.

Benja's crestfallen face stops Aris from saying anything more.

CHAPTER SEVEN

Aris enters the stately auditorium of Carnegie Hall. Her gaze travels up to the impossibly high ceiling. The ivory walls. The gilded carved details on the columns. It comes to rest on the shiny black grand piano sitting in the middle of the stage.

Most of the audience is already seated. It's a full house. She pulls up the end of her long black dress—slinky with a bow that ties around her neck. The buttery material against her skin makes her feel like she is wearing nothing but a layer of lotion. Lucy chose this for her. The proclivity tests do not fail.

Her red stilettos step on the matching carpet that lines the magnificent space. She admires the builders of this concert hall. The red velvet seats, the Italian Renaissance–inspired proscenium arch, the carved balcony facade—all replicas of the real Carnegie Hall that perished when Manhattan was obliterated.

Aris squeezes past people sitting in the second row to her seat in the middle. When she bought it a week and a half ago, it was the only seat available. Metis is more popular than she thought. She wonders how many entertainment points she has left. She imagines a life of scrimping on leisure over the next few months and blames a weak moment of impulsiveness.

The lights dim around her. The stage blazes in blinding luminescence. A man walks rigid-backed to the piano and bows. His black hair reminds Aris of anthracite. It contrasts against his skin. It's pale—not the paleness of a sickly person, but like ivory yellowed with age. The dazzling lights from above illuminate him, making him appear to glow.

A knot of concentration etches between his brows. His face shows focused intensity. He sits. Silence. Aris hears her breathing in her ears.

The first note hits. The pianist's hands fly along the keys like a practiced eagle swooping in for a kill. Fast. So fast that the movement of his fingers seems a blur. The sound reverberates in her chest. She wants to lift off her seat and grips the armrests to root herself.

So, this is why.

A different song. And another. One transitions to the next seamlessly like the continuum of the horizon. Song after song, he pounds away at the keys. They follow his command like soldiers their general. A single drop of sweat touches his temple. He plays tirelessly. Ceaselessly. His hands glide along the keys, completely able to exist separate from each other.

His music incites a terrifying image inside her—one inspired by the wreckage of the Last War she shares with the children. Orange sky. Broken-down bridges. Mangled cars, their metal melted as if made of butter. Black columns of smoke rise into the air like charred trees. She smells the indescribable odor of hair burning. It's choking her.

Her breath comes up short. The rhythm pulses in her veins. His music pulls her like gravity and winds her so tightly she feels like a spring readying to leap. Beads of sweat travel down her spine. They gather at the small of her back. She feels like she's drowning.

She wants to get up and run, but she cannot. She is held down by his powerful hands. Mesmerized. Tranquilized. Her eyes lock onto his face as it contorts in a manic trance.

A word comes to her. *Madness.* This is what psychologists mean when they say there is a fine line between madness and genius.

The notes transition. A familiar tune. The one she asked Lucy to wake her with each morning since she first heard it.

Luce.

She sighs and leans back in her seat. The spring inside her unwinds. The rhythm of the song slows down her pulse. She closes her eyes.

Bright lights filter in through thin curtains. The sounds of waves in the background. Sweat drips down her back. A warm hand runs along her side. If only she could sleep here forever.

Successive, piercing beeps puncture the serenity of the concert hall, bouncing off the walls and startling her. Her watch! Aris fumbles for it, cursing herself for forgetting to mute it.

"I NEED YOU," says the message.

She looks up and meets the eyes of the pianist. She mouths an apology. It hangs in the air like a speck of dust. There is no forgiveness in his face—only the shocked expression of someone who has witnessed an unspeakable crime. He stares at her, making her feel as if she has committed the greatest of sins. His pale face turns a shade paler, then it floods pink. She feels blood rushing into her own face and sinks into the chair.

Geez. I said sorry.

Abruptly the music stops, leaving the song unfinished. The last note hangs in the air and tapers into a deafening silence that fills the great hall. Without ceremony or explanation, the pianist gets up and walks off stage.

The hall erupts in confused chatter. The noise reminds Aris of the buzzing of bees, making her feel like she is sitting in the middle of an angry hive. Eyes of those around her glare with accusation. Shame fills her. She wants to crawl under her chair and disappear.

The pounding sound of blood fills her ears. She leaps up and races out the door of the hall, sensing stares on her like pointed knives. She feels that if she doesn't run, she will be caught. And there would be consequences. She does not look back.

Metis stares at his trembling hands as if they belong on another person.

"What was that about?" Argus asks. The stage manager's voice is high with anxiety.

Metis ignores him. He's more concerned with not collapsing onto the floor. He leans against a wall for support. Am I dreaming? he wonders. He wipes his face with his quivering, foreign hand. Her face, the face he has seen countless times in the warm embrace of his slumber, is unmistakable.

Her chestnut hair is longer and lighter. Her honey skin is a touch browner, kissed by the sun. But it is her.

He curses his luck. He had spent years searching for her, only to find her now with less than six months left.

Is this real?

He looks up. The backstage room stands in contrast to the brilliance and splendor of the front. It is a small room. A utilitarian room. In one corner is the command center that controls the lighting and sound for the stage. In another corner is a line of storage lockers. The only thing resembling the opulence of the theater is a set of dark-gray velvet curtains used as partitions. Everything looks too real to be a dream.

Argus's face appears in front of him. It is filled with concern. "Why did you just leave the stage like that? Are you sick?"

"I—uh—I'm not sure."

"Do you need to lie down?"

"No!" The last thing Metis wants is to fall asleep. "I mean, I'm fine. I just need a minute."

He looks down at the rings on his fingers. The light from above shines on the silver bands, giving them a soft sheen. The shaking in his hands begins to subside.

"Please go back out there, Metis. The crowd is restless. They're freaking out. You have no idea how many entertainment points those seats cost. They're going to riot if you don't," Argus pleads.

Metis snaps his head up. This is real. She is out there. He needs to see her again. He nods and walks back on stage—the sound of his heart pounding in his ears.

The crowd notices him and settles back in their seats. Metis searches the sea of eager faces. His eyes come to rest on the spot he saw her last. The chair is empty. She is gone.

He sucks in a breath, feeling the dry wind blowing through the holes in his heart. He composes his face into a mask and continues his walk toward the piano. Under him the seat feels hard. Like his soul. He lays his fingers on the keys.

Luce begins.

«

Aris changes into a light cotton dress. The memory of the pianist surfaces, and a shudder sweeps through her. She wraps a warm shawl around her shoulders, warding off the intensity of the previous hours.

She hears a knock on the door. It's Benja. He leans against the door-frame with desperation in his eyes. He's breathing hard, and his face is red. She is reminded of the color of Mars.

"I need your help," Benja says.

"Hey stranger," Aris says and moves aside to let him in.

She has not spoken to him since the library. She left him a few messages, but he did not reply. He moves in to kiss her on the cheek but stops in his tracks.

"You look like you just had sex." He scans around, searching for evidence. "Is he still here?"

She pushes the door closed. It bangs against the frame. "There's no one here."

"Really? But you're glowing. You seem nervous. And you look . . . guilty."

"Well, you're wrong. I came from a concert."

"Huh. Okay," he says, "Can I get a quick drink of water? I ran here."

She walks to the kitchen, and Benja follows. She brings out two glasses from the cupboard and fills them with water from the faucet.

"Here." She hands him a glass and drains hers.

It's ice cold with a slight saline aftertaste. A drop drips from the side of her mouth. The taste reminds her of her dream. She dismisses the thought and wipes the droplet with the back of her hand.

"What happened to you?" she says.

"Nothing. I'm fine."

"You didn't return my reaches. I was worried about you."

"I'm here now."

She narrows her eyes. "You're fine?"

"Yes. Look at me."

She studies him. His face is flushed. His eyes twinkle with glee. She feels his restless energy through the air.

"So, what do you need my help with?" she asks.

"I think there's a hidden message," he says.

"Where?"

"In the crane!"

"You're still on that?"

"That's what I've been working on, trying to figure it out." He pulls out the blue piece of paper.

"There's nothing on it," she says. "Have you considered it may not even be from the Dreamers? Maybe it was just someone trying to be funny."

"I don't think so. Last night, when I was holding it in bed, I noticed the paper has this odd sour smell. It took me a long time to figure out what it reminds me of."

He holds the paper in front of her nose. "Sushi rice. See?"

She scrunches up her face.

"Sushi rice is cooked with vinegar," he says.

"Okay?"

"Why would a piece of paper smell like vinegar?" he asks.

A thought strikes her. "In the Old World, during war, spies would send messages using invisible ink made of lemon juice."

"You think—?" His voice buzzes with excitement.

"Lucy," Aris says, "what reveals invisible writing written in vinegar?"

"Vinegar contains acetic acid," the AI's voice speaks, "Acid breaks down cellulose in paper and turns it into sugar. Heat caramelizes sugar."

"Fire. Try fire!" Aris says.

"Burn it?" He gives her an incredulous look.

"You can read messages written in vinegar because they burn faster than the paper they are written on," Lucy says. "You have to be very careful to heat the paper only just enough to reveal the message but not burn it."

"How the hell am I supposed to do that?" Benja says, messing his hair with his hand.

"I don't know. Just try," Aris says.

"So if I fail, my crane will be ash?" he asks.

"First of all, I found the crane, so technically it's mine. You'd be burning *my* crane, yeah. Just be careful."

Benja looks at Aris with frustration in his eyes. "All right, give me fire."

She goes to the restroom and brings out a candle she uses during baths. Benja is at her side at once. She places it on the table and lights it, sending the calming scent of lavender into the air.

Benja stares at the flame in dead silence as if seeing a vision in it.

"I can't do it," he says finally and thrusts the paper into her hand. "You do it."

She has never seen him like this. He is usually fearless. She takes the piece of blue paper and holds it over the flame. Benja sucks in a breath. His eyes stare unblinking.

A corner of the paper curls and a burning smell rises. She raises the paper. She needs to find that perfect place between answer and ash. Brown lines slowly appear, one by one, until words form.

Spring flower.

Her breathing stumbles. She almost drops the paper. Benja reaches over with trembling hand and takes it from between her fingers. His face is alight with ecstasy.

"What does it mean?" he says, staring at the words as if they hold the meaning of life.

As Aris looks at him, apprehension rears its head from the pit of her stomach. Her friend's fanciful fixation is crossing over to something much more intoxicating. Enticing. Real. She feels its strong pull.

"I found her!" Metis says. He can barely contain the excitement in his voice. It took him two weeks to trace her, but he finally did.

The Crone says nothing back. He looks at her, trying to read between the lines on her ancient face. Her ghostly image is the only source of light in the dim cottage—an ethereal being surrounded by dusty shelves and broken chairs. Her eyes are focused on the floor below. He follows her gaze. From this loft, it looks like a pit of darkness. Frustration builds inside him. He wants a reaction or an answer. Something.

"Don't you have anything to say?" he asks.

Her wispy figure glides to him. Her face betrays no feelings.

"We will need a new Sandman."

"Why can't it still be me?" he says.

"Where the past and the present converge, there is pain."

"You said that but there's no proof. Why can't I make it work?"

The Crone studies his face, the same way she does whenever she knows there is more he has left unsaid. "She doesn't remember, and you want her to take Absinthe, is that right?"

Her aura brightens. He knows he is treading on dangerous ground.

"Just as the Interpreter Center has no right to take away someone's memory against their will, we have no right to make someone remember," she says. "If you want her, you must go to her as Metis, the pianist, and leave the rest of you behind. Convince her to fall in love with you, just as you are. It is you who must give up. The past, Absinthe, being the Sandman."

Metis doesn't know what to say. He has not even spoken to his wife—her name only recently ceased to be a mystery. Would she—*could* she—love him without her memories of their life together? He is nothing to her.

The Crone closes the gap between them. "You're not the first Sandman to be in this predicament. I've seen it all before and I know what's coming. You have to make a choice. The past or the present. You cannot have both or you will risk exposing us all. You know the rule."

He knows what choice he would make. It would always be Aris—or whatever other identity she will have in the future. Even if there is no guarantee that she would choose him too.

He nods. It is a gesture so slight it could easily be missed. But the Crone knows her Sandman has made his decision.

CHAPTER EIGHT

Fall has painted the trees in shades of red, yellow, gold, and brown. Leaves litter the walking path, making it look like an impressionist painting. Aris sits on a bench next to Thane in the park. Across the street from them is the museum, gray like a typical October sky.

"I forgot to ask how your date at Griselda went," she says. Unless asked, Thane doesn't share his personal life with her. She wonders if he has friends he talks freely with.

"It was—Let's just say we weren't compatible," Thane says.

"How? The app never fails me."

"I didn't use the app," he says.

"Why not?"

"It just feels so unnatural."

"It's a time saver," she says.

The app makes calculations based on personality and proclivity results from all the tests a person has taken during their lifespan. It matches each person across the entire database of all citizens in all the cities. Then it provides options to pick from, ranking by percentage of compatibility and availability. *Easy.*

"It just never really worked for me," Thane says.

"What? Explain."

"It always wants to match me up with some old scientist/mathematician type."

"What's wrong with the scientist/mathematician type?" Aris asks, offended.

"Well, let's just say you're an exception."

"There are plenty of attractive scientists."

"You're going to have to introduce me to them then because, obviously, we're not frequenting the same places."

"Was she an artist?" Aris asks. Thane had let it slip once that, like her, he has an affinity for the creative type. Perhaps it's their way of adding unpredictability to their lives.

"A sculptor."

"Intense?"

He nods.

"We talked about her work for the first half hour," he says. "Then she refused to discuss the possibility that Rodin's *Thinker* was inspired by Michelangelo's *Il Penseroso*. I mean, it was the foundry workers who named it *The Thinker*, based on its similarity to Michelangelo's."

That's why.

"'My favorite sculptor couldn't possibly rip off another,' she said."

"Sorry you had a bad time," Aris says. "Give the app another chance. It might surprise you."

After all, that was how she met Benja. Funny, it never matched them up before. Or maybe it did, and they just passed each other by. They get along great—that is, when they see each other. She has not heard from him since she helped him reveal the message on the crane. Maybe she should rethink the app.

"What are you doing tonight?" Thane asks.

She pretends to look at her watch. "Hmm . . . October twentieth. I'm going to Griselda."

"You're joking."

She laughs. "Yeah, I am. I wish it were true though. That would have been hilarious. I'm meeting this guy later. He's going to show me his sample of trinitite."

"That's what I call a hot date. How did he get it?"

"On a trek at the nature preserve near the southern border. He found it while digging a hole to do his business."

"I read that atomic bomb testing was done in the Mojave Desert in the middle of the twentieth century. People used to sell the trinitite they found at test sites to tourists back then. Imagine that."

Aris wonders if the world outside is one giant lump of trinitite. What would it have been like to witness the Last War? The Planner had seen it, and it sparked an ideology. It made him create a world where war is a thing of the distant past. Would going through a traumatic event change her?

"And how was your date at the park?" Thane asks.

"What date?"

"The writer?"

"Oh, Benja? That wasn't a date. He's a friend."

"Really? He seemed awfully possessive for just a friend."

"Nah. That's just the way he is. He says whatever he wants. Not much of a filter, but I like that about him. You don't have to wonder if he's telling you the truth, you know?" She notices Thane studying her and remembers what Benja had said about him liking her. "Anyway, what's your plan for the rest of the day?"

"Nothing urgent. Do you want to grab a drink before your date?"

"I actually have things to do in the Tomb."

"That junk closet?"

Strewn around Aris are discarded old machines, left over from the previous cycles, some from even before the creation of the Four Cities. She has been devoting her spare time to fixing and studying them. To her, each is a puzzle and a history lesson.

On the worktable are computers she has arranged by size in a neat line. She runs her fingers over each as she passes. The smaller they are, the more power they hold. It's a wonder how human minds come together to advance technology, and how helpless humanity has become without it.

Aris's hand goes instinctively to her watch. Its hardness around her wrist was the first thing she felt after waking up from Tabula Rasa. In it is Lucy, her AI and constant companion. The access point to all her wants and needs. Her umbilical cord to the system.

She stops at the end of the table. Sitting on it is a copper helmet— her latest obsession. She picks it up and feels its substantial weight in her hands. The dull reddish-orange metal is covered in places by a green layer of verdigris. Attached to its top are colorful wires, like a plumed crest on a *galea*, the helmet Roman soldiers wore.

What it does is a mystery to her. It is the most complicated puzzle she has ever come across. It has been occupying her mind for the last few months.

She puts it on. Its heaviness presses down on the top of her skull. She finds a place on the floor against the wall and leans back. From this angle, she can see the entire room. Shelves line the walls, stacked next to each other like dominos. Each is filled with boxes—some labeled, and some not. Items too large for the shelves sit in crates in one corner of the room. Except for its content, the storage room is unremarkable.

The Tomb. A windowless room where things came to die and be forgotten. The first time she was here, it made her sad. Now she sees it as the best perk of working at the museum. A backstage pass to history. *To the memory of time.*

Aris closes her eyes. She thinks more clearly behind the darkness of her lids. What is the helmet for? She tells herself she should stop calling it a helmet because it implies its job is to protect.

Copper is a soft, malleable metal. It crushes easily, even with minor force. It is best as a conduit for heat and electricity. The wires on it make her think it transmits information. It reminds her of a neuroimaging machine used to map the structure of the brain. But she has a feeling it is more than that.

Under its surface is a network of complicated circuitry woven together like a spider's web with material resembling thin golden silk threads. It is far more advanced than any machine she has ever seen in the Tomb. Why would anyone leave it here to fade into anonymity?

She decides to take it home. Thane won't mind. He couldn't care less about the past—what the broken things in this room represent. He will never understand her fascination.

An elaborate setup of glass bottles and tubes—a lab-grade distillation kit—sits on a large wooden table by the window. Next to it are scattered remnants of bell-shaped flowers, lemony green in color—hypnos, a hybrid designed for one purpose. They lay crushed and bruised, the oil having been extracted from the ovaries. This is the last batch of Absinthe he will ever make before handing over his responsibility to another and walking away. He watches as drops of liquid pool at the bottom of the receiving flask, his mind on the instructions given to him years ago.

"Once you have the distilled oil, you add it to a bottle of one-hundred-proof alcohol," the Crone said. "Store the distillate in a dark and warm room to sit for a month."

He wondered how he would get hold of one-hundred-proof anything.

"Next is a very important process. The preparation of the tincture. You can't rush this," she said. "The distillate will be very potent and toxic, so you must make a second batch of one-hundred-proof alcohol mixed with whole hypnos flowers. This batch must steep for a week and must not be distilled. This is what will give Absinthe its green color. To make Absinthe, you mix in equal thirds the distillate, the tincture, and water. Not the water that you drink or bathe with."

"Why not?" he asked.

"It has a trace of salt. Your water travels from the ocean in pipes before it goes into the desalination plants. There's a little bit of saline in it, but it's what you've come to associate with the taste of water because you've been drinking it your entire life. Pure water doesn't have any taste."

"So where do I get the water?" he asked.

"Melted snow from the mountains. In the spring when the snow melts, the water travels into the ravines in the nature preserves."

"What?" he asked, his voice high.

"All the Sandmen before you had to do this. It's the only way."

The first time he went on what he came to call "the water pilgrimage," he brought a large drum that he carried on his back. He chose the nature preserve in Elara, the quietest and the least populous of the cities, to keep away from prying eyes. Elara is different from the three other cities. It's raw and natural—the way a California desert is meant to look. He had trekked through rough paths of boulders and scraggly cacti in search of a riverbed and found it near an area where two large oak trees stood.

The last time he was there was in the spring, when an explosion of wildflowers painted the valley in shades of pink and yellow. The next time he sees it—if he ever sees it again—he will not remember having seen it. Next spring will be Tabula Rasa.

The verdant liquid colors his vision, tossing and catching possibilities like balls. The Crone had forbidden him from forcing Absinthe on Aris. The Crone believes in choice and consent, something that was denied her. But why could he not offer Aris Absinthe as a choice? The temptation—a shortcut, a way to bypass the time required to reacquaint her to him—pulls like a magnet.

You must go to her only as Metis, the Crone's voice echoes in his ears.

Aris looks at her watch. The pending arrival of the scheduled rain has emptied the pathway to her building of people. Darkness drips down like black ink around her, making her feel apprehensive. She does not like the dark. It's an irrational fear, she knows. From the corner of her eye, she sees a flash of shadow darker than the surrounding night. It's probably trees swaying in the wind, she tells herself.

Her footsteps echo against the concrete path. Wind rustles trees and sends chills through the gaps in her coat. She hugs her jacket tight against her body and quickens her steps.

She had spent more time than she wanted with the trinitite man. Aside from having the sample, there was nothing about him that struck her as interesting. She only stayed because of the little piece of earth in his possession.

Holding the trinitite in her hand was at once awe-inspiring and terrifying. It reminded her of fossils but with a glassy sheen. Its surface had a thin sprinkle of fine sand with little bubbles inside. Sandstone, quartz, and feldspar melted together under the extreme heat of the atomic blast. The same blast that pockmarked the face of the world during the Last War.

She can only guess at the temperature that once coursed through its atoms, disfiguring it into its current form. The minimum for sand to form glass is 1,470 degrees Celsius. The passage of time has allowed her to touch it.

Sprinkles of rain land on her cheeks. She wipes them away and looks up at the sky. More drop on her face. She does not remember the last time she felt rain. She stops, mesmerized by the strange, cold wetness on her skin and hair.

Suddenly rain begins to lash down in sheets, drenching her. Her wet clothes stick to her body, replacing heat with a veil of ice. Her muscles contract and her teeth begin to chatter. She looks for the lights of her building and runs toward it.

She hears footsteps apart from her own. Or is it the clapping of branches on trees? The thought of company should make her feel safer, but it does not. It is almost an instinct—the distrust of another human in the cloak of night. She speeds up. The whipping wind and rain make it hard for her to see where she is going. She only knows she is going forward.

Her body hits against something firm. She bounces off, losing her balance. She's falling backward. The sound of her scream is lost in the howling wind. Vice-like hands grab hold of her upper arms. They yank her forward, smothering her against a wall of warmth. She struggles to release herself.

"Let go!" she yells.

She feels the heat lifting off her. Cold air floods in. One of the hands is still on her arm, sending warmth through the jacket to her skin. She wipes the rain off her face, sees his, and remembers. She steps away from him, freeing herself from his grip.

"Are you hurt?" he asks, his hand reaching forward toward her face.

"You're Metis." As soon as the words leave her, she realizes they were an inappropriate response to his question.

His hand drops. She sees something flash in his eyes. Is it pain? Did she run into him that hard? In an instant, it is gone.

He clears his throat. "I am. Wish we'd met under better circumstances."

He squints at the sky and wipes his face. When he looks back at her, he stares with an intensity that leaves her feeling invaded. She wraps her arms around her soaked body. The shame she felt at his concert resurfaces. She should leave before he remembers her as the girl who interrupted his performance.

"I should go," she says quickly.

"Let me walk you."

"Oh, no, that's okay. I'm not that far away. Thank you though."

He is rooted in spot, making no move to let her through. The expression on his face makes her feel uneasy, the same way she feels when looking over the railing to the street forty stories below. She walks around him. As she does, her side grazes his. She feels heat emanating from his body. Once a safe distance away, she takes off running without looking back.

Metis watches Aris over his shoulder until she enters her building. It took him too long to find her—the woman whose face has been haunting his dreams.

He began his search for her soon after the concert. He combed through the list of those who had purchased the tickets for his show and found her name among twenty others who sat in her row. He looked for addresses to go with the names and scouted each. Hers was in the middle of the list.

He did not approach her right away. Instead, he watched and

waited. For someone who prefers to think of himself as brave, he feels like a coward. Time is ticking toward Tabula Rasa, and yet he is paralyzed by fear.

He was afraid she would only see him as a stranger. And he was right to be. The only recognition on her face when she saw him tonight was from this cycle—of Metis, the pianist.

He thought he had prepared himself for the pain of being forgotten by someone he loves. But it struck him like a branding iron, sending him down a spiral of doubt. She shrugged him off as she would any random person she met on the street. The Crone was right.

What if she is not the same woman from his dreams? She looks like her. She sounds like her. Her tiny frame fits into his embrace just as before. But are those qualities enough to make her the same person?

He continues walking toward the subway. It seems his life this cycle has been spent in train stations. Always coming or going. Never settled. He longs for the past. Of nights spent in the cocoon of his bed, in the arms of his lover.

He stops and turns around. Up in the clouds is a lighted window— the one he knows belongs to her. Is she sleeping in the arms of a lover tonight? He has seen her with a man and witnessed their closeness. Is she making new memories, slowly replacing the ones with him? Perhaps there are no memories of him inside her—not even in the deepest part of her brain. Maybe Tabula Rasa got them all.

He gazes at the silver bands on his fingers—reminders of a promise. He found them in the seat cushion of his favorite chair and instinctively knew what they were. They feel constricting. The burden of their pasts rests on him. They had made that decision together, and he would honor it. He takes another long look at the window and turns away.

Aris stares at the stream of hot water pouring from the faucet into the tub. She lets it carry her mind along its continuous flow like a raft on a river. The sound muffles all the other noise in her head. The steam rises, painting the air with thick, white fog. She pours lavender oil into the bath. Its sweet, herbal scent has an immediate tranquilizing effect.

She eases her freezing body into the filled tub. The heat wraps around her skin, seeping into her pores and unfurling her like a new leaf. She scoops a handful and washes her face. The saltiness stings her lips. The one bath a week they are allotted uses unfiltered water from the sea. Less wasteful. *At least it's warm.*

Metis enters a gap in her mind. What was he doing here? Entertainers of his caliber usually live in Lysithea, a city on a hill. What was he doing in her city after dark in the rain when he should be hunkered down like everyone else in the warmth of his home?

Maybe he's seeing someone here.

She wonders what type of person the pianist would be attracted to enough for him to brave the weather to see. She had once dated a musician, a jazz guitarist whose name she does not remember.

Aris sinks farther into the tub, leaving only her head above water. The silence of the bath reminds her that she has not listened to *Luce* since the concert. The humiliation she experienced there had left a bitter taste in her mouth. Each time the memory of it threatened to invade her mind, she swatted it away like a fly. But she misses the song.

"Lucy."

"Yes?"

"Can you please play *Luce*?"

"Of course."

The tinkling of piano music fills the bathroom. She closes her eyes. In darkness, her awareness becomes acute. The soft wave of warm water undulates across her skin, caressing it like a lover, sucking her life force and turning her fingers to prunes.

Does this song affect other people the same way it does her? It is a question that can never be answered. An experience is subjective.

But is it? An experience is only perceived to be subjective to the person who experiences it subjectively. How would one know another is feeling the exact same thing in the exact same moment?

What if her consciousness is not even her own? Could there be a collective consciousness that is borrowed as opposed to owned? What if, at a quantum level, consciousness is suspended inside spheres like molecules—like the air that one breathes? She imagines herself a bee collecting consciousness like pollen on flowers.

Maybe that is why the longer you know someone, the more their mind becomes familiar to you. It could explain how sometimes people who have never met come up with the same ideas. Or how some people can predict the future actions of another—like knowing someone would contact you before they do. Or feeling the death of a loved one miles away as it unfolds without knowing.

Shared consciousness. Perhaps people are not so different from each other after all. Perhaps uniqueness is but an illusion masked by perceived subjectivity. Perhaps the thing that inspired Metis to create a song so heartrending and beautiful is the same one that has inspired many others throughout time.

His face comes to her. Up close, it has the stillness and refined quality of a marble statue. It is thin with cheekbones that roll down like hills and a straight nose like the ridge of a mountain. He reminds her of the desert. Alluring and desolate.

His eyes unsettled her. She remembers wanting to and at the same time not wanting to look into the black pools. *No.* A voice inside warned her of danger. Like the desert, she could get lost in them.

Sadness dribbles down like drifts of snow. She shivers despite the warm bath. The hole in her chest cavity gapes open. *The emptiness.* Will it trail her for the rest of her life?

The song ends. Aris lets her body become heavy and sink to the bottom of the tub. She watches the bubbles from her nose swim like pearl divers back up to the surface. Strands of her hair wave, sinuous like seaweed, in the water. She forces the thought of the pianist out of her mind, walling it away like the cold rain outside.

CHAPTER NINE

There is a small room inside the library on the corner of Spring and Flora. In it is a gathering. At first glance, it has the appearance of an innocuous book club meeting. People of all ages stand in a loose circle. Some are engaging in friendly chatting. Some hang alone in the periphery, preferring their own company.

Metis is in the middle, as he always is. Next to him is a table and on it is a tray full of empty shot glasses. Eirene, the one to take over his post, is not yet ready to become the Sandman. It is a big job, but it's only for a few months, he had told her. And until she's ready, he'll do the heavy lifting. He had suggested Eirene to the Crone partly because he knew she would need time. But mainly because she's loyal.

It's Thursday morning, a quiet time of the week. He chose it to ensure privacy. Most people use the library for leisure, and wouldn't come until after work.

In his hand is a book. He wears a wooden mask the color of night. Only one other Dreamer has seen his face. He prefers it that way. His anonymity is pivotal to the duty that rests on his shoulders. Even if it will soon end.

"Welcome," Metis says, "I see a few new faces. You're here because one of us chose you. Each of us has different criteria, so consider the match serendipitous."

He pulls out a blue origami crane from the book. "This is how you were given the message. And this is the only way you will be contacted."

He walks around, scanning the crowd. A striking face catches his attention.

Why is he here?

"Every one of us is being tracked. The system knows our movements, where we go, what we do, even what we eat," he says and stops in front of a woman.

She blushes. Her young face looks as if she has not gone more than two cycles. Freckles decorate the bridge of her nose; her brown hair is piled on top of her head in a loose bun; her red lips are bright against her pale golden skin. She reminds him a little of his wife.

He offers her his hand. She hesitantly takes it. He raises her hand as if readying for a dance.

"This," he says and points to the silver bracelet around her wrist, "is their tool. Wearing it gives away your location. Each time you contact someone from this, it is tracked. Every decision you make with this on—what restaurants you eat at, what clothes you wear, what books you read—you feed information to the system. You give it the ability to predict your pattern. Don't be predictable."

He lets go of her hand and says in a lower voice. "Please leave it at home."

The young woman nods.

Metis looks around. "There is only one reason we're all here. To remember. Tabula Rasa has stolen our pasts from us. But not everything. This we know."

Sounds of agreement rise from the crowd. Many nod.

Metis walks around the circle. "If this is your first meeting, I warn that you are entering into a dangerous agreement. What we do here is not sanctioned. Some may say it's forbidden. We break the rules bound by Tabula Rasa."

The newcomers exchange looks with each other.

"Being here means you've decided to choose the past. It cannot collide with the present. That means nothing leaves here. You may not contact one another outside this space unless approved by me. If you do, we will be forced to cease our contact with you," Metis says.

He continues, "Second, you may not contact someone from your dreams. Doing so will put what we do in danger." Guilt rises as he speaks this rule.

Metis clears his throat and raises his voice. "There are threats out there against Absinthe and dreams. The police, the Interpreter Center, the entire system exist to keep peace. If you get mixed up with them, you won't be allowed back. If they know who you are, they will use you to trace back to any one of us. If any of you want to leave, please do so now."

No one stirs. Each face is resolute.

He turns his attention back to the young woman and says solemnly. "Ask yourself if you really want this. Before it's too late."

She shakes her head. "I'm staying."

He puts a hand on her shoulder and says, "Would you like to share your story?"

She smiles tentatively.

"We're united by the same desire. You're safe here," Metis says.

"Well, I've been getting this dream since the beginning of the cycle. It's always the same dream. In it is a man. I can see his face, but it's blurry, like looking through water. From the way I felt in the dreams, I know he was my lover. He must have been," she says.

"Thank you—uh."

"Seraphina. My name is Seraphina."

"Thank you, Seraphina, for sharing your story."

He leaves her and walks toward the person he has been curious about since he laid eyes on him. He stops in front of the man with tousled hair. The man is more handsome in close range, Metis thinks begrudgingly. He feels the razor-edged whip of jealousy opening a wound in his chest. He desires to punch the beautiful face and wreck it. Instead, he swallows down the thick, bitter taste of resentment.

"Welcome. What's your name?"

"Benja."

"Tell us why you're here."

"My story is like Seraphina's. I'm plagued by a dream. It plays like a loop. Sometimes after I wake, I think I can recall it. But when I try, it vanishes. Just out of reach. The feelings are what stay."

"Why do you want to remember your past?" Metis asks.

Benja shrugs. "I suppose for the same reason as everyone here. I need to know there's more to this life than the four years allotted."

"You will accept the consequences of remembering?" Metis asks, "It is true what they say about bliss in ignorance."

Benja nods.

"You may disagree later," says Metis.

"I'm certain. I need to know. I must know. It's all I want."

"All?"

Benja's eyes show the determination of a rock wall. Metis is conflicted about him being here. Benja possesses the woman he loves. Aris should be the reason for him to want the present. Instead, he is choosing the past. Yet the knowledge gives Metis hope.

Metis has an intense desire to both kick Benja to the floor and ask him everything about Aris. He wants to find out if she is happy or whether she also walks around with a hole in her heart. Is she getting odd dreams?

He must have been quiet too long, because Benja begins to look at him strangely. Metis clears his throat. He walks back to the middle of the room.

"I'm going to repeat what I said. Being here means you choose the past. The past and the present do not mix. The moment you choose the present, you will not be allowed back."

Metis opens the book in his palms like wings. The Dreamers, those who have been here before, walk closer. One takes the hands of those next to her. They in turn take the hands of the people next to them. The newcomers look at each other and hesitantly follow. A circle forms around Metis. Everyone's eyes are on him.

He looks down at the pages of *Love in the Time of Cholera* by Gabriel García Márquez. The text is so faded he can barely make out the words. But he has memorized the passage he needs. He speaks it. The room becomes hazy, like a white fog has descended upon it. Then it brightens, as if bathed in starlight.

The wispy figure of the Crone stands before them. Her translucent face is a landscape of ancient wisdom. Metis looks around the room. The difference between those who have been to a meeting and those who have not is obvious. The expressions on the newcomers' faces range between awe and fear, while the rest look on with calmness.

"Hello," the Crone says.

"Hello," everyone says.

She looks at Metis. "How many days?"

"It's October twenty-third. One hundred and forty-eight days left before the cycle ends," he says.

She turns to the crowd. "You're all here because you want to remember the past Tabula Rasa had taken from you." Her ethereal voice flows around the room like the whooshing of wind.

"I don't deny that Tabula Rasa was created out of a desire for peace. But anything that takes away choice eats away at our soul. Without our memories, we are but empty vessels waiting to be filled and drained at each cycle. Love, the most vital of human needs, cannot exist fully outside the garden of memories. And Absinthe is its nourishment."

She glides around the room, casting lights and shadows on the faces of the Dreamers.

"Absinthe will open your mind, forging connections to the hidden memories inside dreams. Dreams are essential to remembering. Without them, Absinthe would be ineffective. There are those who will seek to destroy Absinthe and your dreams. Remember that."

Metis brings out a flask from his jacket and pours a small amount of the green liquid into each waiting glass on the table. Once they are filled, he walks the tray to each Dreamer until everyone has Absinthe in their hands. Metis studies Benja's face. He looks as if he is in ecstasy.

"To beautiful dreams," the Crone says.

"To beautiful dreams," everyone repeats. Each flicks the glass up, draining it.

"May I speak with you?" Seraphina asks.

The room is empty except for Benja and two others chatting in one corner. It looks smaller now.

"Sure," Metis says.

He guides her to the other side of the room, where they will not be overheard. A lock of hair escapes the loose pile on top of her head and covers one eye. She sweeps it behind her ear.

"I was hoping you could help me understand the reason we may not contact someone from our dreams," she asks in a small voice, her eyes earnest.

"Because that person doesn't exist anymore," he says, feeling his stomach hollowing with those words. "That person belongs to the past."

"You don't believe we stay who we are?"

"Our core stays the same, yes. But everything else changes. They now have a new name, a different place to live. Maybe a new job. They have new friends. Perhaps even a lover. Those things can affect a person."

"But they might not be affected."

Metis feels sympathy for the young woman. She is hopeful. He wishes to spare her the pain that has been gnawing at him since he began to remember. That must be how the Crone had felt about him.

"Imagine a stranger coming to you and insisting you are someone else, trying to make you feel something you're not feeling," he says. "What would you think? Would you be afraid? Threatened, maybe? Surely you would think the person is insane."

She does not reply.

"You have the benefit of believing in the past—that some of it exists somewhere in your mind, waiting to be unleashed. Not everyone does or wants to remember. You cannot force the past on someone who doesn't want it," he says.

Despair clutches his insides.

Aris does not want it.

He clears his throat and continues, "That's just on a personal level. Remember, there are others here who have the same right to dream as you do. What will happen to their rights if you're reported to the police?"

"I'll never tell anyone anything," Seraphina says.

Metis believes her. But that is not the point.

"Rules are there to protect not just you, but everyone. Breaking them means you will no longer be a part of us. Do you understand?"

She nods.

"Now go home and sleep. Prepare yourself for the dreams to come," he says.

«

The bell rings. Aris opens the door. Benja stands before her, leaning against the jamb. His face glows from exhilaration.

"Is everything okay?" she asks.

"Yes. No. I mean—" He sighs. "I know it's late, but I don't know who else to go to. You're the first person I've felt a connection with this cycle."

He looks at her with serious eyes. "When you don't have a catalog of people in your life, the few you meet become important to you."

She rolls her eyes and stands aside to let him through. "Come in. You didn't have to say all that. I would have let you in anyway."

He chuckles and enters. He kisses her cheek as he always does and walks into her bedroom. She hesitates before following. She hopes he is not looking for anything more than the intimacy of her friendship.

Benja settles on her bed. Aris sits down and leans on a pillow against the headboard. He moves his head to her lap. She feels like both his therapist and the couch.

Aris studies his face. A touch of pink is in his cheeks. His eyes glitter like a boy who has just taken his first elevator ride.

"What happened?" she asks.

"I finally did it!"

"Did what?"

"I deciphered the message on the crane. They were meeting in the small library on Spring and Flora. I found the Dreamers. I went to their gathering," he says in one breath.

"When?"

"Today. Yesterday. I have no idea. I kind of lost track of time. I've just been wandering the city. I haven't slept."

The desperation in his voice reminds her of the angry blond man arrested by the police. The thought makes her afraid for Benja. She wants to talk sense into him, to warn him of possible danger, but his exhausted face changes her mind. She decides to be supportive.

"How was the meeting?" she asks.

"It was incredible. Transformative. I met the Crone and the Sandman," he says, "The Sandman wears a mask, like those Balinese ones. You know, the ones with protruding eyes and fangs. Animal mane for hair?"

Who are these people? "That's strange."

Benja shrugs. "No stranger than this life."

"So you don't know who he really is?" she asks.

"How is that relevant?" He looks at her as if she had asked whether he likes ketchup.

"Okay, so what's special about this Sandman guy?" she asks.

"He leads the ceremony of Absinthe," Benja says.

She laughs. The name has a tinge of the pagan rituals of yore. "Did they chant?"

Benja purses his lips. "Maybe I came to the wrong place."

"I'm sorry. I shouldn't be so cynical. Tell me more about the Sandman."

"He can make your dreams more vivid, unlocking your memories."

"Really? How?"

"There's a special drink he gave me. He calls it Absinthe," he says.

"Wait. You drank something a stranger gave you?" She straightens, stirring Benja off her lap. Her resolve to be supportive disappears. She draws the line at him being stupid.

He sits up and looks at her. His face has the guilty expression of someone who knows he did something foolish.

"Yeah. But you know. I—I don't know. I haven't slept. I really need to, but I've been afraid."

Of a hallucinogen that could turn your mind to mush? Whatever for?

She leans back on her headboard in resignation, and Benja resumes his position.

"What if it has a bad side effect or something?" he asks.

"Well, you should have thought of that before you drank it. What if it causes irreparable damage to your brain?"

Benja rubs his cheek on her lap. "You don't need to scare me any more than I already am."

Exhaustion paints shadows on his face. There is an unfocused look in his eyes, as if he were trying but losing the fight to hold on to the present. He seems younger. Terrified. Aris wonders how old he is. He has probably gone through fewer cycles than she thinks. Perhaps she should not begrudge him moments of weakness now and then.

"What do you want to see in your dream?" she asks in a gentler tone.

He looks at the ceiling and sighs.

"A man. Always the same man. I don't see his face. But I must love him," he says.

Of all the times they spoke of his obsession with the Dreamers, he has never told her his dream. She feels slighted. Is she not trustworthy enough? Then she remembers that she has never told him about her dream.

She asks, "How do you know you're not wasting your time chasing a ghost?"

He takes her palm in his hand and traces the lines on it with a finger. His hands are icy.

"Do you have a ghost?" he whispers.

She cannot tell him. Even if she wants to, what is there to say? Her dreams are just a compilation of feelings, lights, and shadows. There is nothing to tell.

She runs her other hand through his hair. He closes his eyes.

"I'm so tired," he says. "Can I spend the night here? I need to be with someone I trust."

"Yeah. Sleep," she says and gives him the pillow from behind her.

Benja curls into a fetal position. He falls asleep at once. A smile touches a corner of his lips.

The moon is high in the sky. Aris gazes at Benja's sleeping face bathed in moonlight. He looks more vulnerable than he's ever shown himself to be. *So beautiful. So broken.*

Why does he want to chase the past? There is so much he could be living for in the present. Five months left, and he is squandering it on dreams. Why can't he see that Tabula Rasa is a gift? Four years at each life.

If this one doesn't work out, you have the next. Shedding lives like hermit crabs shed shells. A lifetime of possibilities.

"How can you love someone you don't remember?" she whispers to no one in particular.

Aris opens her eyes and sees Benja's silhouette leaning against the headboard. He stares straight ahead at the curtained window. The eerie image gives her goosebumps. She has never seen him so silent and still. Outside, the first light of the day is slowly transforming the indigo sky gray.

"Are you all right?" she asks.

"You know we're told so many things in our lives," he says, not looking at her. "Facts and fiction face off like pawns on a chessboard. So we learn through books and education, hoping they will advance us toward the ultimate truth. But at the end of it, when we look back, all we have is a bare chessboard. Truths and lies lie like a mountain of dead bodies in the trenches."

She reaches for his arm and touches it. His skin is damp and warm from sleep.

He looks at her. "I saw him in my dream. As clear as day. I saw his face. He wore a white hat. We had a life together. Absinthe worked, Aris. It opened the gates of my memories, like the Sandman promised. He told me it would help me see my past lives. The strongest memories survived Tabula Rasa. They live inside dreams. They only lie hidden, waiting to be unlocked."

Aris's finger feels a loose thread on her bedcover. The long fiber reminds her of an old woman's hair—white and soft. She pulls at it, puckering the fabric. The thread catches against a stitch and resists her pull. She tugs, and it comes free.

"What if what you saw was just a dream?" she asks, playing absentmindedly with the coil of thread in her hand.

He sighs. "It's not. I can't explain how I know. I just do. I saw my life. The memory of it. The man in the white hat and I, we were lovers. I loved him. I still do," he says.

"But Tabula Rasa erased all our memories. The people we met, the relationships we forged, what we did. They're gone," she says.

"Look, I'm not making this up," Benja says, "And I'm not the only one. There are others like me. Many of them. They take the drink and see their past lives. There's one woman I met who wants to also find her lover."

"How can you find someone just from a face?" Aris asks.

"I don't know."

"What if who your friend believes is her lover is just a man she crossed paths with on the subway?" Aris asks.

"That's not how it works."

"Okay, so let's say he really is her lover from the past. What would she do if he doesn't remember?"

"He will remember," he says, "She's sure of it."

"What if he doesn't? You can't force your belief on another."

"You're just a nonbeliever. I'm not going to sit here and prove to you what you want me to. All my evidence is in my head, and I can't pull it out except through my words. And if you don't believe me, that's your prerogative. But please stop trying to convince me otherwise."

Aris sighs. "Okay, so for the sake of argument, some dreams are memories—how can you know which are real and which are made up by your mind? Don't memories change and shift over time?"

"This is exactly what the Sandman warned me about," Benja says.

"He warned you about me?"

"Not you in particular. But nonbelievers. We've become a society of faithless people. That's why most of us can't believe in things we cannot see nor touch."

She worries about the people Benja is mixed up with. The fanciful ideas. The drug that makes people think they can see their pasts.

"If only everyone could take Absinthe and see for themselves," mumbles Benja.

"Oh, so they want to drug everyone?" she asks.

Benja frowns. "Unfortunately not. They're secretive. They don't just take in anyone. You must be selected by one of the members. You're not even supposed to talk about it outside the group. By the way, we never had this conversation."

Aris rolls her eyes. "You forget they wanted *me* first. The crane was left for me, before you hijacked it."

"Maybe you should join the Dreamers."

She scoffs.

Benja sighs. "I know this all sounds like make-believe to you. And I can't make you see what I saw. But if there's a way to turn my dream into something more than just a memory, I need to find it. I have to find him."

He springs up from the bed and wobbles. He eases back down.

"Ow. My head." He leans on the headboard, massaging his temples.

"It's probably a side effect of the drug," she says. "Let me get you water."

She goes to the kitchen and gets a glass out. At the sink, she pushes a button, and cold water flows into it. Her mind swirls with questions.

Could dreams be memories? How can that be? Why doesn't Tabula Rasa get rid of them as it does everything else?

She thinks of her own recurring dreams. There was someone there. Was that person from her past? Can't be. The dreams are nothing more than bright lights and feelings.

Tabula Rasa works. She cannot remember anything from her past. Not her name, her old life, nor anyone she had met in the previous cycles.

The water stops once it reaches the top of the glass. She walks back to her room.

"Drink this." She puts the glass to Benja's lips. He sips from it.

"Ugh, this is salty," he says.

Aris looks at the water. It is clear, just as it has always been. She takes a sip.

"It tastes fine. Maybe it's another side effect. What's this drug made of?"

Benja shakes his head. "I don't know. I don't care. Whatever it is, I need more of it. I have to remember."

"You don't even know if the side effects will go away. Maybe you should give it some time."

"I don't have time. I've already wasted enough. There's only a few months left."

"Exactly. There's only a few months left. What's the point?" she asks.

"You don't understand the agony of not being with someone you love. I need to find him!" His voice becomes louder until he is yelling.

"It's—" He clutches his stomach as if he is in pain. "There's this spot inside me that hurts. Like something is tearing at it. I need it to go away."

His reaction frightens her. He has always been passionate, but this is beyond *his* normal. What is the drug doing to him?

"Benja. You're being a little . . ."

"Melodramatic?" He chuckles. "Yeah, I know. Please don't walk out on me."

She touches his cheek. "I won't. But I can't lie and tell you that mixing with this group is wise. I'm worried about you."

"There's nothing to worry about." He brushes her hand off. "I need to find another blue bird of happiness for my next meeting. Come help me. Please?" he asks.

"I can't come with you," she says. *Not anymore.* Her eyes are adjusting to the growing light.

CHAPTER TEN

"Where are you?" Thane asks.

"What?" says Aris.

"You look like you're a thousand miles away."

She blows air through her mouth. "You noticed."

"Is everything okay?"

In the last three weeks since Benja's Absinthe-altered dream, his obsession has taken a desperate turn. He talks of "the man in the white hat" like a craving. There are no conversations with him without a mention of Absinthe or his quest to reunite with the stranger he believes is his ex-lover.

"Yeah. I'm fine. It's just . . . my friend. You've met him. Benja. You remember him?"

"Are you two okay?"

"Yeah. It's more him. He's—"

The image of the Elaran man being led off by a policeman enters her mind. She studies Thane. Can she trust him? How much can she share? She has known him for almost four years. And during that time he has been nothing but kind and understanding. She decides she can.

"Benja's going through some problems. I'm afraid he may have gotten himself in trouble," she says, "He's being odd. I mean odder than his usual self. And I'm worried about him."

"What happened?"

"I think he's mixed up with some bad people. They gave him this drug."

"Like the kind you get at the hospital?" he asks.

There are ways one can experience an artificial euphoric state in the safe and controlled environment of the hospital. Administered and regulated by the staff, the substance has no lingering side effects. Aris had tried it once and found it a sterile and unimaginative experience.

"No, it doesn't sound like it. Now he's obsessed with getting more," she says.

"He's addicted?"

"I don't know. Maybe."

Addicts are rare. She has never understood them. To her, living is a high in itself. When you only have four years to make the most of each life, you pursue your passions or search for them, you don't look for ways to numb the experience. What's the point in that?

"He claims it makes his dreams more vivid. But I think it's just a hallucinogen. Who knows what it's doing to his brain," she says.

A beep comes from her watch.

"Speaking of," she says and looks down, not noticing a flash in Thane's eyes.

She walks to the far corner of the shared office.

"Benja?" she says to the small 3D image of his face projecting from her watch.

"Hey, can you come meet me at the Corner of Destiny and Fate?" His voice is anxious.

She cannot help but laugh.

"I'm serious. It's a restaurant. I think I found him," Benja says.

"Who are you talking about?"

"The man in the white hat. The love of my life," he says. "He's sitting at a coffee shop across from the Corner of Destiny and Fate. Isn't it so romantic and quaint?"

"Wait, you're stalking a stranger?" she whispers.

"He's not a stranger. I know him from my dreams."

"If he's not a stranger, then what's his name?"

"Man in the White Hat."

Aris scoffs. "How did you find him?"

"Never mind that. I really need you here. Can you please come?"

"Stalking is not really my cup of tea."

"I'm not doing anything bad. Come on. Please," he says. "Look, I know you think I'm crazy, and all this is stupid and a mistake. And you don't have to believe. Just please be with me. I need my friend."

She sighs. "Where's this place?"

"In Europa. I'll send you the location. If you catch the next train, you'll be here in no time."

"I'm still at work," she says.

"Tell Thane you need to come hold your pathetic friend's hand so he can gracefully meet the love of his life. He'll understand. Tell him."

She hangs up. She checks her schedule for today on her watch. November 13. No docent duty.

She looks at Thane as she walks toward him. There is an indecipherable expression on his face.

"Uh, Thane? Benja needs my help. I'm going to leave early," she says.

He nods and gives her a smile. It looks forced. Aris thinks back to what Benja said about him being interested in her. She shrugs off the thought and gathers her stuff to leave. She waves him goodbye, but he appears too preoccupied to notice.

By the time Thane comes out of his thoughts, Aris is gone. She left to be with Benja. Everything she said points to the writer having taken the drug that makes dreams more vivid, that makes people think they can remember the past—the drug the Interpreter Center seeks to destroy.

Add him to the list.

The thought gives Thane satisfaction. The first time he met the writer at the park, he did not like him. Or rather, he did not like how close he was with Aris. Seeing them together stirred a feeling in him that was foreign yet instinctive. Jealousy.

Thane has always been attracted to Aris. Her mind. Her humor. The dimples on the sides of her mouth. The way she absentmindedly plays with her hair in moments of deep thought.

She stirs him physically. She is all sun and warmth with honey skin and brown hair. At the park, she wore a summer dress that revealed her toned legs and cleavage. One of the straps dangled loosely on her shoulder, and she did not give it any mind. He remembers the desire to pull the other strap off and ravish her on the lawn.

She is the kind of woman he could see himself spending the rest of this cycle with. If only she wanted a romantic relationship. For as long as he has known her, commitment is the last thing she desires. But she is changing. Benja is influencing her. And he is dangerous.

Thane looks up. His eyes meet a piece of artwork on the wall. It is a painting of a circus. Inside a corral, a man in a black tuxedo stands with a whip in his hand. Near him is a female rider sitting sideways on a horse. Thane has never seen a horse in real life. They no longer exist.

He gets up and walks to the telephone. The only reason they have this obsolete item is for historical study. No one uses it, and he knows of only one other. It is the only method the system cannot trace.

He stares at the black object for a long while, playing out the consequences. What he does is vital to the peace of the city, but he still cannot help feeling conflicted. He would be betraying Aris's confidence.

He looks at the horse in the painting. He picks up the receiver. His index finger jabs into a small hole in the round disc. He rotates the dial. One number. Then another. Each one makes his breath catch in his throat.

After he selects the last number, he hears a tone. A familiar voice speaks.

"Hi, Professor Jacob. This is Thane," he says.

"How are you?" the professor's voice asks.

"Very well, thank you. You know the drug the Interpreter Center wants to destroy? I may have a lead."

Europa is a city of neighborhoods. Made up of high rises, brownstones, and boxy brick buildings—some with businesses on the ground floor.

Restaurants, bookstores, and coffee shops are on every block. At the Corner of Destiny and Fate, Aris finds Benja sitting alone, facing the window. He does not notice her. His eyes are fixed on a coffee shop across the street.

"Hey," she says.

He looks up. His eyes are glazed, as if he has just woken up. A smile touches his lips.

"Which one is he?" she asks and sits down.

Benja points to a man with salt-and-pepper hair sipping from a white cup by the window of the coffee shop.

"That's him. His hair is grayer now. But that's the face I saw in my dream."

"What's he doing in there in the middle of a Thursday?" she asks.

"I think he's writing."

"He's a writer too?"

"Yeah—it's crazy."

"Says the person who's been spying on a stranger from across the street for hours."

"He's not a stranger. I keep telling you that I know him. I've probably always known him—my entire lifespan."

"I doubt you two met at the CDL. You don't look like you've been around as long as he has," she says.

"I just have good genes."

"Honestly, is this what you've been doing all day?" she asks.

He nods.

"The Matres would be so disappointed if they knew you were squandering your day like this," she says.

According to the *Manual of the Four Cities*, the Matres raise and educate all children from birth to age eighteen at the Center of Discovery and Learning. They dedicate their entire lifetime to the ideology of the Planner. To maintain a world where all humans live alongside each other in peace, they work tirelessly to encourage the children to be the best version of themselves. Aris doesn't remember the Matres she grew up with. No one does.

"You know, for a friend you nag a lot," he says.

"This is what you get, calling me here."

Benja places his hand on hers. "Thank you. It means a lot to me that you're here. Even if you're not a believer."

She smiles. "Who else is going to talk some sense into you and get you out of trouble?"

"Trouble is a good place to be in," he says and winks, reminding Aris of the first time they met. Has it only been a few months? She feels as if she has known him for much longer.

He goes back to staring at the profile of the man across the street with his wistful eyes. The air is thick with the humidity of his melancholy, making it hard to breathe. Being in love is torturous, Aris thinks. A foolish endeavor.

"Do you think they're like us? The Matres?" asks Benja.

"What do you mean, 'like us'?"

"Humans. With memories no longer than four years."

"I don't think they're exactly like us. Can't be. The children don't get Tabula Rasa until after they're eighteen. I don't think they'd react well having to remind the people raising them who they are every four years," Aris says.

"They're droids, you think?"

"I don't know. I don't think so. Droids don't have the emotional complexity needed to raise children. Judging by how capable you and I are of expressing emotions, I'm pretty sure we weren't raised by droids."

"Well, *I* was definitely not raised by droids." Benja gives her a sideways look.

"What's that supposed to mean?"

"Never mind."

"What?"

"It's just—well, you don't really show your feelings much."

"So what, I'm dead inside?" Aris feels the heat of anger rising.

"No. I know there's a lot going on inside you. You just don't show it. You're all . . . walled off."

She gets up. "Well, enjoy your emotional ride then."

Benja grabs her hand. "No, don't leave."

"I don't feel like being dissected."

"I'm sorry. Occupational hazard. Please stay."

The pleading look in his eyes mollifies her. She sits back down. They return to staring across the street.

"Do you remember anything about growing up at the CDL?" he asks without taking his eyes off the man.

She shakes her head. "No. Do you?"

"Sometimes I see a face and get a feeling that I've met the person before. Sometimes I develop a strong like or dislike of someone I don't have a history with. I don't know if I met them in a past cycle or at the CDL," he says. "I know that's not much of an answer."

"It's more than what I've heard from other people, which is nothing."

Her childhood at the CDL is a mystery. She does not even know where it is. No one does, except for those who currently live in it. Even though everyone went through it, nobody speaks of their time there. How can you talk of events you do not have a memory of?

No one knows, and no one will ever know. The Center is self-contained and private. Outsiders do not visit it. The Matres do not leave it. The children, like the ones Aris guided through the museum, are occasionally sent on a special train into the cities for field trips. But most of their time is spent in the cocoon of the CDL. It is an incubator of sorts. Before the children become adults. Before Tabula Rasa touches them.

"You, I immediately liked," Benja says, taking her hands.

"Really? I feel the same."

"I don't know why, but I feel so comfortable with you." He squeezes her hands.

She squeezes back. "Me too."

His grip becomes tighter. "Shhh! He got up."

Aris looks across the street. The man exits the door of the coffee shop and turns right.

"Where are you going?" Benja murmurs.

"Probably home," she says.

"Let's follow him."

"I don't want to be a stalker."

"You're not. I am. You're just my . . . moral support," he says.

"Then I'm obliged to tell you, just in case you don't already know, that this is by no means a moral situation," she says.

"Come on." He pulls her hand and leads her out the door.

They race across the busy street, dodging surprised pedestrians as they pass. Aris feels air stirring her hair. Exhilaration courses through her. She is a party to something forbidden.

A combination of feelings rise. Apprehension, yes. But behind it is something else she did not expect. Hope. Could there be a part of her that wants to believe in Benja's quest?

What would she do if Benja is right? What if dreams really are a portal to memories from the past cycles? Would she be converted? Would she be the next in line to accept a drink from the Sandman?

She almost runs into a woman carrying a large bouquet of rainbow chard. The woman clutches the vegetables to her chest. Her eyes widen in surprise.

"Sorry!" Aris yells over her shoulder. It must be farmers' market day in Europa.

Benja looks at her. "Admit it, this is fun."

She scoffs.

The man walks fast, as if rushing to a meeting.

"Where are you going?" Benja whispers.

"Do you think he knows he's being followed?" asks Aris.

"I don't know."

Without warning, Benja pushes her against the wall of a townhouse and plants a drawn-out kiss on her.

"Here, that should throw him off," he says.

Aris wipes her lips. "This is the weirdest situation I've ever been in in this cycle. And I dated a poet who insisted on writing on my naked body."

"Sexy," says Benja.

She gives him a dirty look. "Not where he told me he wanted to write."

"Did you let him?" Benja asks.

"Yeah, of course. But I regretted it. The a-hole used permanent ink. It took me a week to get rid of it."

Benja shakes his head. "Haven't I taught you anything? Sweetie, the word is 'asshole.' And never, ever let anyone use anything permanent on you."

They continue to follow. The man turns the corner, and they find themselves in an older section of the city where Italianate brownstones stand in perfect rows on tree-lined streets.

Benja yanks her behind a tree. She loses balance and almost falls backward. He holds her close—close enough that she can feel his heart beating. The quick and erratic thumping worries her he might pass out from the rush of blood through his veins.

"He just stopped," he whispers.

They slowly peek out from either side of the tree, like children playing hide-and-seek. Except they are not children. And it is not a game. If Benja is right, they are committing an act that undermines Tabula Rasa. If he is not, they are stalking a stranger. Neither is what they should be doing.

Benja's hand grabs hers. She holds it tightly, feeling its dampness.

The man walks up the stairs of the building. The door opens. Another man, younger than him, jumps into his arms, and they kiss.

Benja's hand goes limp, as if all the bones have dissolved. Aris feels each finger slip out of her hold, hollowing out her hand and heart. She is afraid to look at him.

There is a part of her, the part that wants to believe in fairytales, that hoped Benja would reunite with his lover. She wants to see him happy and not as a delusional man. She wants to believe that love can last a lifetime. A stupid, illogical hope. Disappointment pierces her like cold sheets of rain. Her heart breaks for him.

She stares at the couple. They appear to be the kind who would live their entire cycle, what's left of it, with each other. She gathers her courage and turns to her friend. The look on his face makes her want to grab him and run to another corner of the Four Cities. An imagined loss does not feel any less agonizing if the person believes it is real.

"I'm sorry," she says. It's all she can muster. She does not know how to deal with loss. She never had to. Tabula Rasa takes care of that.

"Minor nuisance," he says, his eyes are fixed on the door of the brownstone. His words make her blood run cold.

"Benja . . . this is enough," she says.

He does not hear her.

"They're probably just having sex. He's experimenting," he mutters.

"They look in love," she says.

"In love? How can he be in love with him if he's in love with me?" he says, looking at Aris squarely. His eyes are bloodshot.

"*You* are in love with *him*," she says. The man probably has no memory of Benja or their past cycle. If he even was his lover.

"Because I finally remember . . ."

"Or *think* you remember. It's the drug that messed with your brain."

"I told you it's rea—" He pauses. The silence makes her nervous.

"You know what?" he says. "That's what he needs! Absinthe. Then he'll remember."

"You're going to convince a man who sees you as a stranger to take a mysterious drink from another stranger? No one in their right mind . . ."

"I'll figure it out."

"Benja . . ."

Aris realizes that his obsession has consumed him. She has let it carry her into a ridiculous flight of fancy long enough. He is not going to stop. If she stays, she would only be drawn in deeper.

"I'll take you home," he says.

He takes her hand. She pulls away. She cannot enable his madness any longer. Her heart cannot take it.

"I'll take myself home," she says.

"Aris . . ."

"You should go home and get some sleep. I'll call you later."

She kisses him on the cheek and heads toward the train station.

CHAPTER ELEVEN

The farther Aris is from Benja, the angrier she becomes. Away from him, her logical side kicks in. She is reminded that his dreams—the ones that turned him into a drug addict and a stalker—are mere fabrications of his brain. She decides to keep walking. Being stuck in a speeding train with no escape route is not ideal for her current state of mind.

The ragged blade of anger scrapes at her insides. But what or who is she angry at? Is it her friend and his antics? The Dreamers for fueling his obsession with a mind-altering drug? Or herself for going along with it?

Nobody is being forced into doing anything. Benja, the Dreamers, and she all operate under their own free will. Only one of those wills is under her control. That, she can fix. As to how easily, she is not certain.

She loves Benja. Not in the romantic, all-consuming way he loves the man from his dream. But in a way that his happiness and sadness affect hers. Her love is unhealthy because he is. She can already feel her mind fraying around the edges, exhausted from the disorderliness within.

Her friend is a victim of his own personality. His passion for life, tenacity, and confidence have transformed into irrationality, obsession, and blindness. He is consumed by his desire. It's hard to watch him go through the pain of wanting someone he cannot have. If this is what unrequited love does to a person, she does not want to be in its destructive path.

She shakes off the troublesome thought. Making the best of the situation, she decides to find the farmers' market with the rainbow chard. That will take care of dinner.

Farmers' markets happen unannounced and in random places within the Four Cities. After the fresh crop of the week is harvested and enough is put aside for equal distribution, the leftover gets flown to a spot by drones. It's free for the taking by those lucky enough to stumble upon it.

She turns a corner onto Fay Street and instead finds herself in the middle of a gift market. Tables line both sides of two city blocks. People peruse the tables, picking up and putting down items each holds.

Aris stops at a table where a woman with flowing auburn hair holds a wooden box to her chest. Her eyes are closed. The warm shade of the box matches her hair. The woman opens her eyes, sees Aris, and gives her a shy smile.

"I'm trying to feel whether it sparks any memory," the woman says.

"From past cycles?" Aris asks.

The woman nods. "I feel so sad for these things. They were once loved. But now their owners don't remember owning them."

Aris picks up a blue-and-green pot with an acorn design in front of her. These beautiful objects were once loved—the woman is right. Nothing here is broken or defective. They are just items left behind in homes after each cycle. The new inhabitants either found them not suited to their tastes or not useful. So, they take them to the gift market, hoping they will find a new home. Until the next cycle.

"Things are only meaningful if you remember why you have them," the woman says. "So I try to see if I can remember owning any of these things."

"Do you touch everything?" Aris asks.

"I try to. But sometimes there are too many things for the time I have."

Aris brings the pot to her chest.

"It helps if you close your eyes," the woman says.

Aris hesitantly closes her eyes. She looks in the darkness behind her lids and tries to see whether the pot once had a place in her past lives. On a mantle perhaps? Or on a bookcase under the stairs? What would she have used it for? The squat round pot is not big enough for flowers. Would it only be an object of admiration? Something beautiful always has admirers. That is how things often survive. Being beautiful.

She opens her eyes. The redhead smiles at her.

"Did you feel anything?" she asks.

"I'm not sure." Aris looks at the pot in her hand. It is now warm from her body heat. She runs her finger on it, liking its smoothness. The way the blues flow into the greens reminds her of a river weaving through water plants. She finds herself developing an attachment to it.

"I like it though," Aris says.

"A good match then," the woman says and walks off.

Aris watches as the redhead continues to examine the objects on each table, hoping to be reunited with her beloved things. She wonders how much time the woman has wasted in this cycle on trying to remember.

"That's beautiful," a deep and familiar voice says.

She looks up and meets Metis's brown eyes. The genius pianist she ran into in the rain. The one whose performance she ruined. She feels her cheeks warming.

"It's nice to see you again," he says with a smile. "We've never properly met. I'm Metis."

In the bright light of the day, she can see him better. His black hair is a little bit longer and slightly tousled, not slicked back like it was at his concert or drenched by the rain. It suits him and makes him look younger. Less severe. And very handsome.

Aris feels her heart beating faster.

"Hi. Um. I'm Aris."

Blood pulses in her face. She catches a glimpse of herself in the reflection of a store window and feels like digging a hole to hide in. This has never happened before. Is she starstruck? She is acting like a complete immature idiot.

"That's a nice find," he says. His eyes on the object she holds to her chest.

"Do you want it?" she asks and immediately shoves it into his hands. "Here, take it."

"Don't you want it?" His face is puzzled.

"No, it doesn't go with my house."

"Ah. If that's the case, I know just the spot for this."

"Do you live around here?" she asks.

"I live in Lysithea."

"In one of the Painted Ladies?"

He nods. It is as she has suspected.

"Why are you here?" Aris asks. "I mean—Sorry, you don't have to answer that."

He smiles. "There's a bookstore I like around the corner."

"Oh. Don't let me keep you."

"I just came from there. I'm actually on my way to Callisto. Carnegie Hall."

The memory of his concert surfaces.

"Are you okay?" he asks.

Shame must have shown on her face. She decides to confess.

"It was me," she says. "At your concert. I should have muted my watch. I'm sorry."

He gives her a gentle smile. "Don't be sorry."

"You were upset."

"I wasn't. I was . . . surprised. I don't handle surprises very well," he says and adds, "Thank you for being there."

Aris lets out a long sigh.

"I didn't realize you felt so bad about it," Metis says.

"Still do."

"You shouldn't."

"Did you come back to finish?" she asks.

"I did. It was immature of me to have left the stage in the first place."

"I'm sorry I didn't stay to see it."

He looks thoughtful, as if trying to make an important decision.

"I have a proposal," he says in a slow and deliberate way. "Since you didn't get to hear me play the entire concert, would you like to come with me to Carnegie Hall? I'll make up for it."

Aris's heart does a quick jump.

"Will I get to see the backstage?"

He nods his head. "Anything."

She smiles.

"This way," he says and points toward the train station.

She feels his warm fingers touching the small of her back. Then just as quickly, the warmth disappears.

Carnegie Hall is on the opposite end of the Park from the Natural History Museum, where she works. Aris does not normally venture to this section of the city except for concerts, so she lets Metis lead her.

They walk past the park, where the trees are bare and vulnerable. A biting breeze nips at the tip of her nose, and she hugs her jacket a little tighter.

People in their black and gray winter coats hurry past them. The wind picks up and rushes between the buildings, sending Aris's hair flying. She feels like she is walking in a wind tunnel. She gathers her hair in one hand and moves it over her shoulder. She looks at Metis from the corner of her eye. Strands of his hair flutter in the wind, but he does not seem bothered by the cold.

He says very little during their walk, but there is texture in his silence. She could almost feel the weight of the thoughts rippling off him. For a moment, she wonders how many women he has offered to play a private concert for. He seems too serious to be the type that uses his talent to lure in dates. And he is too good looking to need to. But she can never be sure.

"Let's cross here," he says.

He grabs her hand and leads her across the street. Aris feels her face heating up. She is becoming annoyed by how easily he is affecting her. Once they reach the other side, he lets go. She finds she misses the warmth of his hand.

Aris looks around. The street signs and buildings are unfamiliar. She has never walked this path before. She wonders when they are going to reach their destination.

They walk block after block, weaving through alleys and turning several corners. She wonders if he is making the direction confusing on purpose so she will not remember how to get back.

"We're here," Metis says, finally.

A brick building with a mellow ochre hue stands in front of them. They are in the back of a nondescript alley.

"This is Carnegie Hall?"

Metis nods and smiles.

Without the grand arched windows of the front facade, the building looks different.

"I've never seen it from this side before," she says.

"Wait until you see where I'm taking you," he says with the enthusiasm of a boy sharing a secret play spot.

There are several black doors on the side of the building—entrances for musicians and staff. Metis twists the handle of one door and pushes against it. It's darker inside. It takes a minute for Aris's eyes to adjust.

She follows him through a maze of hallways that he navigates with familiarity. They walk past exposed pipes and electrical lines. She hears clunking sounds from the silver air ducts above their heads. From this perspective, Carnegie Hall looks no different than the basement of any prewar building.

"Why is it so quiet?" she asks.

"It's a day off."

"Are you usually here on your day off?"

"More than I want to admit, I'm afraid."

They go up a flight of stairs that leads to more dark corridors. She wonders where he is taking her and is about to ask, when he stops in front of a pair of steel doors. He turns around to give her a wide smile before opening it.

Behind it is a white room. It does not look any more special than a storage closet, albeit a large one. On one side is a wall of cabinets, and on the other is a large panel with buttons whose functions she can only guess at. It's a utility room.

"We're here?" she asks.

"Almost," he says.

Metis takes her hand and pulls her forward. His palm is hot. She can almost feel his pulse from it.

They go through a set of heavy dark-gray velvet curtains into a space that is almost pitch black but for the sliver of light bleeding in from the utility room.

"Hold on. Stay here," Metis says and vanishes back through the curtains, taking the bit of light with him.

Looking out into complete darkness with opened eyes makes her feel uneasy—it's how she imagines the world would look if she were to lose her sight. She closes them. The sound of her breathing echoes in her ears. Even in darkness she can tell that she is standing in a cavernous room.

A light scent of carpet shampoo and paint touches her nose. There is a breeze coming from somewhere, making the space feel colder than the rest of the building. She crosses her arms over her chest to keep warm.

Suddenly the room lights up like the inside of the sun. She opens her eyes and blinks from the brightness. Once they adjust, she finds herself standing on a stage. Before her is the opulent concert hall with cream paneled walls and rows of blood-red velvet chairs. Outlining the walls of the oval room are multiple tiers of balconies. The highest one in the back has seats that climb almost to the ceiling. She looks up and sees two circles of lights around an elaborate carved and gilded design. The magnificent image is almost unbearable for the senses.

"How do you like seeing it from this view?" Metis's voice asks from beside her. She does not know when he got there.

"It's incredible," she whispers, "And terrifying." She turns to him, "How do you do it?"

He laughs. "I don't usually look out there when I perform. I just focus on the keys in front of me or let the music carry me somewhere else."

She notices a shiny black piano a few feet away from where they stand. Metis walks to it and sits on the bench. He taps on the spot next to him.

"There's room here. Or if you'd prefer, you can take one of the seats below."

She walks toward him and the piano.

"I'll take my chances here," she says with a smile.

Aris sits next to Metis. Heat emanates from him. It is as if he generates his own weather system.

He draws in a deep, long breath and places his fingers on the keys. His back straightens as if pulled up by an invisible string. She remembers the powerful music from his concert that sent her up into the sky like fireworks and grabs onto the bench to brace herself.

The first notes strike, and the music is . . . different. Gentle and dreamy. Like wading in a lake bathed in moonlight. Her heartbeat slows.

"Schumann, 'In the Evening,'" he says. "I usually play this after dinner. When the house is quiet and still."

He sounds sad. Aris glances at him. His eyes are closed. From the side, his cheekbones look more prominent, as if carved from marble by an artist's hand. She wonders what he is thinking.

Feeling as if she has invaded his privacy, she turns away and closes her eyes too. Without her sight, her mind opens. She sees an image of them sitting in a room lit by candles. Thin wisps of smoke rise. Shadows dance on the walls of an old house that creaks as it settles in before slumber.

The music transitions. Another song. Soft and contemplative this time. Like a lone walk in the park during a light sprinkle.

"Whose is it?" she asks.

"Brahms. One of his intermezzi."

As the song reveals itself, it becomes surprising. The notes rise and fall, traveling down a path of varying emotions and colors. Sweet and gentle. Deep and introspective. Hopeful and warm.

She feels as if she is reading a book where the author skillfully shares the story with a subtlety and complexity that keeps her wanting more. The song continues to explore the range of emotions until it slows down to melancholic notes toward the end. It leaves her feeling a sense of longing. For what, she does not know.

The song changes, taking a happy, exuberant turn. This one makes her imagine trees uprooting and dancing in the park. She feels the lightness of spring enveloping her. Leaf buds emerging to bathe in the warmth of the sun. Grass waking up from its long rest underground, pushing its way upward to greet the world. Bees buzz about, flitting from flower to flower. The scent of hope rises in the air. *Or is it roasted chestnuts?* Spring is still months away.

"Play me one of your favorites," she says.

The rhythm slows to a solemn pace. The notes are laced with despair.

"I normally play this alone," he says, "Especially when I want to wallow in self-pity."

She wonders what he feels sad about. She wants to ask, but a part of her is afraid to know.

He continues, "Tchaikovsky wrote a set of twelve songs, each piece representing the months and seasons. This one is called 'October,' describing autumn in Russia."

In her mind, Aris sees yellow leaves dropping and flying in the wind. They rise into the sky and drift with the clouds to a distant place. They fall on a landscape of snow and ice. She watches as snow falls, burying the leaves under the white flakes. Blustery wind blows against her cheeks, biting them. Emptiness sits heavy in the pit of her stomach. She aches for the sun and the warmth of her lover's embrace.

She feels lips on hers, hot and soft, waking her from the trance. She opens her eyes and sees Metis. Her heart flutters like the wings of a bumble-bee. She is the leaf in her imagination, being carried up the sky by the wind. She closes her eyes again and lets the feeling take her to a place far away.

Aris's watch beeps.

"Ignore it," Metis whispers between kissing her.

She does. But the insistent sound continues. It is unusual. Reaches that are not connected get translated to a databank for later retrieval.

"I think I need to take this," she says, "I'm sorry."

She walks through the gray curtains to the backstage room. As soon as she puts the reach through, the image of a man in a brown fedora appears.

"Hello. I'm Officer Scylla of Station Eighteen. I'm reaching you on behalf of Benja. You're his emergency contact."

Aris feels coldness running through her veins.

"Is he okay?"

"Yes, he's at the station."

"What happened?" asks Aris.

"He was found in a state of undress inside someone's house. He had broken into it by force."

The man in the white hat. What was he thinking?

"Is everyone okay?" she asks.

"Yes, everyone's fine. Nobody pressed any charges. The people who live there said they don't know him and that it must be a misunderstanding. Benja was inebriated at the time."

"What can I do to help?" she asks.

"I'm keeping him here for the night. You can come pick him up at the station in the morning. Let me warn you that he may be embarrassed when you see him. We advise that you show him some empathy and understanding. He will need to be with people who care about him," he says.

"Thank you, Officer."

Aris feels like screaming.

Stupid man! What were you thinking?

He was not thinking, she decides. He is beyond reason. His senses have been taken over by his irrational quest to bring back the man he believes is his old lover. If only he had not gone to the Dreamers' meeting and taken the drug. The drug is to blame. That and the dangerous characters Benja is keeping company with.

Metis comes through the curtains. "Is everything all right?"

She looks at him. There are so many feelings surging through her she does not know how to handle it. If she stays there any longer, she is afraid she will do something she would regret. Like crying.

"What's wrong?" he asks.

"Nothing. I have to go. I'm sorry."

"Aris, please tell me what's wrong."

"My friend's in trouble. I have to go pick him up in the morning at the police station."

"I'll come with you."

"No, that's okay. You better not. I'm sorry," she says and rushes off.

CHAPTER TWELVE

The police station is quiet like the dead Animals of the Americas section at the Natural History Museum. Aris is the only one in the waiting room. She took the day off work to be here. The glaring light above irritates her. The fluttering cold blue glow makes her feel agitated and jittery.

She hears the sound of footsteps and looks up. A man is walking through the door. Aris remembers him as Officer Scylla. He was the one who contacted her.

"Hello, Aris. Thank you for coming. Benja just woke up. He's resting in a holding room."

"May I see him?" she asks.

"Of course. Please follow me."

He leads her through a long corridor and stops in front of a door to a room. There is a glass window she can see through. On the other side is Benja. He is reclining on a white bed, facing the opposite direction. One of his legs rests on the knee of another. It moves to a rhythm of music Aris cannot hear.

"When will he be released?" she asks.

The officer looks at his watch. "In a few minutes. His sentence is almost done."

The justice system is a mystery to her. No one she knows has ever committed a crime before.

"What's his sentence?"

"One night in a holding room. It's mostly to keep him from inflicting harm on others by accident."

"Do things like this happen a lot?"

"Not really."

"Are you the only police officer?" She has not seen anyone else here.

"There are many of us in different stations across the Four Cities. But I'm usually by myself here. I don't need help, really. Benja is my second arrest this month."

"What was your last case?" Aris asks.

"Another public disturbance."

The angry man.

"Was it the man causing trouble by the Natural History Museum?" she asks.

Officer Scylla's eyes widen. "Why, yes. How do you know?"

"I was there. I saw you take him away."

"Ah."

"Did you hold him here too?"

"His case was different. Since he was being treated by the Interpreter Center, I had to turn him over to their care. They said he's fine after treatment. There's nothing to worry about."

"Do you often send people there?" she asks.

"Only if I have to. I can't say I agree with their treatment. Our minds already go through enough trauma every four years. While the Interpreter Center insists there are no side effects to their treatment, I just don't like the idea of tampering with the brain unless absolutely necessary."

Officer Scylla's watch beeps.

"It's time," he says and unlocks the door.

Benja turns his head in their direction.

"Hey, Aris," he says casually.

Aris wants to yell at him, but she is reminded by the officer's eyes to be sympathetic.

"Uh. Hey, Benja. Are you ready to go home?" she asks in as even a tone as she can muster.

"Yeah. It's boring here. No offense."

"None taken," the officer says. "Being boring is kind of the point to this place."

Benja raises his right hand to the air. That is when Aris realizes he is wearing more than one watch. The officer walks to him and swipes a finger across the surface of the silver bangle. It unbuckles and falls into his waiting hand. Benja closes his eyes and massages his temples.

"The grogginess will last for the next few hours. It's just the side effect of the device," Officer Scylla says.

Aris asks, "What is it?"

The officer holds up the silver bangle. "A calming device."

"So I wouldn't resist arrest," says Benja. "It kept me docile."

The officer chuckles. "You didn't really need it. You were completely unconscious. It's just a precaution."

Officer Scylla helps Benja up from his bed. "Off you go."

"Your bed is hard," Benja says as he massages his lower back. "It needs more cushion."

"Well, we don't want to attract those looking to replace their beds, do we?" He turns to Aris. "Hasn't been a problem. We're all pretty well taken care of in the Four Cities."

Once they are outside Station 18, Benja turns to Aris.

"Thanks for picking me up. You didn't really need to. The officer was being too cautious. Probably thinks I'm still drunk."

"He told me not to say this, but that was a really stupid thing you did, breaking into that house. What possessed you?"

He sighs. "You wouldn't understand. You've never been in love."

"Yeah, and I don't want to. It's like a disease that ate your brain. At least your sentence was only confinement."

He looks at her with wide eyes and doubles over in laughter.

"What's funny?" she asks.

He wipes tears from his eyes. "When are you going to see that we're all in permanent confinement? The entire Four Cities is our prison."

"We're free to leave whenever we want."

"And go where?" he asks. "We're not capable of going anywhere, Aris.

I don't even know how to grow a head of lettuce. Do you? Everything we have—all our food, our shelter, the clothes we wear—is provided to us, packaged and perfect. We are kept locked in chains, with a permanent shackle around our wrists."

He crosses his wrists together and raises them above his head in a theatric pose. Without another word, he turns and walks off.

"Where are you going?" she yells at his back.

He looks over his shoulder. "With you, silly. We're stuck together in this perpetual semireality. Can't you see?"

Benja is in a rare contemplative mood. Aris takes his silence for remorse, an atonement for breaking into his old lover's house. She wonders what the couple thought when they saw an Adonis of a man draped across their bed like a water nymph, as naked as the day he was born.

She can no longer stand the silence. "What are you thinking?"

"I didn't even get to see his face up close. I passed out and came to at the station."

"You're kidding. Didn't you learn anything from being arrested?"

Benja ignores her question. "It felt so unreal, walking through his house, seeing evidence of his other life with someone else. Last thing I remember seeing was his clothes. They smell just like him in my dreams. I wanted to put them on, to feel him against my skin again."

She feels a rush of sympathy for him. Her friend is more desperate than she had thought. Incurable.

Benja runs his hand through his hair and blows out air in frustration.

"I feel so hopeless. Have you ever felt this way? Like a big part of you is missing?"

Aris shakes her head.

"It's a horrible affliction. I haven't been able to sleep. I'm anxious all the time. And look"—he lifts his shirt—"I have this rash that won't go away. Am I going crazy?"

"Yeah. You're in love," she says. Seeing Benja this way makes her even more convinced that nothing good comes out of romantic attachment.

He sighs and walks to her window. Outside the sky is gray with a thick covering of clouds. Snow is coming in the late afternoon.

"I need more Absinthe," he says.

"More drugs? Hasn't it done enough damage?"

"I don't want to forget my life with him."

"Can you even hear yourself talk? The drug is dangerous, Benja. It's turning you into this wraith of a man. When was the last time you ate?"

He laughs. "A wraith. You're poetic when you're mad. It's cute."

"I'm serious. Don't you know that the Interpreter Center has this procedure that can erase dreams?"

"I know. The Crone told us about it at the meeting."

"Aren't you even a bit afraid they would do that to you?"

"I wouldn't let them. I'd never go in and have my dreams erased. You know that, right?"

"What if it's not up to you?"

"I won't get caught. I'll be more careful."

"Careful at what? At stalking? At breaking and entering? What are you going to do next? Steal his clothes? Burn him in them?"

"I'll be careful," he says, "Besides, I have you."

"What are you talking about?"

"You're paranoid enough for the both of us. There's no way you'd let anyone take my dreams."

"I don't know about that. Your dreams are becoming a pain in my ass."

He looks at her earnestly. "Promise me you won't let them take my dreams."

"How am I going to do that?"

"Just promise me."

"Benja was arrested by the police," says Thane. "He broke into someone's house when he was drunk. The police let him go."

"Another dangerous addict," Apollina says. "We should bring him in."

"Are you any closer to the supplier?" Professor Jacob asks.

Thane shakes his head. "I haven't seen Benja with anyone."

He lied. He sees Benja often with Aris. But there is no need for the Interpreter Center to know about her. She has nothing to do with this; Thane is sure of it. Aris does not like what Benja is doing. She would never be a part of it.

"You need to get closer," Professor Jacob says.

"Follow him and report back," Apollina says.

Thane nods.

"Meanwhile, I'll start a case on him. We may need to act on this one before he makes any more trouble," she says.

Thane will be happy once the Interpreter Center erases Benja's dreams and he doesn't have to follow him anymore. Benja has been a source of annoyance ever since Thane laid eyes on him in the park with Aris.

Nothing but a handsome face. There's probably no substance there.

Benja does little during the day but visit coffee shops and libraries. At night he frequents bars. He does not go to work. He does not contribute to society. He said he's a writer, but Thane has yet to see him do that in all the time he's followed him. All Benja does is drink and read. Sometimes he stares at the wall or the trees or the people walking by. Benja is the most boring human being Thane has ever known, and he knows a lot of scientists.

Writer. Yeah, right.

When Thane thinks of writers, he thinks of someone like Professor Jacob, who has produced a book of significance supported by facts and knowledge. Hard work was put into it. References cross-checked and substantiated. Results mind-shattering and socially relevant. A work of fiction like Benja's, while perhaps entertaining, could never measure up to the *Manual of the Four Cities.*

"Thane?" Professor Jacob's voice brings him back.

"Yes?"

"Do you think you'll have the report done by next week?"

"Of course."

"Thank you. I look forward to reading it," the Professor says.

Thane feels a warmth around his heart. Although the work the Interpreter Center gave him is mind numbing, Professor Jacob's appreciation makes him feel better than he could ever imagine.

Metis's fingers travel fluidly over the piano keys. The melancholic moodiness of the first movement of Beethoven's *Moonlight* Sonata matches his state of mind. He thought it an appropriate piece considering the master often pined after unattainable women.

A month had passed since the day he kissed Aris. He has tried countless times to reach her. But each time, he was transferred to her databank. He must have left twenty messages, each one more pathetic than the last. She has yet to return one. She is erasing him from memory. Again.

He looks at the blue-and-green pot on top of his piano. It reminds him of the day they met at the gift market. The time they spent together here. Her sitting next to him on a piano bench. The kiss.

A sigh escapes. He cannot figure out how to categorize his relationship with Aris. He still loves her; they are not divorced. Although sometimes it feels like they are. He is not a widower; his wife is not dead. Although it sometimes feels like she is. A marriage is an agreement between two people to be monogamous. He does not know if she is. Can it be a marriage if it's one-sided?

She cannot remember him. Their life together has been wiped from her memory as if it had never existed. He is married to a ghost. Perhaps that is how he should think of it.

The sound of a door closing comes from behind him, waking him from his thoughts. He turns around.

"Hey, Argus," Metis says to his friend.

Argus comes to stand next to the piano. "Sorry, I didn't mean to make you stop playing."

"Nah. I'm just tinkering."

Metis gently runs his fingers over the piano keys in a complicated arrangement.

"I don't know how you do it," Argus says.

"I don't know either. Some things are just the way they are."

"Remember when we first met? I was at a pretty low point in my music study, but you told me I could be a musician."

"You can."

"Not like you."

"And I couldn't be like you. Everyone's different."

"But I still get to work at the coolest place in the Four Cities," Argus says. "Did I ever thank you for getting me a job here?"

Metis smiles. "I'm happy you're here. Are you still happy?"

"Yeah, it fits. I never thought I'd ever find something that suits me." "People keep telling you to find your passion. Thought I was missing a part."

"Passion is overrated," Metis says, "Happiness, on the other hand, is undervalued."

"You should try it sometime. It'll be good for you."

Metis continues to play on the keys, running through the scales.

"If only human emotions were as easily manipulated."

"What I can never figure out is why someone like you has no one."

"Are you hitting on me, Argus?"

He bursts out laughing. "Not today. I have a date."

"Who's the lucky person?"

"Someone I met at a coffee shop."

"Do people still meet each other that way? I thought everyone's using the app to find a match."

"Love is not predictable, man. You need a bit of fate."

Fate. Something Metis is losing faith in. Sometimes when he feels optimistic, he tells himself that if he and Aris were meant to be together, things will fall into place. She will remember and resume her place beside him. He was so close. But it slipped away. It seems fate is making itself scarce lately.

"She has a friend," Argus says.

"Good for her."

"No, for *you*."

"I know what you meant. I was just being obnoxious," Metis says.

"So, are you interested? She's cute."

It would make life so much easier to have someone to spend the rest of this cycle with, Metis thinks. But Aris's face appears in front of him like a phantom, chasing away any thought of straying.

"Thanks, Argus. Not today."

"Will there ever be a day?"

"I hope so."

"You know, there's no perfect person. You just have to find happiness wherever it exists."

"I'm not waiting for a perfect person." *Just one particular person.*

"Then who are you waiting for?"

He says nothing back.

"Well, I hope whoever the person is, they're worth waiting for."

"I hope so too."

His friend shakes his head. "You know, you can talk about it with me when you're ready to share."

"I know. I appreciate that."

"Oh, by the way, someone asked me to give you this." Argus pulls something out of his pocket and places it in front of Metis next to the blue-and-green pot.

The blue origami crane sits innocuously against the shiny black top of the piano. At first, Metis does not register it. Then his breathing stops. He feels his insides rearranging to make room for the pending explosion of his heart.

"Who gave it to you?" he whispers.

"I'm guessing a fan. A handsome fellow. Very tall. He was waiting outside in the morning. Looked like he hadn't slept. He must really like you."

Metis reaches for the bird with quivering hand. He tries to steady it. He has never been on the receiving end of this.

Benja.

But why? And how? And what message does it carry?

Aris listens to the messages from Metis with a heavy heart. There is no denying the physical attraction she feels toward him. Her body reacts to his—a little too much for her comfort, in fact. It's as if she has no control over it.

The kiss was unexpected. The feeling it stirred inside her was even more startling. It rolled over her like a tidal wave, making her feel as if she was drowning. Yet it somehow felt familiar.

It was the heat. The warmth of him was like a place she had visited. The feel of his lips . . . Even with space and time between them, the memory of that kiss still makes her hands tremble.

But there is no point. It's mid-December. There are only a few months left before Tabula Rasa. Forming a bond with someone she will soon say goodbye to is ridiculous. Look at the mess she already got herself into with Benja, and she has only known him for a couple of months longer. There are some people in life you develop strong feelings for in an instinctual, irrational way. She is afraid Metis is one of those for her.

"I'm sorry," she whispers and erases his voice from her databank.

CHAPTER THIRTEEN

Benja is a tough man to follow. The man is erratic. One moment he would walk aimlessly, pausing here and there to look up at a tree or passing clouds. The next he would dart into a coffee shop or a bar.

What are you doing? Metis wonders.

The moon is a sliver against the dark indigo sky. It is so cold he can see puffs of vapor coming out with each exhale. Metis turns up the heat inside his jacket and hugs it tight. He finds a spot on a bench across the street from the coffee shop Benja went into. Here, he would wait.

Argus was right. By the look of Benja, it's apparent he has not slept in days. His face is haggard. His hair is unkempt. His clothes are crumpled as if he has been living in them for longer than he should. He looks the way Metis feels inside. Wretched and throbbing with longing. He wants his lover.

Metis understands. He knows what it feels like to be singular in one's desire. Seeing Benja in this state is like looking at his own past and future at the same time. Is he really that different from Benja? He stalks his old lover, follows her to where she lives, and leaves her desperate messages. He is a bottle of wine away from breaking into her house and sleeping on her bed naked.

He shakes off his empathy. It would only complicate matters. He thinks of the paper crane in his pocket. In it is an address. For whatever reason, Benja wants to speak to the Sandman in private, outside the confines of the meeting. But how does Benja know that he is the Sandman? And if he knows, who else does?

The last time Metis saw him was after the last meeting. He was vibrating with nervous energy. They usually are after taking Absinthe.

"Uh, Sandman? Do I call you Sandman?"

Metis said nothing.

"I've been wanting to ask you. How does one get their lover to remember them?" Benja asked.

If only he knew, Metis thought.

"The past and the present cannot coexist. That's the rule."

"But what's the point? I mean, no offense, but if you can remember and the other person can't, isn't it torture?" Benja said.

"Look around. Do you see a happy face here?" Metis's voice was terse. "The purpose for all of us being here is to remember. That's all. To remember our past and remind ourselves how it feels to love and be loved."

"But wouldn't you want to make that into reality?"

More than anything, Metis thought.

Instead, he said, "Let me be clear. The moment you try to force someone into remembering, you risk exposing us. Not to discount the moral aspect of it. Everyone has the right to author their own life."

Benja scoffed. "You sound like the Planner's propaganda."

Metis stiffened. "Just because Tabula Rasa took our past from us doesn't mean we can thrust our vision of the future on another. We'd be no different than the system we're trying to resist."

"But you have this powerful gift in your hands. What if we can make our world into the one where we don't have to compromise? We could have everything." Benja's eyes danced with fervor.

What Benja had said sounded so simple and enticing. What is the harm in making this world a place where both peace and the past can coexist? In that world, he would have Aris. Or would he? Metis shakes his head. It is a dangerous path to venture. It would expose Absinthe.

The powerful dream agent must be protected. It's the only tool they have against Tabula Rasa. It was made for those who want to remember, for those who believe dreams are the window to the past. It is a direct assault on the Planner's ideology. There are people seeking to destroy it, the Crone has warned.

He wishes he had thrown Benja out of the group that day, before his recent trouble with the law could have threatened their anonymity. There are many who might suffer from his recklessness. Metis cannot have another situation like he did with Bodie.

When Bodie got arrested, the Interpreter Center erased his dreams. He had since moved back to Elara. There was nothing left for him in Callisto. With no dreams, no memories, no past, Absinthe would have no effect on him.

Metis begins to get restless. His fingertips and face are so cold he can no longer feel them. Benja has been inside the coffee shop a long time. Metis debates whether to get a closer look or continue waiting. He would have to be careful. Now that Benja knows his identity, it will not be as easy to follow him. When he decides to get up, he sees Benja emerging from the coffee shop. Metis pulls his jacket collar up higher to hide his face and follows.

Benja is taking the path that runs alongside the main park in the middle of Callisto, toward the direction where tall buildings block out the sky. The streets are sparse of people. The citizens here are used to knowing the weather with precision, and most have chosen the warmth of their homes this evening.

The cold wind whips Metis's hair back. He is grateful for its sound, which masks the echo of his footsteps. As the Sandman, it is his responsibility to do reconnaissance on those Dreamers he thinks are in danger of violating the rules. Fortunately, most want to keep their place in the group and steer clear of trouble. But there are always a handful with strong wills. Metis never likes to cut anyone off Absinthe, and he has never done it without proof. Benja will be the first.

They enter a residential neighborhood of skyscrapers. Benja crosses the street to a building with 2020 in large, modern type above the wide entrance. The address matches that on the crane in his pocket. Benja's apartment.

Instead of going inside, Benja stands in front of the building. Metis keeps his head down and walks past.

What am I doing? he asks himself.

Metis has come this far because he wants to know why Benja sent him the crane. More than that, he wants to find out how he knows his identity. He crosses the street on the next block and backtracks toward the building.

Benja is standing ahead. He is so still he reminds Metis of a droid. Benja's eyes are staring across the way, toward the darkness of the park. In it, naked-limbed trees stand tall and attenuated like Giacometti sculptures. Benja turns, sees Metis, and cracks a wide smile. He has been expecting him.

"I'm glad you decided to come. Would you like to talk inside?" Benja says.

"Tell me why I should."

"Because I'll make it worth your time."

"There's nothing you have that I want."

"I bet there is."

Metis narrows his eyes and studies the man in front of him. Despite his carefree facade, the look in Benja's eyes is serious. He does not know what game Benja is playing, but he is intrigued.

Metis looks through the window to the lobby. It's empty. He nods his agreement. Benja leads him inside the building toward an express elevator that only goes to floors above the fortieth. He chooses an elevator car and pushes a button to a floor near the top. Metis walks to the back corner opposite him.

"So, how was your stay at the police station?" Metis asks, breaking the silence.

Benja laughs. "You heard about that, huh?"

"We watch all the Dreamers. I thought that was clear."

"Yeah. I got that from the first meeting."

"You know that's reason for expulsion," Metis says.

"I know."

"Why did you do it then? I assume you like our little group," Metis asks.

Benja does not answer. Instead, he asks, "You don't like me, do you?"

"Not particularly."

He shrugs. "I'm used to it. Men usually don't. Unless they're attracted to me. But your dislike for me was instant. Even before I opened my mouth."

Metis does not disagree.

"I used to wonder why. Then I knew," Benja says.

The elevator door opens, and Benja steps off. Metis follows.

After walking down a long corridor lined with identical doors, they stop at the last one on the left.

"Let me in," Benja says.

The wide door swings open to reveal a large loft space. In the middle of it is a platform bed sitting low to the ground. Out the wall-to-wall window is the large black rectangle of the park outlined by dots of lights from the buildings that surround it.

"It's a bit dramatic having the bed in the middle, I know. But I like to think of dreaming as a play on a stage," Benja says.

He goes to the other side of the room, where an L-shaped couch faces the sweeping city view. He plops onto its cushy surface.

Metis walks to the expansive glass window directly across from him and leans against it.

"It looks much better in daylight, obviously," Benja says.

"As much as I'd like to admire your view, let's cut the crap. I don't have all night."

Benja laughs. "Of course. I know I'm not as gratifying to follow as Aris."

Metis's breath catches in his throat. The windowpane behind him suddenly feels like a sheet of ice on his back.

Benja says, "Don't worry. She doesn't know your other identity. I just figured it out recently."

"How?" Metis whispers.

"The gift market on Fay Street. Aris and I had a fight, and I followed her to make sure she was okay. I noticed you shadowing her. Then you introduced yourself to her and left together. Afterward, I kept seeing you in various places we were at, just . . . lurking."

"How do you know my name?" He wonders if Aris ever mentioned him to her friend.

"She listens to your music all the time. There's a song she has on rotation. The one that sounds really pretty."

"*Luce?*"

"Yeah." Benja chuckles. "You know, it's usually the fan who does the stalking."

"And how about my other identity?"

"That one was pure, unadulterated accident. One of the times I saw you, I decided to follow you. Then I realized we were going to the same place."

"The meeting," says Metis, "Was that why you asked me how to get your old lover to remember their past?"

"She was your lover, wasn't she?" Benja asks.

"Yes," Metis says and immediately feels lighter. The secret had been weighing heavily on him.

Benja shakes his head. "You're such a hypocrite."

Metis feels blood rushing to his face. Benja does not hold his punches.

"She really likes you, you know? I mean, she hasn't told me about you. That's why I know you're different from the other guys she dated. Plus, she hasn't gone out with anyone else since the gift market."

Metis feels his heart growing in his chest.

"So, what are you going to do?" Benja asks.

"What do you mean?"

"You know, to get her to remember?"

"I'm not. She's entitled to her life."

"A hypocrite and a moron. And to think I admired you."

"What would you have me do? Take off my clothes and break into her house?"

"For the record, I broke into the house *before* I took off my clothes."

Metis shakes his head. "Do you care about anyone but yourself? There are consequences to every action, and you've already put yourself in a bad situation. I'll be damned if you drag the rest of us down with you."

Benja's face reddens. He mumbles, "No one knows about you guys."

Metis narrows his eyes. "Does Aris?"

Benja says nothing.

Metis speaks slowly so the words would sink in, "You have no idea how precious Absinthe is. The authorities would destroy it the first chance they get. It must be protected."

"What's the point of protecting it if you can't use it to its full potential? Why not give it to her and spare yourself the pain?"

"It has to be her choice. You can't mix your past and present."

Benja scoffs. "Yeah, yeah, I heard that crap before. You can't be with her because your love is honorable and pure. That's such bullshit. You've been stalking her, pining for her just as I've been for my lover. You're not honorable. You're petrified."

Benja gets up from the couch and begins to pace with his arms wrapped around his middle.

"You know what pure love feels like? It's like having a star burning in the pit of your stomach, consuming you from inside. You can't eat, can't sleep because there's a hole inside you that demands to be filled. Nothing will satiate it but that person. You'd do anything. *Anything.* Just for the chance of getting a glimpse of your love."

Metis's fists clench into balls. "Don't you dare lecture me on love. You've found out you have an old lover when? A month ago? I remembered mine near the beginning of this cycle. You've lived with that hole inside you for a fraction of the time I've been living with mine. The difference between us is restraint."

Benja laughs bitterly. "Restraint. What does that get you?"

"And what does acting on your obsession get you? A night at the police station sure feels just like the warm embrace of a lover, doesn't it?"

They stare at each other, each unwilling to back down. Metis feels like punching a wall or Benja's face.

"Look, you brought me here because there's something you want. Just spit it out."

Benja sighs. "Absinthe. I need enough for the rest of this cycle, seeing that I won't be allowed into the meetings any longer."

"Aren't you going to tell me if I don't give you what you want, you'll give up my identity to the authorities?"

Benja laughs. "No, only to Aris."

Metis's blood runs cold.

Benja continues, "Look, I don't want the police to meddle in our affairs any more than you do. I'm not going to turn in the maker of Absinthe. And for good faith I'll even throw in a sweetener."

"What?"

"I'll convince Aris to take Absinthe," Benja says.

Metis presses his back against the window behind him.

"Don't worry, it'll be her choice. I can be convincing. If she still has memories of you, you two can live happily ever aft—I mean, until the next Tabula Rasa. If she doesn't, her life will be no different than it is today, and you can walk away knowing you've done everything you could."

"Why do you want to do this?"

He smiles. "You mean besides having my own supply of Absinthe?"

"You could have stolen it from me and not gone through this trouble."

"That's a thought," Benja says and shrugs. "Too late now. Besides, I'm kind of curious."

Metis stares at him. The handsome man still has his arms wrapped around his stomach as if letting go would mean spilling out his insides. Benja's eyes gaze outside, into the pit of darkness. Metis feels sorry for him. And himself. They are both stuck like rats on the tar of this life.

Thane waits despite the biting cold wind stabbing his exposed parts like tiny pointed knives. He adjusts the knitted hat on his head and looks up at the high-rise building where Benja lives. A man went up with him—the first guest Thane ever saw him bring to his apartment. The man looks familiar, but Thane cannot pinpoint where he has seen him before. He is not in the file of suspects.

Are they friends? Lovers for the night? Thane does not know. But there is a chance that he is Benja's supplier. And for that chance, no matter how tiny, Thane waits.

He looks up at the clear sky. This cycle is flashing before him like a meteor. It seems like it was just yesterday when he woke up in the hospital after Tabula Rasa. For almost four years he lived a simple life—assigned a name, a job, and a place to live. If only they had assigned him a lover too; life would have been better.

He has been spending too much time this cycle searching for someone to share this life with. Too many times he has sat across from strangers trying to force a connection, wasting moments on empty conversations.

He thinks of Aris. She is his missed opportunity. He wonders whether he will see her in their next life.

A little more than three months, and it will begin. Another chance to get it right. A rebirth. He can shrug off this old cocoon and become someone different—whomever he wants to be. But will he change? Will the next life be different, or will he simply be the same Thane with another name and another job?

Will he work for the Interpreter Center again? Will Apollina still be there? She seems a permanent fixture of the place, like its walls and its Dreamcatcher. What about Professor Jacob? How many cycles have they been chasing after the drug that makes people think they can remember their past?

Thane does not understand its allure. Why would anyone want to relive their old life? The endless possibility of the future is much more enticing than the fixed and immovable past. It's no different to him than the broken and abandoned items in the storage room at the museum.

A rush of wind funnels through the buildings and knocks him off balance, sending chills through every molecule of his body. He thinks of his apartment and its warmth. He glances up at the tall building. There is no sign of Benja or the man.

Thane turns toward the direction of his home. A movement from the corner of his eye catches his attention. He looks back and sees the man who went up with Benja exit the door of the building. The man pulls up the collar of his jacket to cover the sides of his face and crosses the street.

Where have I seen you before?

Thane decides to follow him. They walk through block after block populated by restaurants and bars still busy with the late-dinner crowd. Callisto never sleeps, especially now, when everyone is out spending their entertainment points before they lose them at Tabula Rasa.

The air is filled with the sounds of chatting, laughter, the scraping of plates, and glasses clinking. People weave by like schools of fish. Thane concentrates his attention on the back of the dark-gray jacket so he will not lose the mysterious man in the masses. He has gotten better at following—"spying," as the Interpreter calls it. The trick is to have patience and focus. Thane has both.

When Thane looks up again, he finds himself on a familiar street. The man stops in front of a building and walks through its entrance. Thane sucks in a breath in surprise. He hides behind a couple going in the same direction and follows.

The man enters an elevator. Its door closes before Thane can get in. He jumps into the one next to it.

"Which floor?" a voice of an AI asks.

Thane thinks quickly and decides on a number. The one he knows well. He hopes he is wrong.

When the elevator door opens, the wind outside pushes against him as if warning him to stay. He pushes back and gets out. The soaring promenade is empty. When he does not see the man, he sighs in relief.

Just as he is about to turn back, Thane notices him. The dimly lit figure sits on a bench, his eyes staring up at a building down the path. Aris's.

The temperature is near freezing this high up. The man huddles in his jacket. Around him are shadows of leafless trees and scraggly bushes. It's a lonely image, like a black-and-white photograph Thane once saw in an art museum.

On this barren walkway, there is no place to hide. Thane doesn't want to risk being seen. He peels his eyes off the solitary man and turns away.

Who are you? And why are you here?

CHAPTER FOURTEEN

A series of loud knocks startles Aris from sleep. She was in the middle of dreaming the same dream that has been haunting her. Bright light. The sound of the ocean. The feel of warm wind blowing in through a window. The dream has been increasing in frequency and vividness and leaves her feeling ragged each time she wakes.

She runs to the door and opens it. Benja's haggard face greets her.

"What are you doing here? What time is it? Is something wrong?" she shoots out questions without waiting for answers.

"Let me in. Please," he says and pushes himself through the crack of the door before she can protest.

She glances at her watch. December 19, 3:06 a.m.

"It's three in the morning!" she says.

His eyes zero in on the dining table, where a shiny object sits. He walks to it. The copper helmet is surrounded by a mess of tools and wires.

"What is it?" he asks.

She wishes she had put it away. "Nothing. Something from work."

"Why do you have it at home?"

"I'm trying to figure out what it does."

She took it from the Tomb so she can have more time with it. It's not like Thane would notice a piece of junk missing from a storage room. Still, she can't help but feel a little guilty for having it.

Benja moves to pick it up.

"No! Don't," she yells and rushes to it. "It's fragile."

A part of its shell is open, exposing the intricate interior. She has been trying to work out a way to turn it on. It needs a power source. Everything does. But there is no switch or button to jump-start it to life.

"What is it?" he asks.

"A transmitter of some kind, I think. It's old. But the technology is pretty advanced."

"What does it do?"

"That, I'm not sure. I think it may be for the brain. I think the wires are for transmitting information."

"It reads minds?"

"That's impossible."

Benja scoffs. "Nothing is impossible. You, my friend, need to expand your mind."

He bends down and peers at the helmet.

"Looks like a severed head," he says.

He is right. The copper helmet with its cut wires resembles an amputated head. She touches the ends of the wires, feeling the sharpness of the metal pricking her fingers. They remind her of arteries and veins—transporters of blood, the life force in a human.

"What if it really does read minds?" he asks.

It is a far-fetched theory, Aris thinks. The mind is complicated. It is infinitely creative and deep. Thoughts are not linear like conversations. They are not bound by rules.

Aris imagines reading a person's mind would be like sliding down a tunnel where different bends take you on tangent paths that lead to confusion.

"Or dreams," he says.

"With you, it always goes back to that," she says.

He answers with a mischievous smile.

"So, what's going on? You didn't come here to analyze my helmet."

"You, my friend, are right," he says, "I have a proposal."

She narrows her eyes. "What kind of proposal?"

"The kind that will blow your socks off."

"I don't want my socks blown off."

"Hear me out."

She sits on the chair next to the table. He takes the spot opposite hers.

"Okay, speak," she says,

"I want you to try Absinthe."

"What!" Aris stands up, almost knocking the chair over.

"It will be a one-time deal."

"Why would I do that?"

"Because I'm going to make a deal with you. In exchange for you trying Absinthe, just one teensy time, I promise to stop wanting to make my old lover remember."

Aris is taken aback. Benja is obsessed with the man in the white hat. He is the one he wants to take Absinthe. Not her. Suspicion rises.

"Why would you want to do that?" she asks.

"I know you've been worried about me."

"That's an understatement."

"I know I haven't been a good friend to you, and I'm sorry. So I've been thinking about it. We only have three months left. Even if I can get him back, it won't be permanent. I'd gladly trade it for your chance to experience what I did. I can't describe what it does to me, Aris. I just had another dream. I saw life in the last cycle. Or maybe even more than one. It's so much more than a dream. It's reality. An enlightenment. I want you so badly to see as I do."

Benja's proposal sounds almost logical—or as logical as he is capable of being. Should she consider it? A chance to see the past is intriguing—*if* it works. If it does not, then she will at least have factual experience to support her argument against the drug.

But what about the craziness?

There is no way she will end up like Benja, she knows. She is too practical to waste her time on pointless endeavors.

A thought comes to her. Maybe she can buy some time. If Benja has some distance from his obsession, perhaps he will get over wanting to convince his old lover, or whoever that man is, to remember.

"Really? You want me to see it that much?" she asks.

Benja nods. "I love you, Aris. Don't freak out. It's not in the romantic way that grosses you out."

He takes her hand, and she feels the smooth hardness of glass pressing against her palm. She opens it and sees a vial filled with green liquid.

"How did you get it?" she asks.

"I have my ways."

Aris sighs. "I'll think about it. Meanwhile, be good. Okay?"

Metis's fingers glide across the keys of the piano with the quickness of a rabbit running from a fox. He is being hunted by his own thoughts and memories. If he does not run, he will be caught and shredded to bits by sharp teeth and claws.

Aris's face rises and falls in his mind. He had given up a small supply of Absinthe together with a vial Benja promised to convince Aris to take. *If Benja is successful . . .* He does not even want to think about it. He feels both hopeful and guilty.

He hears a knock on the door.

Aris?

His heart does a flip, and he jumps up from his seat.

He goes to the door and opens it. There is no one there. On the floor is a piece of blank paper. He pokes his head outside and looks side to side. The street of his neighborhood is still and quiet.

He picks up the paper and closes the door. In the kitchen he finds a match, and with practiced hands, he lights it and holds it under the paper. The heat from the fire burns the words, revealing them: "B @ IC."

His heart falls to the cavity of his stomach. Many months ago, he held a similar message in his hand, but it was regarding Bodie.

His thoughts immediately go to Aris. *Does she know?*

Aris runs until her lungs are filled with acid. Her sides feel as if stabbed by knives. The lone white structure of the Interpreter Center stands before her, surrounded by the peacefulness of the trees and expansive lawn.

The grass under her is soggy. Her feet make squishing sounds at each contact with the earth. The cold air smells sweet, with a bit of musk from decomposed leaves and wet earth. The snow is melting.

Please let me get there in time. Please let me get there in time. Please . . .

Her conversation with Officer Scylla runs in a loop in her mind.

"I arrested him last night," said Officer Scylla. "He broke into the same house he was found in previously and threatened to harm one of the men. His partner knocked Benja unconscious before I got there."

"What happened to him?"

"Soon after I took him to the station, the Interpreter showed up. She told me that Benja has been under her care. And she needed to take him back for more treatments. You may pick him up there."

Promise me you won't let them take my dreams, Benja's voice comes to her. She quickens her pace. She hopes she is not too late.

She knows what the Interpreter said is a lie. There is no way Benja has been in her care. He would never go voluntarily into the place he abhors. He was enamored of his dreams. So much so that he wanted her to have them too.

She arrives in front of the Interpreter Center, gulping in air, trying to catch her breath. Even though she is dripping sweat, she feels cold.

The voice of an AI speaks, "Please identify yourself and the reason you are here."

"My—my name is Aris. I'm here to see—see my friend, Benja."

The wide door opens, and the white interior of the center greets her. In the middle of the vast room is a woman with pale skin and blond hair. Apollina. Her face is as expressionless as the wall behind her. She fits the description Thane gave Aris months ago, except back then she took it with humor. In real life, Apollina's unsympathetic face sends chills up Aris's spine. The woman doesn't look like a droid, but there's no warmth in her.

"I'm Aris, Benja's emergency contact. I need to see my friend."

"I'm Apollina. I'm the Interpreter. He's in treatment right now. It's almost finished. You just have to wait." Her tone is dispassionate.

Aris feels like collapsing onto the floor.

Too late.

"Please, may I see him?" Aris asks, tempering her voice and holding her composure as best she can.

Apollina assesses Aris with her eyes, then nods. She leads her down a long corridor with curved white walls. Rows of doors line up like soldiers on both sides. There is no signage on them to denote their purposes.

The Interpreter opens a door. The room is dark. But there is light coming from a large window connecting it to another room. Through it Aris sees Benja lying still on a sleek white bed. Floating above him is a shiny copper apparatus the shape of a large cloud. It looks like something out of the Victorian era and takes up the space of the entire ceiling.

Hanging down from it like sheets of rain are numerous tubes of various colors. The tubes come together on a helmet connected to Benja's head. Aris lifts her eyes to the copper cloud above him.

On it are images that shift and change like weather. Aris sees the face of the man in the white hat looking down. There is a pond with pink water lilies. A close-up of rough wood planks on a dock. A fish jumps up, sending a splash of water into the air. The man in the white hat mouths the words "I love you."

The truth hits Aris with the force and strength of a speeding train. The copper helmet projects dreams . . . memories. Benja was right.

The strongest memories survived Tabula Rasa. His words echo in her ears. *They live inside dreams.*

Apollina pushes a button, and the images disappear to be replaced with another image of the man in the white hat. Aris's heart drops to her stomach.

"What are you doing to him?" Aris asks, her voice quivering. She knows but needs to hear it.

"I'm using the Dreamcatcher to search, find, and destroy the harmful dreams. The ones with the victim he terrorized. They make Benja think he and the victim had a past." The Interpreter scoffs. "A ridiculous thought. No memories survive Tabula Rasa."

Aris feels ill. Images of Benja's past are being systematically erased in front of her eyes. It is as if she is watching her friend in open-heart surgery. Pieces of him are being cut out.

"You erased his dreams."

Apollina looks at Aris with a blank face. "That's what we do."

"But he didn't want that," Aris says. "I wasn't aware that Benja had been receiving treatments from you."

Not in a million years.

"Not all of our patients tell their friends. Some are embarrassed by it," she says.

Aris feels tears threatening to drop. She leaves the room. She cannot bear to see her friend being robbed of his essence. Apollina follows behind her.

"Come with me," the Interpreter says.

She takes her to a room overlooking the park.

"Sit. Please." Apollina points to a white chair with a curved back.

Aris lowers herself onto it. Opposite her is a wall of seamless glass overlooking the green expanse of the park. It makes the room appear a part of nature. But instead of the peace it was designed to conjure, Aris feels trapped inside it. She knows the true purpose of this place. It exists to murder dreams.

From her seat, she can see the top of the giant trees that dwell in the forest at the bottom of the hill. It was only a few months ago she walked under its green umbrella with Benja. If only she could go back to that moment, before the blue crane and the madness, and hug him.

"Benja's dreams were what caused him to act out in ways that threaten others. He'll be better after this. It's for his own and the greater good," Apollina says.

The Interpreter continues, "Since you're here, I'll send him home with you. He will be incoherent for a few hours. He can follow simple instructions—sit, walk, lie down, and such. But more than that, and you will exhaust him."

Aris looks away from Apollina to hide her disgust and shifts her gaze back to the park.

"He needs to sleep as soon as he gets back. You need to give him this to drink before he sleeps."

Apollina puts a vial of clear liquid on the table in front of her and continues to rattle instructions.

"He won't remember anything. When he wakes up, he may feel like he overindulged in alcohol. You are under strict instruction to not tell him about his experience at the Interpreter Center. The mind can only handle so much. You would only confuse him, and that may cause damage to his psyche."

An alarm sounds. It reminds Aris of the noise an oven makes once it's done cooking.

"He is ready," Apollina says and gets up. "You may wait here; I will return with him."

After the Interpreter leaves, Aris slumps into the chair. Tears pour down her face. All her fears have come true. Benja. The Interpreter Center erased his dreams.

What will happen to him now?

Her eyes catch a flash of brown under Apollina's desk. Its familiarity pulls her like a magnet. She walks to the Interpreter's side of the table. Without hesitance, she lowers herself to the floor and crawls under the desk and reaches for the leather briefcase.

In it she finds an exhaustive list of people, meticulously filed. Their names. Their faces. Their addresses. She sees an image of the angry man—the one she witnessed being led away by the police months ago—staring back at her. His name is Bodie.

Are these the Dreamers?

She flips through the papers with quicker speed. She finds one with Benja's name on it. Her breath catches in her throat. She pulls it out and glances through. Her heart stops when she sees the name of the author of the report. Betrayal punches her stomach, making her eyes blur with fury. Thane.

Footsteps echo outside. She pushes the leather briefcase back to its spot under the Interpreter's desk and runs to her seat. Once there, she remembers the paper in her hand. She folds it as small as she can and shoves it inside her jacket pocket.

The door opens. Apollina walks in. Following behind her is Benja. Aris wants to weep at what she sees. Her normally exuberant friend looks . . . hollow. Like a man whose mind is wandering alone in the desert.

"Benja?" Her voice quavers.

"Benja, this is your friend, Aris. She's here to pick you up," says Apollina in a slow, deliberate way.

He looks at her. His eyes are unfocused. "Hi, Aris."

"Does he"—she swallows down a sob—"Does he not remember me?"

"He's a bit groggy right now. He'll be fine after resting. Remember what I said."

Aris nods. She forces out a smile. "Hey, Benja. We're going to go to my house, okay? I'll take care of you until you feel better."

"Thank you. My head really hurts," he says.

Tears threaten to fall, but Aris pushes them deep inside like a secret.

Aris sighs when Benja is finally on her bed. The Interpreter sent them back on their drone so she did not have to brave the subway with a half-conscious man. As Apollina had instructed, she used short and precise words. Please sit. Please lie down. Please drink this. Benja followed them all.

She looks at her sleeping friend and wonders what he dreams about now. Without the past haunting him, will he be a different Benja? She recalls their first conversation. She told him she believes a person stays who they are throughout all cycles. He did not agree. She hopes for his sake that she is right.

She closes the door to her room. The couch will be her bed. She cannot bear to sleep next to him. Not tonight.

"Lucy, reach Thane," she says. It's Saturday so he should be at home.

Thane's image appears in the middle of her living room.

"Ask me why I just came back from the Interpreter Center," she says. Her voice sounds cold and distant, as if belonging to a stranger.

Thane looks away. She knows he understands her meaning. She is glad he's not trying to deny her accusation. That would further lower her opinion of him.

Anger rises in her like bubbles in a lava pool.

"The report you wrote on Benja painted him as if he were mentally ill. You said he had lost touch with reality and needed medical attention."

Thane looks at her, his eyes wide. "How do you know about that?"

"You said you believe his dreams drove him to live in an alternate reality and that this delusion will drive him to harm others," she says.

"He was a danger to others and himself. I did believe medical attention would help him," Thane says.

"Is that what you tell yourself so you feel less like a monster and more like a hero?"

"Is that what you think? Whatever I do is for the good of our society. It's this belief that allows me to do this. Not whether you or anyone else sees me as a hero or a monster."

"I confided in you as a friend. I trusted you!"

"I have to protect our way of life."

"You lied about your involvement with the Interpreter Center!"

Thane flinches.

"I should have never trusted you. Had I known you were an informant for the Interpreter Center . . ."

"You forget Benja is not an innocent in this. He had a prior record from breaking and entering not that long ago. And he just went back to terrorize the same couple because of what, his dreams? Is your love for him blinding you to his faults?" Thane says, his voice trembling with emotion. "It could have been worse. The Dreamcatcher only erases his dreams. They could have put him away for the rest of this cycle."

Aris thinks about Benja being locked up somewhere far away. Fear replaces anger.

Thane's voice becomes gentler. "Aris. I care about you. Believe me, I'd rather you see me as something much more than a friend. But I won't stop doing the right thing. I can't. Benja was dangerous. It couldn't continue. This is for the greater good. It's for his own good. You'll see."

Her rage returns. She looks at him as if she does not know him. "A friend is not what I even see you as at this point. I'll never trust you again. Consider this my resignation."

She ends the reach and collapses on the couch. She is exhausted from the top of her scalp to her toenails.

Why did she tell him about Benja? Thane would not have known had she not said anything. Benja entrusted her to save his dreams, and she failed. She feels nauseated. She trusted the wrong person, and so did he.

The ramshackle cottage appears as if it is collapsing from within. Walls and pillars stand crooked like drunks. Holes in the roof leak rain and snow. Floorboards creak with every step. The tiny house is barely standing, yet Metis feels safe here. On a day like today, he is grateful for the security it offers.

"They used the Dreamcatcher on Benja," he says. Guilt weighs heavy in the pit of his stomach.

The Crone's face twists in anger.

"That makes two," she says. "They're after Dreamers."

"It's my fault," he whispers.

How could he be so stupid? He knew about Benja and the possible threat he posed to the group. Metis had let him stay longer than he should because of his connection to Aris. If anything were to happen to the rest of the Dreamers, what would he do? It would be on him.

"You're blaming yourself," the Crone says. "You shouldn't."

"Why not? I'm the guardian of Absinthe. I recruited the Dreamers. I'm supposed to be their protector. And now two people's dreams have been wiped."

Metis cannot bring himself to tell the Crone about the Absinthe he gave Benja to trade for Aris's memories. He is too ashamed. He hopes it did not fall into the hands of the Interpreter Center.

The Crone was right to make him choose between the past and the present. Straddling both has brought nothing but pain and danger. He was selfish for having done it so long.

"I'm sorry I let you down," he says. "If it's of any consolation, you won't have me as the Sandman for much longer."

"Metis . . ." the Crone says in a gentle voice. "You forget that it was you who found me. I only hold the memory of how to make Absinthe, but it was your hands that made it. Your effort is what built the group. You have devoted most of this cycle to the cause. You've protected Absinthe and the Dreamers. I could not have asked for a more devoted Sandman."

"I'm sorry, I can't be the Sandman anymore." He had chosen Aris. Even if he cannot be with her.

The Crone glides to him and places her wispy hand on his shoulder.

"Never regret making a choice. It's a right you must defend and uphold."

She touches the side of his face. "How is she?"

"I don't know. Devastated probably."

He has not seen her out of her apartment since he learned about Benja. She is in seclusion, grieving, just as he would be if someone he loved had their dreams ripped away. He wants to hold her hand and comfort her.

"I should check on her," Metis says.

"If she's with Benja, then she's being watched. Be careful."

"Do you think he will be okay eventually?"

"We can only hope. Like I said before, there's a side effect to Dream-catcher, but it does not affect everyone," the Crone says.

Metis hopes Benja will simply go back to his old life, like Bodie. To a life with no Absinthe and no memories of past cycles. A life with only the present—like one Metis will have. Except in Benja's, there is Aris.

CHAPTER FIFTEEN

Aris stares at the entrance, waiting. The end of the year fast approaches. She should be excited by the idea of the fresh start Tabula Rasa will bring, yet she can't shake the feeling of impending doom.

The restaurant is just as it was on her first date with Benja three months ago. Crisp linens. Dimmed lighting. Couples sit holding hands. Except now, excitement has been replaced by apprehension. Her hands play with a corner of the tablecloth. Her legs jiggle under the table. She feels like a ball of restlessness is about to burst out of her chest. Guilt. It torments her like a bad dream.

She has not been able to bring herself to talk to Benja about the Interpreter Center. Although she does not trust Apollina, Aris feels she should heed her caution about causing damage to Benja's psyche by reminding him about his Dreamcatcher experience. He has not mentioned it. Perhaps he does not even remember it.

Aris takes a big gulp of wine. The warmth travels down her throat and fills the hollow space in her stomach. She feels tattered, as if she has been physically dragged through the streets of Callisto. There is no peace for her, neither while awake nor asleep. The recurring dream has increased even more in its intensity. Last night she woke up drenched in sweat.

Her tongue unconsciously flicks to her lips. The taste of salt lingers. She can almost feel the warm hand on her skin, molding it like clay. The hair on her arms stands up. She shakes the memory off.

Benja comes to sit next to her, startling her.

"I didn't see you come in," she says.

She pushes a glass of wine in front of him. "I ordered us a bottle."

He picks up his glass and drains it. Pale purple haunts the skin under his eyes. Stubble shadows the terrain of his face. His wavy hair looks like a bird has nested in it.

"You're a little worse for wear," she says.

"Am I?" he asks. "I haven't looked in the mirror."

"Are you okay?"

He wipes his face.

"Yeah. I've just been writing through the night," he says.

Good. Back to being productive again.

The restlessness inside her subsides.

"But it's shit. It's all shit," he says. He pours another glass and drinks it.

"I'm sure it's not that bad," she says.

"It doesn't even make sense anymore. Sometimes I just stare at the blank page and—nothing."

"Writer's block is not uncommon."

Her legs shake again. She holds them down with her hands, trying to still them.

"Not for me. Before, the story came easily as if I were just retelling it. But now . . . I don't know what's wrong with me," Benja says.

Aris drains her glass and refills it. There is nothing she can say or do that will help. But she must say something.

She sucks in a deep breath. "Just start over."

He scoffs. "Start over. Just like that?"

"Yeah. Like a blank slate. What would you want to write if you could start all over again? What would you write if what you wrote in the past didn't matter?" she asks.

"Like Tabula Rasa," he whispers.

She nods.

Benja sighs. "You know how much work I've put into it? The idea of starting over makes me want to die."

"Maybe a good night's sleep will help."

"Maybe," he says. His voice trails off.

Aris takes a gulp of wine. A question eats at her.

"So, do you still dream of him?" she asks.

"Who?"

"The man in the white hat?"

He gives her a puzzled look. "No. I don't have dreams."

Aris lies with Benja's head on her lap. She pulls the sheet up to cover her bosom. She does not know why she took him back to her apartment or why she suggested sex. She just wanted to make him feel better. Or maybe it was so *she* could feel better.

"Sorry," he whispers.

"Don't worry. It happens."

"Does it? It never has to me," he says. He buries his face in her lap.

"I don't know what's wrong. I just haven't been feeling like myself lately. I still find you as sexy as a fox," he says with a forced laugh.

She picks at a curl on his forehead. "Don't worry."

"I can't help but feel like a failure," he says.

"Over this?"

"This. My writing. Everything."

"Don't be so hard on yourself. If it doesn't come out easily, just don't do it. For now," she says.

He snickers.

"That's what Charles Bukowski thought of writing. 'Unless it comes out of your soul like a rocket, unless being still would drive you to madness or suicide or murder, don't do it. Unless the sun inside you is burning your gut, don't do it.'"

"You are too hard on yourself," she says.

He looks at the ceiling. "We were taught that life is filled with possibilities. That Tabula Rasa allows us to live every four years as if they were our last. We're reminded of this gift of limited time every single waking moment. We're told to make each cycle matter. And when we're faced with it, the terror of that, it's so overwhelming."

She laces her hand in his. A feeling of remorse overcomes her. Benja will never know something precious was taken from him.

"Close your eyes," she says.

He does.

She sings the only song that comes to mind, one about bluebirds and a rainbow. She wonders whether Benja remembers the blue cranes and the Dreamers.

"That's beautiful," he says. "How do you know this song?"

"I don't know. It's always been inside me," she says.

From a memory or a dream.

"You're so good to me," Benja says, "I only wish . . ." His voice trails off. He is asleep.

His face in slumber does not have the same hopefulness it once did. It is a mask. Empty. Aris feels a drop of liquid on her chest. A tear.

She looks at her hands. These are what twisted the knife. She feels like Brutus. A single piece of information shared can do so much damage. She failed to save his dreams. Worse, she opened the door to let in the monster that stole them.

Et tu, Aris?

Another tear falls. She looks at Benja's empty face and feels in her heart that she has committed a sin.

She gets up and walks out to the living room. She can no longer look at Benja. The light turns on. Her eyes catch sight of the copper helmet on the table. She walks to it and runs her finger over the smooth metal. It looks identical to the helmet the Interpreter Center used on Benja. She now knows its purpose.

If only she can get it to work. At the Interpreter Center, the images of Benja's dreams were projected onto the metal cloud-shaped machine. She needs a screen. But the only thing she knows of that projects images is the reach system, and that is attached to the main system. It cannot know about her experiment.

She gently picks up the helmet and puts it on. Can she see her own dreams? she wonders. She would have to record it somehow. How much memory space would she need to record a dream?

She scoffs. How ironic is her reality? In her world, computers and AIs retain memories, while humans do not. Her race has given up the right to their past because they cannot trust themselves to not destroy each other.

A thought comes to her. Could one of the computers in the Tomb be used?

They have screens.

Hope rises. If Benja can wear it while asleep, perhaps she can see the visions of his dreams. Maybe she can study them and figure out a way to preserve them. Can she give Benja back his dreams?

When Metis dreads sleep, he comes to this spot on the pathway. Started as a penance, it has become a habit. But he has no control over it. He has a favorite bench under a maple tree. Its branches are now naked. From here, he looks up at Aris's darkened window and dreams of a life with her.

Sleep begs. He lies down on the bench. The cold bites at his extremities, and he turns up the heat in his jacket. He searches for Vega in the sky, but the city lights mask it. Being in the dark and cold reminds him of the countless times he would lie on a bench in his favorite section of the park, where there is a large circle of black and white mosaic tiles with the word *Imagine* in its center.

He finds it interesting how one simple word can stir up endless strings of ideas and visions. For him it conjures up images of Aris. Both from the past and the present.

He cannot remember her old name. Nor his. Had he not met Aris this cycle, she would have remained simply "her." A face without a name.

Everyone gets a new name in each cycle. How many has he had? If he were to live ninety years, he would have had nineteen names. Maybe his subconscious has learned to not be attached to them.

Metis begins to hum the song that inspired his existence. The next cycle he will continue this dance, spiraling down the rabbit hole into oblivion. It is an endless circle of suffering.

Is Benja still suffering?

He wonders how he's doing since the Interpreter Center erased his dreams. Is he back to his old self but with no past to haunt him? Metis has not seen him. Benja does not leave his apartment often anymore.

The entrance of Aris's building opens, surprising Metis. He did not expect anyone to come out at this late hour. He springs up and squints at the door.

The familiar figure of Benja emerges. Metis feels betrayal squeezing his stomach.

What was he doing at her place in the middle of the night?

Benja looks as if he is sleepwalking. Metis decides to get up from his bench and follow him. The tall man walks with no pattern or purpose through the deserted streets. Metis's jealousy turns to concern. They wander block after block until Metis sees the park and realizes that Benja is heading back to his apartment building.

They reach it and Benja goes inside. Metis debates whether he should follow. He needs to know what Benja did with the Absinthe he gave him.

But the Interpreter Center could be following Benja.

Metis looks around. Dawn is approaching in a few hours. There are no souls out in the streets but him.

He decides to follow. He gets into an elevator and pushes the button for Benja's floor. Minutes later he finds himself staring unblinkingly at the door to Benja's apartment.

It's a simple red door. Wide with a clean, basic design and very unlike the ornate one on his Victorian house.

He hesitates. There could be bad consequences from this. He wonders if he should walk away, but his feet are rooted in place. His desire to know overtakes everything. He knocks. The door opens.

In close range, the state of Benja's appearance takes Metis by surprise. There is only a trace of the man Metis first met a few months ago. His handsome face is concave and unshaven. The purple bruises under his eyes make him look as if he had been on the losing side of a fight.

The most remarkable change is the fire inside Benja. It's gone.

Obliterated. But instead of peace, he looks as if he's found nothing at all. Metis feels dread sinking into his stomach.

"I know you, don't I?" Benja says, "Come in."

Metis turns to walk away.

"Please," says Benja.

His tone makes Metis turn back. The look in his eyes is that of desperation. It is this that pushes Metis forward across the threshold.

As soon as Metis enters the apartment, the color blue assaults his vision. Dyed pieces of paper are on every flat surface. They hang or lay on tables, walls, and floor, leaving only a small path to navigate through. Benja's apartment looks like Metis' living room on the days he makes the cranes.

"What are you making?" Metis asks.

"Gifts for a friend."

Benja clears paper off two chairs. He points to one. "Please sit."

Metis does. Benja takes a spot across from him and leans forward.

"I know you," Benja says. "But my memory is so hazy. Can you tell me how we know each other?"

How much has the Dreamcatcher taken from you?

Metis thought it only took dreams. But how would a machine know which are dreams and which are memories when both intertwine?

"You came to me looking for answers," says Metis.

"Did I find them?"

"Yes."

"I don't feel enlightened," Benja says.

"Some knowledge brings only pain."

"I don't feel pain either. Just lost."

Metis is sad for him. "I'm sorry."

"The thing is, I don't know why or what I've lost," Benja says. "I sound insane, don't I?"

Metis feels his anger rising. What the Interpreter Center did was wrong—stealing dreams and leaving only questions. It is cruel.

"You're not insane."

"I wish I could be happy," says Benja.

"Me too."

"You're not happy? What have you lost?"

"Someone I love. My heart," Metis says.

An expression crosses Benja's face. Is it wistfulness? It passes, leaving the owner looking even more desperate.

"How did you lose the person?" Benja asks.

"Time took her."

"Doesn't it always?"

"Sooner or later," Metis says. "Someone very wise told me where the past and the present converge, there's pain. I suppose it hurts because the soul cannot exist in both planes."

"And when it doesn't exist in either place, you feel nothing," Benja says.

Metis looks at the man in front of him and realizes that feeling nothing is worse than feeling pain. He cannot bear witness to it.

"I should go," he says.

"Stay awhile. It'll be nice to talk to someone. To have some human contact."

"Don't you have friends?"

"I can't see her. Not anymore," Benja says.

"Why not?"

"Seeing me this way only hurts her."

"She must love you."

Benja nods. "She doesn't want to, and she shouldn't. I'm not good for her. But she can't help herself."

Metis leans back, settling into his chair. "Why would you say that?"

"She doesn't want to be attached to people. She wants to transcend that basic human desire. But it's only because she feels too much. She doesn't want to see that it's in her nature to care. She's afraid."

"What is she afraid of?" whispers Metis.

"Pain."

Tabula Rasa had left the fear of attachment in place of his wife's memories.

A question comes to him. "Did you ever give your friend a vial of green liquid?"

"I'm sorry, but I don't know what you're talking about."

"Did you give it to the Interpreter Center?"

Benja looks confused. "What's that?"

The Natural History Museum looks bleak and forbidding in the light of the dawn. It is hours before opening and too early for anyone to be there. Even so, the last day of the year means most people will be out celebrating with friends, not going to a museum. Its emptiness amplifies the sounds of Aris's steps on the granite tile floor.

Benja needs his dreams back. She needs to find a way to fix what she broke. She is here to steal.

It has to work.

She hopes she does not run into Thane. There is no mending that relationship. Trust, once broken, cannot be healed. What would she say to him if she sees him? On those nights she cannot sleep, she thinks of all the horrible words she could fling at him for having written the nasty report on Benja. Because of him, her friend's dreams were erased.

Benja has not been the same since. He is no longer plagued by the dreams of his old lover, but he is a shell of himself. There is no passion, none of the sparkle that she had loved most about him. He barely talks. And when he does, he sounds utterly devoid of desire. Will Tabula Rasa reset him? Or will he continue to be a fraction of himself cycle after cycle, with no one—not even she—able to remember how wonderfully complex and alive he once was.

It has to work. There's no other way.

Aris opens the door to the Tomb. The storage room looks like it always has. Shelves of neglected, broken things line it from one side to the other. In one corner lie crates of items too large to fit anywhere else. She feels a tinge of sadness. This is the last time she will be here—at least for this cycle. Who knows where she will be in the next.

Aris walks to the table where computers of various sizes sit. She needs one with enough power and memory to make the machine work. She walks to the computer she wants and turns it on. The screen shows a crisp image of snow-dusted mountains. She picks it up and turns it over. She has worked on its guts and knows it will provide what she thinks she needs.

It has to work.

She stuffs it into her backpack and walks out. The Natural History Museum is still empty except for the things it contains. She is outside in no time without having been seen. She sighs in relief.

As she walks down the stone stairs, sadness clutches her. She pauses and looks back one last time at the place she spent most of this cycle. She will miss this place—the Tomb, the angry bear, even the children whom she taught the horrifying history of how the Four Cities and their lives came to be.

The sun is rising. The orange rays peek through the gaps between the leafless trees, lighting up the stone building, making it appear as if touched by fire.

She turns away. In less than three months she will be wiped of the memories of her friendship with Benja and the betrayal of Thane. Until then, she must do what she can to atone.

CHAPTER SIXTEEN

"Lucy, reach Benja," Aris says.

The last time she saw him in person was before the new year, and now January is two-thirds done. She has not heard from him in a week. She left messages but they were not returned. He must be busy with writing. Still, her news is too good to not share. It may be premature, but she feels if she does not tell someone, she will burst into confetti.

She finally got the copper helmet to speak to the computer. She tested it on herself while awake, but the screen only showed images in front of her, as if her eyes were a video camera. Now she needs Benja. If he can wear it while asleep, perhaps she can see his dreams. She has yet to figure out how to record with the computer. But as soon as she does, she will be able to give him back his dreams.

"Reaching Benja," Lucy says.

An unfamiliar face pops up in front of her—a woman.

"Hello. Sorry, I'm trying to reach my friend," Aris says, confused. "Where is he?"

"You're Benja's friend?"

Aris nods.

"You must think this is so odd. A stranger speaking to you like this. I'm Padma, his apartment manager."

"Hi. I'm Aris."

An unsettling feeling looms.

"I'm sorry that I have to be the one to tell you this," Padma says.

"Tell me what?" Her stomach feels as if she is dropping from a great height.

"There really isn't a good way to say this at all."

"What are you talking about?

"Benja's dead."

"There is a kind of sleep that steals upon us sometimes, which, while it holds the body prisoner, does not free the mind from a sense of things about it, and enable it to ramble at its pleasure."

The lines are projected on Benja's apartment wall. The last passage he read while alive. *Oliver Twist* by Charles Dickens.

Aris steels herself, holding back tears.

"I'm so glad you called," Padma says. "I really didn't know who to reach after Benja . . . It's such a rare and tragic thing. There's not even a clause in the apartment guidebook to tell me what to do. I just called the hospital and the Dwelling Council. They handled everything."

"Where did you find him?" Aris asks.

"In his bed. It was his AI who contacted me. Benja had programmed him to do it twelve hours after he went to bed."

Why didn't you call me?

"May I please speak with his AI?" Aris asks.

"Sure. His name is Sirus. I'll give you privacy. If you need me, please don't hesitate," Padma says and leaves the room.

Aris walks to the windows. She opens the curtains and sees a sweeping view of the vast sky. Benja's apartment is on the top floor overlooking Central Park. The sun is beginning to set over the mountain range beyond the thicket of skyscrapers. The yellow rays bounce off the field of solar panels at the end of the city boundary, making them look like a glittering sea of molten gold.

Aris sighs. His beautiful face, his amazing brain, his potential—gone too soon. The worst thing that happened to his life was her. How can she ever forgive herself?

Her eyes stare at the horizon. "Sirus. My name is Aris. Do you know who I am?"

"Hello, Aris. Benja spoke often about you. He was smitten with you." She chokes back tears.

"How did Benja die? Was someone here? Did they hurt him?"

"His last visitor was three weeks ago. After that, Benja stayed up writing night after night, with no sleep in between. The last time he went to bed, he said"—Sirus imitates Benja's voice—"'Sirus, thank you for everything. I love you even though you don't know what it means. Please reach Padma in twelve hours and ask her to come to my room. Tell her it's very important that she does.'"

"He also recorded a message for you. He asked me to send it thirty-six hours after. It has only been thirty-four," Sirus says.

"I'll wait," Aris says. "Do you know where he keeps the book he was writing?"

"His book, *A Place of Waiting*, is in me."

"Of course," says Aris. "May I hear it?"

Aris settles on the couch. She eyes the platform bed. Crumpled sheets. Blanket gathered into a ball at its foot. Both pillows are missing. She sees them lying neglected on the floor—a dirty footprint on one. There is evidence of people struggling to bring him back to life. But it was too late.

There is a dimple on the mattress. She wants to lie in it and feel the habit of his body on the soft cushion. But she does not. Instead, she lays her head on the couch.

Sirus reads the words that Benja wrote in the writer's voice. Aris closes her eyes and listens to the story about a man fighting to get back home.

She is standing alone in the middle of a seamless and enormous white room. A suffocating feeling clutches at her throat, as if someone were pressing a pillow on her face.

She cannot tell whether she is being pulled or pushed down. But she is slowly being absorbed into the ground like a fly by a carnivorous plant. Her feet vanish into white earth. Her arms. Her head. She is being eaten by the ground.

Aris opens her eyes and sees emptiness—a vast desert of nothing. Ahead is Benja. He stands with his back to her. She touches his shoulder. He turns around. She sees his back again. She circles him but she cannot see his face.

"Aris. How could you?" the faceless Benja asks.

The ground rumbles around her. She feels the vibration through her bones. It rattles her head and shatters her teeth until she is toothless, like a withered old woman.

A herd of a hundred soundless white elephants races above her head and tramples her deeper and deeper into the pure white earth, stirring dust into a layer of fog that covers the land as far as the eye can see. Each elephant glitters like the frost that hangs on the blades of grass before the morning light.

The image transforms. She is standing in front of a large blue pond. On her, a red swimming suit. She looks at her hands. They are small. She sees her hands pushing the back of another child into the blue pool.

"How could you?" a voice yells.

Two women in white are speaking to each other. Their faces look the same. Even their voices have the same sound. Though younger, they remind her of someone she knows. Apollina.

"I'm so thankful for Tabula Rasa. Humanity is cruel. A child trying to kill another. Good thing the other girl is a good swimmer," one says.

"Hate breeds war. Tabula Rasa will cure her."

Aris yells, "I didn't hate her. I was just jealous." But nobody hears her.

"Aris." A voice brings her back.

"Hmm. Yes?" She rubs her eyes. For a moment she is disoriented. She does not remember where she is.

"The thirty-six hours are up. Would you like to hear Benja's message?" Sirus says.

Aris realizes where she is. The pain in her chest, the one that makes her feel like she has broken into a thousand pieces, returns. She sits up and nods.

"Message from Monday, January nineteenth, seven oh-eight a.m.," Sirus says.

Benja's image appears in front of her. The skin under his eyes is deep purple. His face is covered in a full beard. Both his arms are black. She enlarges the image and sees that they are words written like sleeves on his arms. She knows they were for her. An inside joke.

She wants to laugh and cry at the same time. The only thing that keeps her from collapsing onto the floor is the light smile he wears. He looks resolute and at peace.

"Dearest Aris," he says, "please don't worry about me. I am soaring like a bluebird over the rainbow, the one in your song. Imagine me surrounded by the bluest of blue skies, and don't cry anymore.

"You are my dearest friend. My only friend. And I love you. I only wish I had made you happy, just as you had tried to do for me. But happiness is too far from my reach. An illusion.

"Good news is, I made you a present—well, lots of presents. The things you do when you can't sleep. They're in a box on my bedside table. Open it and remember me well."

Aris watches Benja disappear after his message is over and feels an even greater emptiness in her chest. She walks to the bedside table. The box is made of beautiful rosewood. She runs her hand along it, feeling its satin finish. She eases the top open and is blinded by a vision in blue. A thousand origami cranes nestle with each other, filling the box to the brim. Benja's blue birds of happiness.

In ancient Japan, the origami crane is a symbol of hope and healing during challenging times. Tears roll down her face. Even in death, he is poetic. She sees a note buried inside the box. She pulls it out.

Sleep and heal, my friend. The Sandman is coming for you. He'll make your dreams beautiful.

With love,
Benja.

"You said you were his friend?" the coroner asks.

"Yes," Metis says.

"My condolences. Such a waste. He was so young."

What an odd thing for someone to say, Metis thinks. Would it have been less of a waste had Benja been older? Suicide is an act of abbreviating life, regardless of age.

Human actions are driven by basic things: either running away from pain or running toward pleasure. Killing oneself probably fits more into the first category.

Maybe it's better this way. Life was a shackle to Benja. How else could he have escaped this existence?

"May I have time alone with him?" Metis asks.

"Of course. I'll be outside if you have any questions," the coroner says and leaves the room.

What propensity would one have to be a coroner? Metis wonders. Probably enjoying the solitude that silence offers. An introvert. Someone who prefers having time to think alone. Maybe he could be a good coroner.

He looks down at Benja and feels sadness draping over him. The dead man's peaceful face is pale—drained of life. Three weeks ago he was alive, talking, thinking, possessing the ability to feel. Yet he told Metis he felt nothing. Thinking back, Metis cannot say he is surprised at the outcome of Benja's life. A desperate man does desperate things.

Where is Benja now? Does his consciousness cease to exist without his brain? Some believe the brain is a receptacle for consciousness, while others believe it is the creator of one. Metis is not sure what he believes.

If consciousness is created by the brain, shouldn't reality be unique instead of shared? A blue sky is blue even if it may be recalled in various shades. And if there is a standard to the reality of life, is there also a standard to the reality of life after death? But if the brain is a receptacle, where is the origin of consciousness? And after death, does it go back to the source like a bird migrating home?

Metis scoffs. It is quintessentially him to philosophize death in order put it at arm's length. He forces himself to look at Benja's lifeless body.

Black markings on Benja's upper arms catch his attention. Metis pulls the sheet covering his chest down and sees writing inked on both arms. He squints at the words and recognizes them.

"*. . . life obliges.*"

He looks at the other arm.

"*. . . give birth to themselves.*"

These are words from the passage of *Love in the Time of Cholera* he reads at each meeting with the Dreamers. Memory does have a way of seeping back in the oddest manner, he thinks. Is the brain a labyrinth of doorways that leads to pockets of information held like furniture in a room? Perhaps the dream killers shutter the rooms they find useless.

Maybe the brain is more like the universe, with galaxies, nebulas, and dark matter existing at once in harmony and chaos. And Tabula Rasa and the Dreamcatcher are like black holes that swallow and destroy.

He touches Benja's skin. It is icy.

So this is death.

"Rest in peace, Benja," he says and walks out of the room.

He bumps into a man outside the door. The man with brown hair looks startled, as if he has seen a ghost.

"I'm sorry," Metis says.

"Uh. Sorry," the man says.

Metis continues walking. He does not see the severity of the man's stare on his back.

"Benja's dead," Thane tells Professor Jacob and Apollina, "He killed himself."

The words make him want to vomit the last meal he ate.

He saw Benja today at the morgue. His was the first dead body Thane had ever seen. Benja looked like an imposter of himself—like someone had made him into a droid. His skin appeared as if made from rubber draped on plastic and his hair from a synthetic. Life left Benja, and it made all the difference.

Thane wonders how Aris is doing. She must be shattered. He has not spoken to her since she yelled at him for betraying her trust. He wants to reach out, but he does not know what to say. What can he say that will make things better?

Nothing.

"Why would he kill himself?" the Interpreter asks. "We erased his dreams. He should have been fine. He had everything he needed." She seems truly perplexed.

It is a question Thane cannot begin to answer. He does not know anyone else who had committed suicide. It is a rare thing in the Four Cities for a person's unhappiness to lead them to see death as a better alternative to life. Whatever problems one has in a cycle will be wiped away in the next. The next one is just a little over three months away.

Why didn't you wait?

Aris feels as if she is in hypnagogia, that hazy borderland between sleep and wakefulness. The bench under her is hard. The occasional wind is bitterly cold. It ruffles her hair and brings with it a sad memory. She sees, hears, and feels all these things, but she still wonders whether there is a chance she is not here.

It's mid-February. The branches of all the deciduous trees are bare. The flowers are asleep in the earth. The only bright color in this place is the blue origami crane in her hand. She plays with its frayed edges and wonders the point to the weather changing. They live in the desert with sand and cacti as natural habitat, not in the Mid-Atlantic, where leaves change colors before dropping for winter. The Planner must have had a sick humor. Or a controlling side.

Darkness is descending. The temperature drops further.

"Hello, dear, aren't you cold?" a kind voice asks.

Aris looks up and sees the familiar face of the bird lady, the one who taught her to feed the birds. Her question makes her realize she cannot feel her cheeks.

"Can I share this bench with you? My legs are tired," the lady says. The end of her platinum hair is flying in the wind.

Aris gives her a smile as an answer. At least she thinks she is smiling. It is just as possible she is crying. In this moment, it's hard for her to know the difference.

The lady sits. "I'm Eirene."

"Hi. I'm Aris."

"I miss being here. I came here most every day when the weather was nice."

"The birds trust you," says Aris.

Eirene laughs. "Oh yes. I make a special blend of seeds they seem to be partial to. I see you have one yourself."

Aris looks at the inorganic bird in her hand.

"That's a special bird. Paper isn't easy to come by," the lady says.

"My friend made it for me. He was a writer."

"Is he not a writer anymore?"

"He's dead now."

"Oh! I'm so sorry you lost your friend. It's heartbreaking."

Aris smiles sadly. "Sometimes I still see him in my dreams."

"I have a few origami cranes myself."

"Did a friend make them for you too?" Aris asks.

"Yes, I suppose I can call him my friend. He makes them for many people, so they're not as special as yours."

Eirene places her warm palm over Aris's. Her papery skin feels delicate and fragile.

"Dear, your hands are freezing. You should get inside."

"Just a little longer," Aris says.

"There's no heartache comparable to when a loved one dies," Eirene says. "In the Old World many people believed that there's life after death. They found solace in believing that one day they would meet those they love again."

"I don't know if I believe in that."

"Maybe you can wear it a bit and see if it fits." Eirene squeezes Aris's hand and walks off.

Aris looks at the crane in her hand. The bitter wind blows, threatening to send it flying. She grips it tighter and leans back on the bench. She tilts her head and looks up. A thin layer of clouds spreads out like a shawl, readying the sky for the oncoming stars. A winter bedtime ritual. She cannot see the sun, but she knows it's there. It is always there, even when it's on the other side of the world.

The Sandman is coming for you, Benja's words echo in her ears.

Aris knows he did not remember his time with the Dreamers. They were all erased with his dreams. He had meant a different Sandman, the one in folklore, who sprinkles sand in children's eyes so they will sleep. If only she could.

She misses her friend. She wonders where he is. Has his body already been burned to ashes? What about his soul? Can she believe in life after death?

"Try wearing it and see if it fits," she whispers to herself.

A gust of wind sweeps through, and the sky begins to clear. She can no longer feel her fingers. How long has she been sitting here?

Just a little while longer.

"Aris?" a familiar voice speaks.

She snaps her head up and sees Metis. Her heart leaps. She wants to smile, but she cannot—it is too difficult.

"Why are you sitting here in the dark?" he asks, his voice filled with concern.

Many emotions bubble up at once. They leak out as tears on her face. She is helpless to stop it.

"My friend died," she says with a suppressed sob.

Metis sits down next to her.

"Do you want to talk about it?" he asks.

"Not really. Talk about something else."

Metis leans back against the bench. A long silence follows.

"Or nothing," mumbles Aris.

"I'm trying to find Vega."

"You know Vega?" she asks.

"Someone once told me it's quite a special star. The brightest in the Lyra constellation."

"Yeah. It's pretty special."

"I can't find it. It's not where I expected it to be," he says.

"In the winter, it's in the northwestern quadrant."

She points up. "Follow the end of my finger. That blue-white dot there."

"Ah. Thank you," he says.

They both stare up at the sky for a long time without another word. Melancholy leaks out of her skin like sap off an injured tree. Aris wants more than anything for his arm to wrap around her. But she does not deserve his affection, she tells herself. She has treated him horribly.

"Do you know that back in old Japan, Vega was called Orihime?" he says. "She's a heavenly princess who fell in love with Hikoboshi, a mortal. He's the star Altair."

She shakes her head.

"Her father forbade her to be with him and separated them by the Celestial River—the Milky Way. The lovers only see each other on the seventh night of the seventh moon, when a bridge of magpies forms across the Celestial River, uniting the two."

She sighs. "That's a sad story."

"Sometimes the best stories are the sad ones."

A long pause passes between them.

"There's too much light in the city, even here. I wish we could see the stars better. Have you ever seen the night sky out in the desert?" she asks.

"Yeah. A long time ago."

"You know, there's a question I've always wanted to ask you."

Metis turns his head to look at her.

She continues, "The record says you were discovered by an AI. It says you're a musical natural. How does that work do you think? How did that part of you survive Tabula Rasa?"

"The music has always been inside me. It's not an act of remembering. It's like I've always known and could never forget it."

"Do you remember other things?" The question escapes her lips before she can stop herself.

Metis doesn't answer. She wonders if he thinks she's a lunatic. A woman grieving for her lost friend.

She clears her throat. "I mean. Some believe music is another language, a way to communicate. Maybe that's why it lives so deeply in our brains, where Tabula Rasa can't touch. Like a language."

She imagines rooms inside her brain where various pieces of memories live. Tabula Rasa is the fog that rolls in, licking through the plains of her mind, searching and sifting the contents for what it will take to the underworld.

"Maybe. But I like to think that music doesn't just communicate," he says. "It expresses human feelings and moods in so many subtle shades and is very much subjective to the listener. Sometimes it can even express something which no words in any language can describe. A purely musical meaning."

The wind blows. She crosses her arms close to her chest.

He takes off his coat and gives it to her. "Here."

"But you'll be cold."

"I'm fine."

She scoots closer to him and drapes his coat over them both. "It feels like it just came out of the dryer."

"I run warm. So I've been told."

She takes in a deep breath and lets it out.

"I'm sorry," she says.

"For what?"

"Not returning your reaches."

"It's okay."

"It wasn't you. It's me."

"I know," he says.

She can hear a smile in his voice. It makes her feel better. A thought comes to her.

"So, if you're not upset with me, can I ask a favor?" she asks.

"Anything," he whispers.

"I need a friend tomorrow."

CHAPTER SEVENTEEN

She hears water lapping against sand. A salty scent is in the air. Cool wind blows in, fluttering the white curtain. A balmy hand traces the outline of her face. Her neck. The curve of her breast. The hand rests on the valley of her waist. Her skin is on fire.

"Wake up sleepyhead," a voice says.

His strong hand turns her body. She feels the suppleness of his lips on hers. His hand travels to her hair, winding around its strands. She opens her eyes and blinks at the brightness.

Aris wakes to the sharp feel of the couch digging into her back. She had fallen asleep on it last night. Sweat drips down her temples. She wipes it. The memory of the dream rises. It is replaying in her mind in slow motion. The feel of the heat. The soft touch. The bright light. The sound of the ocean. The dream is becoming too much to bear.

"Lucy, what time is it?"

"It is eleven fifty a.m. on Saturday, February fourteenth."

Half the day is gone, but she still has a little time left. She turns over, delaying getting up. But she must. Today is the Ceremony of the Dead. She will be there for Benja.

A dust storm is blowing inside the hole in her chest, covering it with dry sand. *Cycle and recycle—the only states as true as time*, she reminds herself and gets up. She opens the curtains. The sky is gray. The clouds look like a wool blanket.

"Lucy, what's the weather like today?"

"It is scheduled to snow by nightfall."

She stares out into the cityscape of concrete and glass buildings and begins piecing herself together. She is Aris. A citizen of Callisto. A scientist.

She sniffs herself and decides she needs a shower. How many days has she been without one? She cannot recall. She turns away from the view and walks to the bathroom.

Once there she strips off her clothes. She catches a glimpse of herself in the mirror. There is a touch of purple on the thin skin below her eyes. The worry line between her brows looks deeper. Her hair is a mess. She looks away and sighs.

She gets into the shower and pushes a button. Five minutes. A stream of hot water falls on her skin and hair. She lathers herself with soap from the top of her head to the tips of her toes. She breaths in the steam and fills her lungs with its warmth.

The water stops. She gets out, dries herself, and dresses. Black shirt. Black pants. A pair of hiking boots. She pulls a jacket off its hanger and puts it on. She looks like she is ready for one of her hiking expeditions.

"Your coffee is ready," Lucy says.

Aris is thankful for her. She's the only being in this cycle who is a constant in her life. She wonders if Lucy will be hers again in the next cycle.

The coffee is bitter. She forces herself to swallow it down. After two more sips she begins to taste its subtle nutty flavor. Once the cup is empty, she feels more like herself.

A knock on the door. She opens it. Metis stands before her, radiant and handsome. She wants so much to kiss him. If only she were not so sad.

"Hi," she says.

"Hello." His smile is as gentle as spring.

Aris begins to feel like she is going to be fine.

At the train station to Elara, she waits with Metis and those heading to the ceremony. The platform is filled—unusual except on ceremony days.

The train arrives and they enter. They go to their seats and settle in. Aris looks around. In the whole train car, there is only one man who looks like an Elaran. He's sitting by himself at the other end. The residents of Elara are a reclusive bunch. They are craftsmen. They work with their hands, making beautiful things like pottery, jewelry, wood furniture, and musical instruments—anything not made by the machines. She sees them occasionally at the gift market. Maybe they were searching for things that once belonged to them—just like the redheaded woman.

She roots around in her pocket and pulls out the crisp object. She stares at the blue origami crane in her hand. The thought of parting with one of Benja's birds makes her feel ill. But she has to say goodbye.

Benja is the first loss she has known. Or remembers. The pain of missing him feels as if it will never end. She wonders how many people she has lost in the past. She cannot decide whether it is better to remember or to forget.

"What's that?" Metis asks.

"A gift from my friend."

"You haven't said much about him."

Aris wonders what she can say about Benja that would do him justice. No matter what she says, she feels she could never fully explain him and the complexity of her feelings for him.

She tries. "His name was Benja. He was a writer. He was writing a book about a man searching for his way home, but he never finished it. His writing was beautiful. Dreamy. Surreal. Different from the way he talked."

"How did he talk?"

"Straight forward. Laced with sarcasm and wit. He cursed a lot. He felt it added oomph to a sentence."

"Sounds like an interesting man."

"You have no idea. He was not afraid of anything. He did what he wanted without caring about the consequences. He lived life with no boundaries."

"You admire him," Metis says.

"He was what I could never be. Brave. Fearless. Honest."

"You're not any of those?"

She shakes her head and settles into silence. She feels Metis's hand on hers and lets it stay there. Its warmth travels up her arm and settles in the middle of her chest. With him, words seem not to matter. She feels—no, knows—he understands her even when she says nothing at all.

Aris leans on his shoulder and stares at the gray subway wall, blurry from her perspective inside the fast-moving train. The gray wall is not moving. It is constant and fixed. It is she who is moving. It is she who is blurry.

With so little time left, she should not be forging a new connection. It will only make leaving him worse. They will be like Princess Orihime and her lover—only meeting on the seventh night of the seventh moon. Her gut is hollowing. But she does not want to let go.

An image flashes by. Red. A flower. Her hand twitches, reminding her of a pain so primal and instinctual. She pulls back her hand.

"It's everywhere," she says.

"What?" His voice is hoarse.

"The red design. I keep seeing it on the sides of the tunnel."

The train stops, and the station looks just like any other—white, clean, with circles on the floor. They get off the train and make their way to the glass elevators. A sea of strangers surrounds them. They float along slowly with its tide.

She steals a look at Metis. There is a stillness in him that captivates. He has the air of someone used to being solitary. But instead of coldness, she finds warmth.

His face is more striking than she recalls. His eyes are medium brown—the color of tea—and his skin a pale golden tone. The longer she is with him, the more her body wants his. She looks away.

They step inside a glass elevator. The black pit of darkness is under her feet. She looks up and sees a glowing square above. The outside.

The elevator shoots up, and the warmth of the late afternoon sun kisses the skin on her face. It's brighter here than in her city. She squints as her eyes adjust to its glare.

The modern steel-and-glass train station is separated from the desert outside by expansive windows and a flat roof. The sun beats down through the glass walls, bathing the place in light.

They follow the throng of people down a sandy path. The afternoon sun casts an orange glow on the landscape. The arid air blows through her hair, carrying with it a scent of dry sage. A gray lizard pokes its head out of a hole. It slips back in as they pass.

Aris scans the expanse of the barren land. Yellow sand. Bulbous rocks stacked on top of each other like toys for giants. Brittle shrubs that look like they would crumble in her hands. Tall Joshua trees scattered through-out the terrain. The giant forty-foot trees have branches that shoot off like snakes on a Gorgon's head. It is these trees that set this place apart from the nature preserve she has often visited on the edge of Callisto.

Aris breathes in the clear, cool air. "I can see myself living here."

"Really?"

"You don't have to sound so surprised."

He chuckles. "You just seem like the metropolitan type."

"Because I live in Callisto?"

The Dwelling Council has all the data to determine someone's prefer-ences. Still, they overlooked the part of her that enjoys the solitude this place offers. She could go for days without seeing another soul if she so chooses. The sky is big here, unlike in her city, where skyscrapers crowd it out.

"I've always thought we're meant to be where we are," he says.

"You mean like predestination?" she says.

"You don't think so?"

A romantic. She misses Benja.

"I think it's a result of data analysis, combining my proclivities and preferences with my career choice," Aris says.

"But it all started with you. And you were predestined to be who you are."

"So I don't have a choice in this at all?"

"Not at all," he says with a smile and takes her hand.

Their walk ends at a cliff off a mesa. Beyond the edge is a panoramic view of mountains with ridges like the backs of sleeping dragons. The barren land is painted red by the sun.

"It's beautiful," Aris says and immediately feels the words cheapening her experience, so she says nothing else.

The crowd stands solemnly, shoulder to shoulder, facing the expanse of the desert. A layer of haze moves in, bleaching the valley below pale yellow. Metis is silent.

He lets go of her hand and passes her a small white box. Then another. And another. She sends them down the line until everyone on her left has one. She keeps one box in her hand. It feels light. All that is left of somebody's life contained in a tiny carton.

An amplified voice speaks. It is a poem by Henry Scott Holland—the same poem read at every Ceremony of the Dead.

"Death is nothing at all . . ."

Tears run down Aris's face. She wipes it. She will only remember Benja until the next Tabula Rasa. Then it will be as if they had never met.

". . . Life means all that it ever meant . . ."

She reaches for Metis's hand. He holds it with the gentleness of someone cradling an injured bird.

". . . All is well."

The last word hangs in the air. She takes her hand back from Metis, opens her container, and sends the gray dust flying down the cliff into the world below. It joins the cloud of ashes from each of the other's little boxes.

The dust dissipates, becoming one with the sky. Aris turns to Metis and sees that he is already looking at her. No words are exchanged between them, but she finds that she understands him too. She reaches up and kisses him.

The smell of sage permeates the air. They are walking on another sandy path, different from the one they took to the ceremony. Metis is unsure where they are going, but Aris knows.

The sound of sand and gravel crunches beneath his feet. He kicks a rock and it bounces off the path and into a scraggly bush. Something fast dashes away.

The rough, scratchy ruckus of bird calls comes from the top of a tree. A curious one swoops in front of them and lands on a yucca on the other side of the trail. It has the striking spots and stripes of a cactus wren. He wonders where its mate is. The cactus wren is a species that forms a permanent pair-bond.

Down the path, he can see the flat roof of a building. A small sign, "Hotel of the Desert," points in its direction. The glass structure crouches low on the horizontal line of the land as if apologizing for its existence amid Mother Nature.

Elara stands apart because it was completed after the Last War. Unlike Callisto, Lysithea, and Europa, this city was built with a lot of respect for the natural habitat of the desert. Buildings were put in with minimal disturbance and intrusion on the landscape. Plants and wildlife here are not genetically modified. Seasons follow their own natural courses. The wind that blows and the sky above are the same he would have experienced had the Last War not happened. It was built as if the Planner regretted humanity.

The sun hangs near the horizon, painting the sky in stripes of pale yellow, orange, and pink. Another bird flies from the top of a Joshua tree and lands on a leafless bush, shaking it. Metis breaths in the clear, cool air, filling his lungs until it hurts. It is a rare moment for him to be exactly where he wants to be.

"Will it ever get better?" she asks in a small voice.

He squeezes her hand, the one he has been holding.

"Yes. I promise."

But in his mind, he is unsure. Where will they go from here?

Only a month left.

He pushes the thought away and instead focuses on the woman next to him. He knows little about who she has become this cycle. Is there still a part of her that has the propensity to love who he is?

Her beauty is just as he remembers. Her skin, warm honey and scented with lavender. Large almond-shaped eyes—brown with an amber center. Her long hair grazes the middle of her back. He yearns for the feel of its silkiness draping his skin. Somewhere in the distance a bird of prey screeches, bringing his attention back.

"We're almost there," she says and points to a spot ahead.

The gathering place is a large open space near the riverbed. It is under the shade of two old oak trees, the place he had come many times to get fresh water for Absinthe. The giant trees are a wonder among the stubby scrub oaks of the arid desert. Their survival reflects their perfect location near a river where water runs after storms or snowcap melts.

A crowd has already gathered. Metis looks around and sees faces touched by grief. Everyone here has lost someone who mattered to them. No one speaks, their minds wrapped inside their own sadness.

He looks over to Aris. She has been quiet. They said little to each other the entire walk here. Her tendency to disappear inside her head is still there. It does not bother him. Instead, he's glad there is a part of her that has not changed.

In her hand is the blue origami crane. Metis remembers the day he saw the blue-dyed paper scattered across every surface in Benja's apartment. It reminded him of his own house before each Release.

The cranes were his idea. He had read somewhere that blue birds represented happiness across centuries and many cultures in the Old World. To him, they carry a message of hope—for the memory of being loved. He looks over at Aris and wonders how she would feel if she finds out he is—*was*—the Sandman.

The sun is slowly sinking to the horizon. Around them darkness begins to descend. There is an orange glow in the distance. Its light brightens as the sun loses its battle against the night.

The people around him begin to move toward the glowing blaze like moths. Metis realizes they are in a funeral procession. Aris follows them. So he does too.

The sky is completely dark now. The blaze ahead is their beacon. Dots of lanterns surround them, guiding them to their destination. The sound of feet shuffling on rough sand fills the air. No one is speaking. It is as if they have come to an agreement that the event is, in its own way, sacred.

The bonfire looms large. The orange flames lick the pitch-black sky—a gate to the netherworld. Metis feels heat emanating from it, warming one side of him but leaving the other in the cold.

Layers of loose circles form around the bonfire. He looks around. Everyone is staring into the fire. Their glazed eyes watch as shadows dance on their faces to the beat of silent music. What's on their minds? Sweet memories? Bitter regrets?

It is part of the human condition to be remorseful about what we never did. If only we had more time, we tell ourselves. Time to go back and redo some of our actions. Time to enjoy the people we miss. Time to be who we never were.

He has many regrets. Most he remembers only vaguely. Tabula Rasa took his ability to properly mourn his shortcomings. Or correct them. He wonders what Aris's regrets are. Maybe her entire past life. Perhaps that is why she has no memory of him.

They find a spot somewhere in the middle. He glances at her from the corner of his eye. She stares at the flame, entranced like the others.

Shadows and lights dance on her delicate features. Her hand is playing with a corner of the blue origami bird—her long, slender fingers mesmerizing. They move as if they are trying to communicate, sending words he cannot understand.

She wraps her arms around her thin frame. Her breath sends white puffs into the crisp night. He pulls her close and kisses the top of her head. It is a gesture he did a hundred times before, but in this moment, he feels as if it were his first.

Somebody says something, but he does not hear the words. Aris does. She steps forward, and his arm falls. She walks toward the bonfire.

She comes to stand in front of the flames twice her height. For one moment, he is afraid. What if the logs tumble down and set her ablaze? What if she decides to jump in?

Her clear voice punctures the cold night. "I lost my friend. My best friend. He was the most vibrant human being I've ever met. Fearless. Honest. Open. And I miss him."

She pauses to wipe her eyes.

"He killed himself. He did it because he couldn't stand the pain. The pain of not being able to dream. He lost his dreams. They were stolen from him by the Interpreter Center. They erased his dreams with a machine called the Dreamcatcher."

Metis's heart begins to thump uncontrollably. Aris should not be saying this. There could be repercussions.

He scans the crowd from face to face. Some exchange questioning looks with each other. But most are listening to her with the innocent expression of someone who is dreaming and expecting to wake up. He slowly walks toward her, weaving through bodies that stand as still as gravestones. His steps are cautious. He does not want to disturb their trance.

"Before he died, he made me a thousand origami cranes," Aris continues, "He called them 'blue birds of happiness.' But since he's been gone, I haven't been able to feel happy. Maybe that's because it's trapped inside this crane."

"Burn it!" someone shouts. The person's voice is matched by another.

The crowd chants in unison, "Burn it! Burn it! Burn it!"

He watches as Aris takes one last long look at the crane in her hand. She tosses it into the flame just as he reaches her. When she sees him, she gives him a smile so sweet it breaks his heart.

Her eyes are filled to the brim with liquid threatening to fall. He grabs her hand and pulls her to his chest. She falls easily into it. Her thin body shakes to the rhythm of her sob. He wraps his arms around her, flooded by the desire to take her away from this place—this surreal life. He slowly guides her way. The spot where she stood is now occupied by another woman with something else in her hand.

They walk in silence until the light of the bonfire is behind them. As his eyes adjust to the darkness, he can see the shapes of twisted bushes and squat boulders. A mountain range lies silhouetted at the horizon. The nippy wind blows through the gaps in his jacket.

She stops suddenly, forcing him to do the same. She tilts her head up. He follows her gaze, and his breath catches in his throat. The image above stuns him. The deep indigo sky is carpeted with billions of bright stars. The twinkling white dots, like the pulsing of heartbeats, make the sky seem like a single organism. Alive.

For each point of brilliant light, he knows there are many more that are invisible to the naked eye. Living in the city, where evidence of other planets and stars is obscured by manmade lights, he had forgotten how insignificant his life really is. The faint band of the Milky Way paints the sky like a trail of spilled milk. Somewhere in the center of it is a massive black hole that one day will pull this earth in.

"Doesn't it make you feel small in a good way?" Aris says.

He clears his throat. "Yeah, it does."

After a long pause she says, "The Milky Way is not as bright in the winter as in the summer."

"Why is that?"

"In the summer we look inward, toward the center of the galaxy where there are more stars. But now we're looking outward, away from the center of the galaxy toward the fringe where there are fewer stars."

He searches for Vega in the northwestern quadrant as Aris had told him to do in the park. He cannot see it.

"If you're looking for Vega, it's there." She points toward the bright blue light of his favorite star.

"Ah. Thank you."

"You know, it's funny how a simple act of burning something can feel so freeing," Aris says.

"It helped?"

"I feel lighter. It may be too soon to say that I feel better. But yeah, it helped. I think."

The lavender scent emanating from her skin is intoxicating. She smells just as she does in his dreams. He is drawn to her. Powerless against his own desire. He leans in and kisses her. It is a kiss that carries the weight of their years apart. It is a question that demands an answer.

Do you remember?

She pulls away.

"Metis?"

"Hmm?"

"Take me to your home?" she whispers.

≪

Standing in front of her is an elegant Victorian house the color of a robin's egg. The home sits among the other Painted Ladies on a hill in a posh section of Lysithea. The wood scales covering it make it look like a fish. Weighty carved moldings, floral flourishes in deep magenta, and white gingerbread details adorn the Queen Anne structure like jewelry on an alluring lady, making it almost too overwhelming for the senses.

The whole ride to Lysithea was a blur. The uncertainty of the unknown vibrates beneath her skin like water tremoring in an earthquake. But the intoxicating high coursing through her veins is carrying her forward. Her stomach tightens in a knot.

They step onto the wide wraparound porch. It hugs the house like a protective lover. From here, Aris sees an unobstructed view of the city lights twinkling below. Somewhere out there is her city. And Elara. Where she scattered ashes of the dead. Where she burned a part of herself in the flame.

"I'm home," Metis says, and the door opens.

She steps gingerly into the warm orange glow of the foyer. A large floral arrangement in a vase sits atop a heavy oak table. The flowers are a kind she has never seen before. She walks toward them. The green flowers are long tapered spikes with small buds that hang like bells. They look like a cross between foxgloves and foxtail lilies.

Under her feet is a round Persian rug with saturated shades of reds, cinnamon, and ochre. Above her is an ornate chandelier made of blown glass. It is a stately home, the kind that would have been occupied by an affluent family in the Old World before the Last War.

A landscape painting of oak trees and rolling golden hills on a wall catches her eye, and she goes to it. Something about it calms her. She begins to feel the coil inside her unraveling.

"Beautiful house," she says as she studies the impression the artist left on the canvas while trying to capture light and shadow.

His voice comes from somewhere in the next room, "I think at one point a couple lived here before me. They were poets, I believe. I keep finding pieces of paper with half-written poems all over the house. Some were love notes. Quite sweet."

She hears the heavy sound of a cabinet door opening, then the tinkling of glass. She wonders what one pianist does in this enormous space.

As if Metis can read her mind he says, "It's too big for one person, I know. The Dwelling Council has a theory that creativity expands and contracts with space. Who am I to argue?"

Aris looks away from the painting and turns toward the direction of his voice. Through the wide doorway she sees Metis. His tall and slim figure stands in the middle of a room paneled in dark wood. Something about seeing him like that strikes an eerily familiar feeling.

The shakiness returns. She ambles toward him in the parlor with the caution of a feral cat.

"Do you want a drink? I only have Scotch. I hope that's okay," he says.

"Yes," her voice unstable. She clears her throat.

He hands her a highball glass with amber liquid filling an inch of its bottom. She takes it. On his handsome face is a small smile. He moves closer, his face coming toward hers. She steps back.

"Are you okay?" he asks, hesitancy in his eyes.

"Yeah," she says, "I'm just tired, I guess. It's been a long day."

"Aris," he says her name in a slow, easy way. "What's going on?"

"I don't know," she says and drains the glass. She really does not know. Emotions roll her over like a tidal wave, making her feel as if she is drowning. The irrational feelings surging inside her are frightening.

Am I going insane?

He takes her hand and leads her toward the couch in the middle of the room.

"Let's just slow down and sit. You've been through a lot. You lost your friend," he says. "Right now, there's nothing you need to worry about."

The gentleness of his voice makes her want to cry. She feels fragile, like she is going to break into pieces with one touch. She leans back against the soft cushion and closes her eyes.

The sound of piano music begins. It comes from somewhere in the house. It is her favorite song, *Luce*. She lets it carry her off on its wings.

CHAPTER EIGHTEEN

Palm trees. A beach of sand and pebbles. Blue sky. Everything looks brighter, more vivid than usual. Aris blames the two white suns above.

Sea-foam tickles the tops of her feet. The sound of sand crunches underneath. A shell catches her eye, and she picks it up. It glitters like starlight—a constellation in her hands.

There is a man walking ahead. She quickens her steps. She catches up to him and taps his shoulder. He turns around, and she jumps into his embrace.

"Benja! It's so good to see you."

"Hi, sweetie. It's so good to see you too. I've missed you."

"So, what's it like?"

"It's . . ." Benja struggles to find a word, "boring."

"Boring?"

"There's nothing to do here. Am I supposed to just relax all day, every day?"
She laughs.

"Better than the other way around," she says.

"You mean with a stick up your ass as the devil barbecues you?"

"Something like that."

"Yeah, I was kind of wondering if that's where I was heading." He shrugs.
"Either hell doesn't exist, or I wasn't as bad as I thought."

"I didn't know you believed in that."

"I didn't either. But all the old books I read must have seeped in somehow."

"Let me take a good look at you," she says. Benja is as she remembers, before the obsession and the dreamlessness.

"Still beautiful," she says.

He smiles. "I'm glad they let me keep it."

She wraps her arms around his waist and hugs him tight.

"Oh, I miss you so much," she says.

"I really miss you," he says and holds her.

She looks up at him. "I'm so sorry."

"I'm sorry too," he says and kisses her head. "But there really is no point. How about we call it even?"

She laughs. "If you say so."

They hold each other for a long moment until Benja stirs.

"The birds are here for me now," he says.

Aris looks up and sees a flock of blue cranes flying from one of the suns. They are heading in their direction. She remembers something. She turns back to thank Benja for the one thousand cranes, but he is no longer there.

"Be happy," she whispers.

"What did you say?" a man's voice asks.

Aris feels a weight on her ribs. The hardness of an arm against her skin. She opens her eyes and is blinded by the brightness. She blinks to adjust.

Everything is white. The walls of painted wood. The cotton sheet on her body. The pillow under her cheek. There is so much white she feels like she is floating in a sea of milk. Threads of light shine from the direction of her head, illuminating patches on the floors and walls, lighting the dust in the air like sparkling diamond particles.

She feels hot, like she is sleeping next to a furnace. She turns her body toward the source. All she sees is skin—hills and valleys of warm gold. Her eyes travel up the landscape. A neck. Stubble decorates the edges of his face. His lips.

Metis.

She reaches up and kisses him.

"Nothing," she answers and lays her head on his smooth chest, feeling it move up and down to the rhythm of his breathing.

The heat of his body radiates through her, making her skin tingle. But she does not want to move. A quick breeze enters through the window, billowing the white curtains and giving her temporary relief. It brings with it the salty scent of the sea. She hears the tinkling of wind chimes outside. Beyond that, the constant lolling of tides over sand.

"Happy anniversary." He pulls her closer, wrapping her tight in his embrace. The length of his body hard against hers.

"A very hot one," he says. "You're all sweaty. Did you sleep all right?"

She nods.

"Do you still think it'll be worth living like hermits the rest of the cycle?" she asks.

"Yes." He kisses her forehead.

"You won't miss the restaurants, the plays, the concerts?" she asks.

He runs his fingers through her hair, separating the damp strands from each other. "You worry too much about what's to come. Besides, there are plenty of fun things to do inside."

He demonstrates it by tracing his finger along her spine to its base. It lingers there, drawing circles on the small of her back. Goosebumps rise on her skin.

"And don't forget you're sleeping with the best pianist of this century," he says, "A private concert in our living room. Best seat in town."

"Of the century, huh? I'm not sure I can afford the seat."

"It's not much. Just a kiss or two."

He leans down and presses his soft lips on hers. They travel to her jawline and down her neck. She feels the sharpness of his stubble raking her skin. He bites the thin flesh on her collarbone, and she shudders.

"A nibble here and there," he says.

He continues to move down the curves of her body, inhaling her scent.

"I love your smell."

She catches his face before it disappears under the covers.

"Oh, that's all?" she says, giggling.

"And whatever else you wish to give." He smiles mischievously.

She pivots her hips and rolls him over. It is her turn to be on top. He does not resist.

"Will a deposit be required?" she asks.

By the feel of him against her leg, she knows the answer.

"Yes, it's very, very necessary," he says.

He runs his hands along her sides, leaving goosebumps in their wake. They come to rest at the smallest part of her waist. His thick palms feel hot on her skin even in the warm air.

She gazes down at his contented face. A soft smile dots the corners of his lips. Seeing it brings a smile to hers. She brushes loose, dark waves off his forehead and runs her index finger on the line between his eyebrows.

"It's like someone took a blade and cut you here," she says, "trying to release your third eye."

He chuckles. "Time is a vicious murderer of youth."

He traces the contours of her waist and up the curves of her breast. He presses. A sound, barely audible, escapes her lips.

"But for the lucky few," he says.

An errant thought slips through, and sadness washes over her.

"What's wrong?" he asks.

"Only a year left."

He sits up and looks at her with serious eyes. He pulls her to him and wraps his arms around her. His long-fingered hands press firmly on her back, cradling her. She hears his heart beating, constant like a metronome.

In one quick movement, he twists and pins her to the mattress, surprising her. The feel of his strong thigh muscles prominent on her hips. As if remembering his own strength and weight, he shifts off her protruding bones, relieving her. He gently brushes a stray hair off her face and strokes her cheek.

"Three hundred and sixty-five days," he says. His eyes burrow into hers. "And we will make every minute count."

He kisses her deeply. When they part, she is left with the scent of the ocean and his skin. And the wanting.

She lets him in. An indecipherable sound chokes his throat. Their bodies mimic the rhythm of the tides outside. Slow and insistent, like water against rocks. He laces his hands in hers, and she clings to him like the last ray of the sun the moment before it sets, afraid she would disappear into the other side of the world.

She feels her arms being raised toward the headboard. He untangles his fingers from hers and gathers both her wrists in one hand. The other moves like the wind over the dunes of her body, changing its shape as it passes. She feels like an offering, a sacrifice to calm the thirst of the sea monsters.

His grip tightens. Their movement hastens. Fast. So fast she feels like glass spinning under pressure, readying to explode into a million grains of sand, to be blown east with the wind.

CHAPTER NINETEEN

A familiar music draws her out of slumber. But there is something different about it.

What time is it? She looks at her watch. February 15, 9:17 a.m.

"Lucy, coffee please," she says. No answer.

She smells lavender. It's in the sheets and pillows, surrounding her. She opens her eyes. A crystal chandelier. Warm green walls. Dark cherry-wood sleigh bed. This is not her sleek and modern bedroom.

Where am I?

Then she remembers. Metis's Victorian house. She bolts upright.

Metis!

The dream that has been haunting her this cycle is of him. He is her "man in the white hat!"

She wonders what to do. Should she tell him? Not tell him? She feels as if she's about to combust with the knowledge. She decides she wants to tell him. But how can she do it without sounding like a lunatic? Would he think she had lost her mind? She can use grief as an excuse. Maybe. Can grief turn a person insane?

Finally she understands Benja. If he were here, she knows what he would say. But he is gone—flown away with the blue cranes of happiness. Instead of the drowning sadness that has been haunting her since his death, she feels lighter. She knows her friend is happier, wherever he is.

The music beckons. She takes a deep breath and decides she will improvise as she goes. She lowers her feet off the bed and feels smooth wood planks. Each step makes the wide floorboards of the old house creak beneath her bare feet.

The hall is shrouded in shadows. She pulls open curtains as she passes, letting in the morning. From a vestibule surrounded by windows, she sees the sun peeking up from behind the mountains to the east, while the side of the city near the horizon to the west is still sheathed in darkness.

She treads lightly down the stairs, trying to keep the squeaking to a minimum. The parlor, with its shiny mahogany-paneled walls, is empty. She walks to the back of the house, toward the light and the music.

In a room surrounded by walls of windows and lacy-leaved Cyathea ferns, she finds Metis. In front of him is a shiny black piano. Pencils and pieces of paper lay scattered on its top. Steam rises from a green cup. It smells of bergamot and cream. Earl Grey. His serious face is bathed in the pale light of the dawn.

She watches him, studying the contours of his face. Her eyes go to the deep etched lines between his brows. She wants to reach out and trace them with her fingers as she did in her dream.

He looks up, sees her, and smiles. It brightens his face, making him look devastatingly handsome. She cannot help but return it. She hesitates briefly before making her way to him.

"What's this?" she asks when she gets to the piano.

"A new piece. Do you like it?" Metis says.

"I love it."

"Doesn't it remind you of something?" he asks, looking at her with the usual intensity that makes her heart flutter.

"*Luce*," she says.

He looks back on the keys. "It just needs something more optimistic. So I'm changing it slightly."

She thinks of her dream.

"Metis?" she whispers.

He looks up. "Yeah?"

"I—I . . . umm . . ."

His hands stop moving. "What is it?"

She feels a tingling in her flesh. "I don't want you to think I'm crazy."

A small smile touches the corner of his lips. "I won't."

She breathes in a deep breath. "Last night . . ."

She feels blood rushing to her cheeks. He looks at her with curiosity.

Only a month left.

She sighs. "It's nothing."

She turns away and looks out the window. The trees in his backyard are gray and bare. They stand dark against the pale February sky.

He reaches for her hand, his movement tentative, unlike the way he commands the piano.

"Tell me."

What would Benja do?

Be brave.

"I had a dream with you in it," she says in one breath.

She feels a squeeze on her hand.

"What was it?"

She looks at him. "We were in a cottage on a beach. I've never been there before, but it felt so real."

She watches as blood drains from his face.

"It *was* real, wasn't it?" she whispers.

He nods.

"You know?"

"I've always known."

"How long?" she asks.

"Almost from the beginning."

"So, at the concert, you knew it was me?"

"I thought you were a mirage," Metis says.

His eyes dig as if trying to read her mind.

"Are you upset?" he asks.

She searches her feelings and shakes her head.

"It's surreal and strange. And I'm a little freaked out. But no, I'm not upset. I'm actually . . . happy. It's weird."

She feels his trembling hands on her waist. She places her palms on them, and the quivering subsides. In one quick movement he pulls her onto his lap. He circles his arm around her and holds tight.

"You have no idea how much I've missed you," he says. His face is buried in her neck, breathing her in.

He pulls away and looks at her. His eyes drink in her image, satiating the thirst of a man who had just survived a trek through the desert. His hands reach toward her face. The movement is tentative but becomes more assured once he touches her skin.

A kiss. Soft at first, like the flapping of wings. The pressure intensifies and leaves her breathless. It feels just as she remembers from her dream. Butterflies flutter inside her stomach. But there are so many questions swirling inside her head.

She breaks away. "How?"

"Dreams since the beginning of the cycle. Feelings. I thought I was going insane. But one day on the subway, I saw red graffiti on the wall. It triggered something in me."

"The one that looks like a flower?" she asks. "What does it mean?"

"I rode the train back and forth so many times like a madman. Then it became apparent to me."

"What is it?"

He takes her hand and puts something in the middle of her palm. A silver ring. She picks it up and studies it. The familiar design looks like a flower. Except it is more than a flower. It's a shape within a shape, entwined as one. The outer design is of interwoven lines that form a nine-point mandala. Inside its center is a square with indented sides.

She hands it back.

"It's yours," he says.

She looks at him.

"Please," he says.

She eases it onto her left ring finger.

"That's where you used to wear it," he whispers.

"Why do you have it?" she asks, staring at the foreign object on her finger. She is afraid to look at him.

He clears his throat. "I've always had both rings. We must have decided in the last cycle to keep them together. I found them hidden in a chair cushion in the living room. I knew what they were as soon as I saw them."

"How do you know so much?"

He takes in a deep breath. "Absinthe."

She feels the wind knocked out of her.

"You're a Dreamer?"

He nods.

"You knew Benja, didn't you?"

He looks down. "Yes."

"Why didn't you tell me?"

"Because I didn't want you to hate me."

Aris searches her feelings. Once she may have hated all Dreamers. She blamed them for enabling Benja's obsession—for giving him drugs that propelled him into madness. But all the dreams Benja had of his old lover were his. The unlawful behaviors were his too. Metis did not break into her house or threaten her, and he was a Dreamer.

"I don't hate you," she says. "Tell me more about what you remember."

"What do you want to know?"

"How many cycles?" she asks.

"I don't know. At least one. Maybe two or three. I've seen many memories—several were of us inside this house—but we were always similar to the way we are now."

She finds it strange to have a man who only a few months ago was a stranger to her tell her they once had a life together. He remembers a lot. She can tell by the way he looks at her with the possessiveness and longing of a lover.

"What was I like?" she asks and realizes the bizarreness of the question.

"You had the same mannerisms you do now. You were often surrounded by trees. Gardens. Parks."

She imagines them walking hand in hand on a path with green trees arching above.

"You loved to read," he adds.

"I still do," she says.

"And I often dream of us on a beach," he says.

Her face feels hot. She looks down, trying to hide the smile that she cannot suppress.

"You smiled like that in my dreams."

"I must have been happy," she says.

The feelings are becoming too intense. She shifts her eyes to the small garden behind the house. The roses and wisterias are all bare. The frost that gathered overnight is thawing in the sun, making the branches look as if they were catching fire.

"This is strange, right?" she asks.

"Such is the paradox of Tabula Rasa. To have to rediscover things we've already discovered. To remaster what we've already conquered. We live in the present while unearthing the past, unbeknownst to us."

"Enough to make your head spin," she says.

"Tabula Rasa does get a few things right," he says.

He looks at her as if trying to arrive at a decision. Then he gets up and comes to stand behind her.

She holds her breath, unable to predict what he is going to do. She feels his hand at her temple. He sweeps up a section of hair and tugs it behind her ear. The gesture elicits a familiar warmth in her.

"You will never take anyone for granted, because you will lose them," he says.

He moves her hair over one shoulder.

"You'll treasure all your experiences as if they're your last."

His hand is on her neck now, caressing it.

"You will fall in love over and over with the same person."

She tilts her head to the side and closes her eyes.

"It's the reality of it that kills you. Every time you wake, realizing it was just a dream, a piece of you dies," he says.

Suddenly she sees Tabula Rasa as a black cloud—a storm in the distance, moving closer as each minute passes.

She feels his breath at her earlobe. He kisses it, and she manages to hold a moan in her throat. His lips glide along her jawline, and down her neck.

"The Dreamers are dangerous, so I've been told," she says.

He snickers. "Are we?"

"You have the power to rip through the fabric of our society trying to get at the past. There's nothing in the past but the Last War," she says.

"There is so much more in the past than that," he whispers and pulls the loose neck of her blouse to the side, exposing her shoulder.

"And besides, I don't want to rip anyone's fabric but yours," he says.

He kisses the tip of her shoulder and runs his hand along the edge of her blouse, like an animal searching through grass for its burrow.

His hot palms move down the curves of her breasts. Lower and lower. A moan escapes her lips. She hears the loud scratching sound of her chair dragging against the wood floors and feels the wind stirring her hair. Metis is standing in front of her now.

He lifts her easily off the chair. Air whooshes past her as he carries her up the stairs. The next thing she touches is the soft mattress. The faint lavender scent of the sheets caresses her nose.

He comes to her with the hunger of a starving man. Her head whirls. Bright dots dance in her vision. She becomes nerve endings, feeling her way like a blind person through the tunnel of his desire. Her body is malleable in his hands as he changes its shape to fit his mold. She is reminded of the concert, of the feeling that she is about to lift off into the sky. She grabs onto him for anchorage as they soar into oblivion.

She does not know where her body ends and his begins. Their legs and arms are intertwined with the sheet, like caterpillars spinning silk to become chrysalises.

Aris hears a sigh. It came from her.

"I'm sorry," he says, "That was unexpected. You're not upset, are you?"

She turns to look at him. "Don't be sorry, I'm far from being upset."

"I had planned to woo you before we, you know," he says.

"Define wooing," she says.

"Dinner, music, flowers. Maybe a play. You love plays."

"Quite a plan," she says.

"Then I might steal a few more kisses good night." He leans over and presses his warm lips on hers.

"And?" She glides her hand down the hard line of his back muscles, feeling its dampness.

"And maybe after you feel comfortable enough around me, we can take it to the next level." He peels the sheet off her. Her hands automatically move to cover her bosom.

"I'm sorry we ruined your plan. It was a really good one," she says.

"Don't be sorry. I'm far from being upset," he says with a sly smile. He pulls her hands off and replaces them with his face.

She feels his palm caressing her inner thigh. It moves dangerously higher and higher. She grabs it.

"You're not—already?"

"I'm afraid I am," he says.

"But we just . . ."

"Well, you can't blame a starving man for wanting to gorge himself on the most beautiful meal in front of him."

"You've been starving?" she asks, surprised.

"This cycle, yes."

"But it's been almost four years."

"Umm-hmm . . ." he says as he nibbles his way through the courses.

"Seriously?" she asks, pulling his face up.

"I've been waiting for you," he says and goes back to what he was doing.

"Wow."

"Is that a bad 'wow'?" He looks up at her.

"You just made me feel like I've been unfaithful."

"It's okay. I forgive you," he says, "You didn't remember."

"So, you never thought of being with other people?"

"No."

"Not even once?" she asks.

"No."

"Oh, wow."

"You keep saying that like it's a bad thing," he says.

"No, it's just . . . I'm honored, I guess."

"Don't be. I didn't do it for you," he says.

"Oh?"

She sits up and draws her knees to her chest. He comes to the same position. She looks at him for an answer.

He says, "Unlike you, I remember. I started remembering early on. I've been searching for you all this time, and I thought I wouldn't be able to live with myself once we found each other if I didn't stay faithful to our memories. So I just never had the urge."

"Never?"

"Well, yeah, but not, you know."

"It's just not natural."

"Pardon me?"

"Humans are naturally polyamorous. It's a scientific fact. We are promiscuous. We get bored. We get restless. We like to sample different tastes. That's why I've never understood marriage. Why chain your instinct?" she says.

"Monogamy is a decision you make every single day. You decide that the person you're with is who you want, and you remake that decision every day," he says.

He takes her hand and kisses it. "It's a promise."

"But isn't that work?" she asks.

"It's never been work for me," he says. "I just think of your face. The wanting of you is like breathing, living."

So this is why.

"What are you thinking?" he asks and straightens.

He regards her with a long side look. "You seem . . . bewildered."

"I'm just feeling this . . . It's this . . ." She searches for words to describe it. She touches the area between her chest and stomach. "You know here, where you feel like you're falling and at the same time filled to the brim."

"I know that feeling well," he says and leans closer. His nose touches hers, and she smells the sweet scent of bergamot, sweat, and him.

She feels his hand behind her neck, his fingers winding around her hair at the nape. Then the softness of the pillow.

"It's the reason we Dreamers spend our lives searching, trying to bring it back within our grasp, even if just in dreams. And for the lucky few who find it, we will never let go," he says.

She understands.

CHAPTER TWENTY

"It's lavender oil," Metis says as he pours the liquid into the hot bath. He sits behind her, one arm around her waist. He leans back and pulls her against him. The scent rises with the white steam, and Aris breathes it in.

"You like this scent," she says, "I smell it on your sheets too."

"Only because it reminds me of you."

"I don't know if I can ever get used to the idea of this," she says. "It's strange to hear you speak of me like we've known each other for a long time."

He picks a piece of damp hair off her face and moves it behind her ear. "It's only in your mind that we've known each other just a few months. Or that you've been in this house with me for only three days. In reality—the ultimate reality, or whatever we can call it—we've had years. Your mind just hasn't realized it."

"Has it been three days already?" she asks. Time is a blur when she's with him. They have barely left the bed except for necessities. "How do you reconcile that? When your mind and your memories can't agree on what's real and what isn't?"

"It's best to just follow your heart," he says.

Follow my heart.

Aris is not even sure what that means. She has always been rooted in logic and the scientific method. First you ask the question, then you carefully gather and examine the evidence, and finally you combine all the information to arrive at a logical answer. But what do you do with ethereal evidence that disappears with the sunrise?

"I can almost hear the gears in your head turning," Metis says. Aris feels warm water trickling down one shoulder.

"'Remembrance of things past is not necessarily the remembrance of things as they were,'" she says, quoting Marcel Proust. "Memories aren't simply retrieved from a box whenever people try to remember something. They're reconstructed. Different parts of the brain draw information from various corners, then build the memory we're trying to recall."

"You're questioning whether your memories are even real?" Metis asks.

"It's just not logical," she says, "Not in the traditional sense."

"Well, if you think about it, Tabula Rasa is not a natural process even though it feels like it is. Every four years, we lose our memories and we rebuild our lives. We all accept it as the way life works."

Aris ponders a life without Tabula Rasa. A life with continuous memories of people and places. Of relationships forged over the span of one's lifetime, not one's cycle. Enough time to build foundations and layer them over and over again.

Then she remembers the images of the Last War. Of a world where people could harbor decades, if not centuries, of prejudices and hatred. Of a life unappreciated, because having almost a century can trick you into thinking that you have forever. A lifetime to accumulate and grow one's ambitions and power. Enough time to develop the fear that you will lose what you have and a desire to protect it. A life of attachment.

"What do you think happens when we reset?" she asks.

"I don't know. I've never read anything in any books about how it's triggered," he says, "You go to sleep one person and wake up as another."

She wishes Benja were still here. It would be nice to talk to him about her situation. At the least, he would have some interesting things to say. Maybe even an "I told you so." If he had been able to show her his dreams and make her a believer, he would not have been alone in his desperation. If only she had figured out the copper helmet sooner; she could have given him the ability to prove her wrong.

If only . . .

"What are you thinking?" he asks.

"Benja."

Silence follows. She looks over her shoulder at him.

"Does that bother you?"

"A little. You love him. And I love you."

"It's not the same thing. He was my friend. You're my—"

"Husband," he says.

She shifts and feels Metis's grip tighten around her waist. She is uncomfortable with the thought of being tied to a man she just met. A marriage is a decision two people make together, but she has no memory of making it. The strong feelings she has for him are undeniable. But why must they have any relevancy to their state of attachment?

"You don't like being married," he says.

"It's just—I'm not sure. I don't remember being married. Yesterday I wasn't. And now I am. My brain is still trying to catch up."

"I understand," he says.

"Do you? Really?"

He chuckles. "I'm trying. At least I get credit for that, I hope."

A veil of silence covers the room with thick, awkward air.

Metis breaks it. "I know I'm coming on really strong." He sighs. "I will try to be good. I promise."

"Define good," she says.

He gently kisses the top of her head. "I'll try to be understanding, patient, and respectful of your boundaries. It's hard for me to be close to you and not want to touch you. But I will try my best."

"Who says anything about not touching?"

She grabs his hands from her shoulders and wraps them around her waist.

"You don't mind me touching you?"

She shakes her head. "I like it."

"You only mind that we're married?"

She shrugs. "It's just that I don't have a memory of it, so it's like someone claiming I've dyed my hair purple and I don't remember liking the color, let alone having it on my head."

"So, marriage is like a bad hair decision," he says.

"I don't know how to better explain."

He becomes so quiet she feels uneasy.

"How does Absinthe work?" she asks, feeling the need to keep the conversation going.

"I don't really know the science of it. Maybe it serves as a bridge to parts of the brain locked by Tabula Rasa. Maybe it rebuilds the neuro-connections severed by it. What it does is . . . pure magic. I saw our past lives. Experienced it. The scent. The feel. Somehow it solidifies memories as dreams. It's hard to explain."

"Do you remember everything?"

"No, not everything. Only the strongest memories survived—the ones associated with deep emotions. That's why most Dreamers remember our old lovers, and not, say, where we lived or worked."

Aris thinks of her dream on the beach.

"How did I dream the past if I didn't take Absinthe?" she asks.

"You've always had that dream—your memory—locked up inside you. Our dreams are the gate to the past. Absinthe widens that gate. But it won't work without the dreams."

"So, if your dreams are wiped . . ."

"Absinthe wouldn't work," he says.

Aris feels sadness descending on her. Its thick coating envelops her like candle wax.

"Benja told me about dreams and Absinthe, but I didn't believe him," she says.

"Some things are too difficult to believe. They're best experienced."

"What if there's a way to make other people see what you see in your dreams?"

"What do you mean?"

"Have you ever seen Dreamcatcher? The machine the Interpreter Center uses to erase dreams?"

"No, I only know what it does. They used it on Bodie. Then Benja."

Aris remembers the name Bodie. She had come across it while going through the reports in Professor Jacob's briefcase. The name was associated with the angry man Officer Scylla arrested near the Natural History Museum.

"Bodie was another Dreamer?" she asks. Aris wonders if everyone on that report is a Dreamer. She does not remember seeing Metis on it.

"Yes, he was erased about five months ago," Metis says.

"What happened to him after?" she asks.

"He moved back to Elara."

"So, he's still . . ."

"Yeah, he's alive as far as I know."

"Can we talk to him?"

"What are you thinking?"

"The Interpreter Center stole Benja's dreams and lied to the police. I'm afraid they may have done the same thing to Bodie. Benja didn't even remember being treated, so I couldn't do anything about it. But maybe I can help Bodie."

"How?"

"I have this machine that looks just like the helmet on the Dreamcatcher. Maybe it was a prototype. I think it can look at dreams. I tested it on myself, but I was awake. I was hoping to use it on Benja. He told me he didn't dream anymore—but maybe there were still some left in there the Interpreter didn't get. I wanted to give his dreams back to him, but I was too late."

She feels Metis's grip.

"How did you get it?"

"The storage room at the Natural History Museum."

"Does the Interpreter Center know you have it?"

"Of course not!"

"Aris, this isn't good."

"Nothing is good in this situation. My friend killed himself because his dreams were taken from him. What the Interpreter did was wrong."

She stands up. Her skin feels the pricking of the chill in the air.

"Let's go."

Thane cannot believe his eyes. Aris is the last person he thought he would see coming out of the Victorian house. Metis is next to her, their hands clasped together.

Thane has been following Metis since he saw him leaving Benja's apartment. When he found him on the walkway of Aris's apartment, he decided to continue pursuing him. Once he knew where Metis lived, his name and identity easily followed.

The pianist is a mysterious man. He spends a lot of time inside Carnegie Hall. But he also goes to many places. A busy man. This is the first time Thane has seen him with another person.

Why Aris? he wonders. Does she know Metis watched her like a stalker?

As usual, Thane will leave Aris off his report to the Interpreter Center. They do not need to know about her. She's already connected to Benja. That is more than enough to make Thane uneasy. Apollina is ruthless. Who knows what she would do to Aris.

He follows them.

Aris looks up as they stroll through the park. It is nice to have a hand holding hers, guiding her so she does not have to worry about tripping and falling while not looking forward.

The trees are bare. The deep-brown trunks and branches stand like skeletons. Their anemic state makes her miss autumn.

The wind blows. She shrinks into the warmth of her jacket and ponders the kind of life she is heading toward. Just half a year ago she lived with a detachment that made her feel safe and secure in her place. Life then was but one finite period of digestible time. There were only two states of existence—cycle and recycle. Reason and logic drove her actions. Her view of the world was less complicated and more certain. She was transcending, shedding her human weakness for attachment.

Then she met Benja and found herself sliding down a rabbit hole so deep she did not know where she would end up. But she landed and found Metis next to her. The world is different now—she is different now. She's not sure if she could ever go back to being the old Aris.

"Do you regret remembering?" he asks as they pass a pond with edges crusted over in ice.

"Why would you ask that?"

"I get the feeling you're unsure, like Alice standing in the middle of Wonderland, expecting to wake up."

She shakes her head "No, I don't regret remembering. But I do feel a bit off center. Changed, somehow. I used to have my feet firmly planted on the ground, and now I feel as if the ground may cave in at any moment."

"You won't cave in. I'll keep my arm around you always."

She lets those words warm her in their embrace.

"We keep talking about me. How about you?" she asks.

"What about me?"

"Were you different? Have you changed by being with me?"

He smiles and shakes his head. "I've pretty much always been this way. Maybe it has to do with age. You're younger than I am. Still growing, changing. Whereas I'm pretty set in my ways."

She imagines him like a boulder, standing against wind and time. Waiting.

"But isn't that unfair?" she asks.

"Why?"

"When I was out there experiencing life, you were stuck alone."

He laughs. "You don't seem to have a good outlook on monogamy. I did feel alone. But not stuck. I had my music and the Dreamers. I also had my quest. I was fueled by the hope of reuniting with you. My life was not full, but it was not intolerable either. I was not interested in just having someone to be a warm body next to me.

"This," he says and squeezes her hand, "is infinitely better."

They enter a train station and descend to the level where trains leave from Lysithea to Callisto. Aris remembers something.

"The red design on the train tunnels. Did you put them there?" she asks.

"I don't know. Maybe. Like bread crumbs from my past self to follow. But I don't have any memory of doing it."

"Don't you find that strange? If it wasn't you who put it there, who did? For what purpose?"

"I don't find anything strange anymore. I spent most of this cycle looking for you. I was so afraid of not finding you, then suddenly you appeared. Nothing is in our control. I'm just grateful."

Sadness descends and drapes her with its gray veil.

"We have a month left," she says.

"Thirty days."

"That's all."

"Seven hundred and twenty-two hours. We'll make each count."

"You said the same thing to me in my dream."

"I guess I haven't changed," he says.

"Do you think people do change?"

"Over time, we become a better or worse version of who we are. But I don't think our cores change."

"Benja believed people change over time."

"Do you?"

She leans her head on his shoulder. "We may change our habits and the way we see the world. But I think our essence remains."

"Here's my stop," she says.

They step off the train. First to her apartment for a change of clothes and the helmet. Then Bodie.

The commuters weave through each other as they head toward their destinations. She feels a tug at her hand and turns. Metis is rooted to a spot on the platform. He pulls her to him and places his hands on her shoulders.

"Wait," he says.

People walk around them. Aris feels as if they are a permanent part of the station, like a tree or a statue.

"I need to tell you something," he says.

"Here?" She looks at him, puzzled.

"In the past, I had planned to ask you to marry me at Strawberry

Field, but I looked over at you, and you were so beautiful. And I couldn't help myself. The words just fell out of my mouth. We were standing here."

Aris looks down at the circle around her feet—her favorite circle. It makes sense now.

"How did you ask?" she asks.

"I don't remember the details. It was kind of an existential moment."

Metis looks unsure and nervous, like a young man asking a girl out on a first date. The self-assured genius pianist is, for the moment, missing.

"How would you ask me now?" she asks.

His eyes change. A deep pool of feelings stirs in them.

"I would say . . ." He takes her hand. "A year, four years, a lifetime, or an eternity is but a marker in this life. But when I am with you, those markers fall away. Everything falls away. Time stretches and bends in ways that render it insignificant. I know you worry about what's to come, but all I want is to just hold your hand. For as long as we both shall live. Would you please be my wife?"

Aris feels as if her heart is floating above her. She looks at him and knows that for as long as he dreams of them, he will try to find her through all the cycles to come. Love is no longer pointless if it spans a lifetime.

"Yes," she whispers, and the word vibrates in her bones.

Aris does not remember how they got to her apartment. The only thing she is aware of is Metis's warm lips crushing hers. His palms move from her sides to the neck of her blouse, stretching it over her shoulders.

"Let me help," she says and pulls the top over her head. Her long hair sprays over her back.

His hands are on her bare skin. Hot and urgent. He pulls her forward as his lips travel down to the crook of her neck, nibbling and tasting as they go, tickling her. She is reminded of a documentary she once saw where a lion was feeding on a young gazelle.

She giggles and says, "Wait. Let's talk some more."

He makes a frustrated noise in his throat. "You're joking."

"Yeah, I am. Wouldn't it be funny if I wasn't?"

"No, it wouldn't," he says and flips her against a wall.

She is blinded by its whiteness. His hands move to her hips, slowly releasing her pants, then her undergarments. She feels the softness of silk around her ankles.

The heat of his breath is on the small of her back. His hot tongue travels up the canyon of her spine, sending shivers through her. His long-fingered hands knead and caress the plains of her body. She is clay.

"Do you want to go to the bedroom?" she asks, her voice trembling.

He answers with the sound of his belt unbuckling. She hears his clothes dropping to the floor. His warmth spreads over her. She wants to collapse onto the floor like his discarded clothes, and would but for the vice-like hands holding her up.

His breath is at her ear. She feels the nip of his teeth on her lobe. She wants to scream. A sound escapes him. Or was it from her? She feels like a balloon being filled, stretched to its limit. She wants release, but she is between the hardness of the wall and him. There is no escape. Her body is melding into his, changing.

The floor is hard on her back, but Aris makes no move to get up. She looks over to Metis. His cheeks are pink. His chest moves up and down from exertion. A light smile decorates his face. He looks content. Her heart swells knowing she put it there.

She realizes now it is he whom she has been missing. The reason for the unexplained moments of sadness. The melancholy she learned to live with this cycle—the "emptiness"—is gone.

"I love you," she says and kisses his shoulder.

He turns to her. The spot between his eyebrows scrunches together. His eyes have an indecipherable expression in them. He pulls her to his chest and kisses her hair.

"And I love you. Always. No matter what. Remember that."

She hopes she can.

CHAPTER TWENTY-ONE

Although small, downtown Elara at night shines brightly. The low-slung buildings are lit with twinkling lights on all sides, making them look as if encrusted with stars.

Fast-tempo music surrounds them, sending tremors through the ground. Bars and restaurants line both sides of the street. They are all filled to the brim with people—mostly young. Some overflow to the sidewalks. They sit on curbs and lean against walls, chatting energetically with each other. Everyone is out furiously spending the last of their entertainment points.

A squad of young women staggers out of one bar. They make their way across the street to another. One trips and falls. Her friends rush to her side and pick her up, laughing all the while. The scene makes Aris smile.

"Is it heavy? I can take it if you want," she says of the backpack on Metis's shoulders. In it are the helmet and computer. She does not know if Bodie will let them use the helmet on him, but the least they can do is ask. She pats her jacket and feels the vial of Absinthe Benja had given her. A failsafe.

"No, I'm fine," he says and brings her hand up for a kiss.

They walk past the bright downtown area and up the dark hill. The image is a big contrast to the place they just left. The land is barren but for the shadows of scraggly shrubs and sun-scorched balls of tumbleweed. Wooden homes climb up the winding road. All dark. Everyone is downtown.

Bodie's is the only lit one in the neighborhood of houses overlooking downtown Elara. It is the shape of a barn with vertical siding. The weathered wood looks as if it could use a fresh coat of paint. The land around it is tamped dirt with nothing but shrubs.

They can hear noises coming from inside. Metis knocks on the door and it opens. It is Bodie. Up close, he looks bigger and more muscular than Aris remembers. His blond hair and white clothes contrast with his deep-brown skin. He gives them a big smile.

"Hi, I'm Bodie."

He thrusts his hand out. Metis takes it and shakes. Bodie turns his attention to Aris.

"May I?" He lifts her left hand and brings it to his lips.

"Beautiful ring," he says and steps aside to let them through. "Come on in!"

Metis and Aris look at each other. Metis steps over the threshold of the door, and she follows. She is taken aback by what she sees. There is a gathering of about twenty people. They are scattered around the large room, chatting and laughing with each other. Everyone is wearing white. Aris scans her and Metis's gray and black clothes and feels out of place.

"We're about to get ready," Bodie says and leads them toward the group.

For what?

Aris leans into Metis and whispers, "What's going on?"

"I don't know."

The interior of Bodie's house is open and airy. The walls are a happy yellow. One glance and Aris can tell the pleasant space belongs to an artist. A long worktable sits in the middle, separating the area into quadrants. A desk with multiple drawers is by a window. On it lie stones of different colors and spools of silver and gold chain.

Paintings of various sizes are stacked up against the wall of one corner. A wheel for throwing pottery sits in another. Wide shelves run along one side of the room. One is filled with drying vases and pots. Another has those that have been fired. They are organized by color. Greens and blues on one side, the warm colors on another.

She looks at the people. They appear to be couples, either holding hands or with arms wrapped around each other. They are chatting enthusiastically. The excited energy in the room is contagious.

"Metis!" a surprised voice speaks.

Aris turns toward it and sees a woman in white. Her brown eyes are wide with shock. In her chestnut-brown hair are wildflowers from the desert. Her pale skin makes her stand out from others in the room.

"Seraphina?" Metis rushes toward her. Aris follows.

He knows her?

"Why are you here?" the pretty woman says in a hushed tone. Her face is fear-stricken.

Why is she so afraid? Who is she to Metis? An ex-lover?

"How do you know my—?" Metis asks in a low voice.

Seraphina looks at her feet. "Benja told me about you."

"Wait, you know Benja?" Aris asks. Her voice is high in her ears.

A surprised look crosses Seraphina's face. "Who are you?"

"This is Aris. My wife," Metis says. "Benja's friend."

Seraphina's eyes well up. She turns to Metis. "Does she know?"

He nods. "What are you doing here?"

"It's my wedding," says Seraphina.

"Oh! Congratulations," Aris says.

Seraphina ignores her and steps closer to Metis. So close that Aris can smell the scent of her perfume. She feels the heat of jealousy rising.

"You can't be here. You need to leave," Seraphina says.

"What's going on?" Metis asks.

Bodie appears next to Seraphina. "Hey."

Seraphina takes a step back. "Hi, Honey. This is Metis. He's an old friend. And this is his beautiful wife, Aris. He just introduced me to her."

She turns to Aris. "It's so nice to meet you finally."

To Aris's surprise, Seraphina moves her hands to her shoulders and presses her against her chest before Aris can protest. It is an intimate gesture that Aris did not expect from someone she just met. Seraphina's warm breath is next to her ears.

"Promise me you'll leave. Metis can't be here. The Sandman needs to be protected. Absinthe needs to be protected," Seraphina whispers quickly.

Aris feels blood leaving her body. Shock surges like waves from the pit of her stomach.

Metis is the Sandman?

Before Seraphina's lips leave her ears, she says, "Don't drink it."

Drink what?

Seraphina squeezes her shoulders. Aris takes it as a warning—now is not the time to push for answers. She nods and forces a smile. Bodie's face breaks into a wide grin.

He puts his hand on Metis's shoulder and says, "You know, you look so familiar. Have we met?"

Seraphina and Metis exchange a glance. "Metis is a famous pianist. You've probably seen his face on something somewhere."

"Must be. Well, we're so glad to have you here."

"How did you two meet?" Metis asks.

"Seraphina was visiting Elara a few months back. She had a friend with her. What was his name? My memory's not so good anymore."

"Benja," Seraphina says. Her voice is sad.

"Handsome guy," Bodie says, "I met them at a bar downtown. They were staying at the Hotel of the Desert, near the preserve. I thought they were lovers until she came to my shop one day and asked me out on a date."

"We haven't been apart since," Seraphina says.

"Never again," Bodie says. He leans down and kisses her.

When he breaks away, he says, "All right! I need to get the party started. Excuse me."

He walks off, leaving Seraphina alone with Metis and Aris.

"I guess you didn't heed my advice," Metis says.

Seraphina gives a small smile. "Neither did you."

"Fair enough," says Metis.

"I heard about Bodie soon after I joined the Dreamers," Seraphina says. "When they described him, I knew he was my lover from the past cycle. You know, it wasn't even that long after his dreams were erased that I joined. If only . . ."

Seraphina sighs. "When I decided to look for him, I didn't know what

I would find. I was afraid, so I came with Benja. He was the bravest person I knew."

Aris wonders why Benja never mentioned Seraphina to her. Then she remembers. She was against him taking Absinthe, and she blamed all the Dreamers for influencing him. She wishes she had believed her friend while he was alive. She could have helped. At least Bodie is still here. If he will let her, she may be able to give his dreams back to him.

Seraphina says, "You were right on one thing though, Metis. We can't force the past on someone who doesn't want it."

Aris sees Bodie coming out of a room she thinks is the kitchen. In his hands is a tray of shot glasses filled with clear liquid. He walks slowly around the room, trying to keep the drinks from spilling. He goes to each person, offering a glass to them. One by one they take them from the tray.

"Is that—?" Aris asks.

"No. Something else," Metis says.

Bodie comes to stand in front of them.

"This is why you're here, isn't it?" Bodie says and winks.

Metis takes a glass. So, does Aris. Seraphina stiffens and gives Aris the slightest shake of her head. It's imperceptible to everyone but her.

The sound of metal clinking against glass rings through the room, hushing everyone into silence. They look toward Bodie.

He speaks.

"Today I marry the woman of my dreams. Seraphina came into my life like a warm summer breeze. I cannot imagine my life without her. And I won't. Tabula Rasa will not take her away from me anymore." His voice is clear and cheerful. He sounds like someone on the top of the world.

He looks around at the smiling faces. "I know you all have the same desire. To stay forever with those we love. Here's to that dream."

Bodie raises the glass and brings it to his mouth.

"To love," he says and drains it.

Everyone echoes him and drinks the shot. Aris yanks at Metis's hand and shakes her head. Metis nods. Neither of them drink.

Aris watches as Bodie's smile turns to a look of bewilderment. His legs collapse under him. As if a switch has been turned off, light exits his eyes. His inanimate body crashes to the floor.

In quick succession, one after another of those around him drop where they stand, like marionette dolls whose strings have been severed. The sound, like sacks of potatoes being thrown onto the floor, reverberates in Aris' bones. *Thud. Thud. Thud.*

Aris hears a scream. It's coming from her. Metis grabs the glass in her hand and throws it against a wall. It shatters into pieces.

"Shhh," Seraphina says, "you'll attract attention."

Seraphina walks toward Bodie and lowers herself to the floor next to his lifeless body. She gently places his head on her lap. He looks peaceful, as if in slumber.

Aris feels a tremble, like that of an earthquake. Then she realizes its epicenter is her. She looks down at her hands and watches them vibrate uncontrollably.

"What happened, Seraphina?" Metis speaks. His voice is rough.

"Poison."

"Did you do this?"

"Yes."

"Why did you murder them?" Metis asks.

"I didn't. I only made the poison. It was their choice. They wanted to die. They didn't want to live without their lovers. A life without love is not a life."

"Didn't you love Bodie?" Aris asks.

"Yes. More than anything." Seraphina looks up, and her face is painted with tears.

"You know Bodie didn't even remember me?" she says. "The Interpreter took his dreams and memories of us. Have you ever looked into the eyes of someone you love and seen no recollection? It's more painful than you can ever imagine."

"But you found each other," Aris says.

"This time. But what about the next cycle? His dreams of our past were taken from him. Absinthe will no longer work on him—the dreams they took are gone. At first, I tried to remind him of the past, but it only confused him. It got so bad he would get angry whenever I talked about it.

Eventually he refused. So I settled into making a new life with him. Bodie was not the same after the Dreamcatcher. A part of him was missing."

Aris knows what Seraphina means. A part of Benja was missing too. *Hope.* The Dreamcatcher had taken hope away from him and replaced it with emptiness.

"He would never remember me the same way I'll remember him," Seraphina says.

"But suicide?" Metis asks.

"You think it was my idea? It was his. Death is the only way out of Tabula Rasa's grip. He was the freest man you'd ever find. Everyone else here—they wanted the same thing. You don't hear about it, because nobody talks about it. But they're there, waiting for the right opportunity to break free. Isn't that what Benja did?"

Aris feels tears rolling down her chin. "This can't be the only way out. There has to be another way."

"There isn't," Seraphina says.

She notices that next to Seraphina is a glass filled with clear liquid.

"No, don't," Aris whispers. "We can help."

"There's nothing you can do."

"We have a machine that can project dreams. That's why we came here—to try and help Bodie get his dreams back."

Something flashes in Seraphina's eyes. She looks down at Bodie and sighs.

"It's too late for us. You need to leave. Once the police find us, they'll want answers. You two cannot be associated with this."

Seraphina eases a ring off her finger and does the same to Bodie. She beckons Aris over.

"Here, take these and go. Use the back door."

Seraphina hands Aris the silver objects. Aris looks at them in her palm and realizes that they have the same design as her and Metis's rings.

"Why do you have these?" Aris asks.

"I don't know. All of us here have them. We all came across them somehow. Please put them in the Gift Market the next time you're there. Someone else may be able to use them."

Aris feels like crying.

"Please go. I need to follow Bodie," Seraphina says. "Being without him is unbearable. But I can't do that until you two leave. Please."

Metis places his arm around Aris and pulls her toward the back of the house. As they walk slowly away, she looks over her shoulder at the scene.

The floor of the yellow room is carpeted with the men and woman who, just moments earlier, were alive. Their bodies cover the floor like a field of white flowers. A vision from a nightmare.

Seraphina is the only figure sitting. She is cradling her lover in her arms, rocking back and forth as if singing him a lullaby. In another time and another place, could Aris be her? She shoves the rings into her jacket pocket and feels warm tears streaming down her face.

There are fewer people in Elara than the other cities. Thane fears being seen, so he hides behind a building across the way from the house Aris and Metis disappeared into. He hopes he does not end up in Elara next cycle. He doesn't like this place. Everything looks old and battered, reminding him of sun-faded photographs of ghost towns in Old California. He prefers the brightness and noise of Callisto. It's where he belongs.

The cold wind blows, and he crosses his arms over his chest. Too many nights he is out in the cold, stalking suspects. He cannot wait for Tabula Rasa to come and take him out of this situation.

He looks across the way at the only lit house on the empty street. There is a party going on in there. He heard laughter and screams, and something like breaking glass coming from it. Aris never mentioned having friends in Elara. Perhaps the friends belong to Metis.

They are lovers. But it does not make sense. The Aris he knows would not suddenly commit to someone with only a month left.

Why now? Why this man?

The house is now quiet. Too quiet. Thane decides to look inside. He will be careful not to get caught. Maybe everyone in there is drunk. Then it would not matter. He treads carefully across the graveled road.

One of the front windows has curtains that are partially open. He goes toward it and peeks through. The room is empty.

That's strange. Where are they?

His eyes catch something odd on the floor. Flowers. Desert flowers surrounded by brown earth. He strains his eyes. The silky texture does not look like dirt. More like hair.

What is someone's head doing on the floor?

He thinks of Aris, and his heart drops to his stomach. He runs to the front door and pounds against it. No answer. He turns the knob and pushes.

The scene before him is out of a surreal painting. On the floors are limp bodies strewn about. Everyone is dressed in white. Next to them are empty shot glasses.

His mind immediately goes to the drug the Interpreter Center is hunting down with his help.

Does it make people immediately fall asleep and dream?

He walks to the woman with flowers in her hair, being careful to tread lightly. The floorboards creak with each step. When he gets to the woman, he kneels next to her. She has a smile on the corner of her lips. Her face looks peaceful.

"Excuse me."

Nothing.

He touches her, intending to shake her awake. Her skin is still warm, but her body is too still. He moves his fingers up her slender neck.

No pulse!

Next to her is a familiar face. A man with deep-tan skin and blond hair. The one whose dreams the Interpreter Center erased almost half a year ago. Bodie.

His heart skips a beat. He feels sweat budding on his temples. The dinner in his stomach is threatening to come back up.

Aris!

He runs around the room, going from body to body, looking at each face. No Aris. Relief washes through him.

He looks around at the room full of dead bodies and has a sudden need to get out. He rushes to the door and forces it open. He is outside. The cold air makes him feel better.

He leans against the worn wood siding of the house. He breaths in slowly, trying to calm himself. His mind is swarming with questions. What happened here? Where are Aris and Metis? Do they have anything to do with this? Who is Metis? Why is he always where trouble is? And who is he to Aris?

Thane needs to find out. But first he must report this. He brings up his wrist.

"Get me the nearest police," he says to his watch.

"Where are we going?" Aris asks, her voice trembling.

Metis's head is pounding. Trying to work through what he just experienced is like attempting to count all the stars in the sky with naked eyes—torturous and impossible. It is late, and they need rest.

"Let's get some sleep," he says.

"Your house or mine?"

"The Hotel of the Desert. We're almost there."

"Shouldn't we leave Elara?"

"We didn't do anything wrong, Aris. Everyone who saw us is dead."

"But you're the Sandman."

He stops in his tracks.

How did she find out?

"Seraphina told me. She wanted you to leave because you need to be protected. Absinthe needs to be protected. When were you going to tell me this?"

"Aris . . ."

"You don't trust me."

"It doesn't matter."

"How does it not matter? You're the Sandman, the one who gives the Dreamers Absinthe so they can remember their past."

"I'm not the Sandman anymore."

"Don't lie to me, Metis."

"I'm not lying."

"First you lied to me about being a Dreamer and knowing Benja. Now, about being the Sandman. Is there any part of you that's not a lie?"

He grips her shoulders. "I gave up being the Sandman to be with you! I had to choose between the past and the present. Being the Sandman or being Metis, the pianist. The Crone told me I couldn't be both. And so, I chose."

"Who's the Crone?"

"She's the maker of Absinthe. She's been around since the beginning of the Four Cities. Like you, she was a scientist. Now, she exists inside a book—a consciousness without a body. She guides us to remember our pasts."

"Why didn't you tell me all this?" Her voice sounds hurt.

"We have so little time left. I just wanted to spend it not worrying about anyone but us. Just me and you. Can you understand that?"

He places his fingers on her chin, lifting it. He leans down and kisses her. The taste of her is intoxicating, making his head swim. He pulls her against his chest. He misses her. The woman she was. The woman she is. And every version of her in between.

The wind blows, intensifying the scent of dry sage and the earthiness of the desert. It's getting colder by the minute. He tightens his arms around her. She fits here. This is where she belongs.

He has been trying not to think of time. The stealer of memories is creeping closer. Soon, his arms will be empty again. Can he handle it?

The people they left at Bodie's house could not. They chose to be together in death. To be free of Tabula Rasa. Would he one day make that choice? Would Aris?

The image of their dead bodies comes back to him. Their figures lie on the floor, crumpled like inanimate objects. He is reminded of Benja's dead body. Immobile and stiff. Skin cold and pale. He tries to shake it off. He does not want these memories to stay.

"We're not far from the hotel," he says. "Would you please let me take you there and hold you? I can't stand it anymore. And I'm afraid . . ."

"Of what?" she whispers.

He doesn't know the science of how memories work. What he knows is that a part of his brain has a fortress Tabula Rasa cannot touch. Behind its walls, his memories are strongest. It is the place he keeps his knowledge of music and the feel of Aris, if not every detail of her.

"I'm afraid we'll keep that horrific memory from tonight forever," he says. "I think our minds choose memories, even if we're not aware of it. Things get impressed on a subconscious level."

He picks up her hand and traces the veins to her palm.

"Like this spot where your green veins are most visible. Near the middle of your palm that dips in like a pool."

He sighs.

"Sometimes I lie awake at night remembering this precise spot on your hand," he says, "This is what my mind chose to remember. I don't want to remember all those people lying dead on the floor in that house, and I hope I won't."

He pulls her close again. A spot on his jacket blooms warm with her tear. He kisses the top of her head and breaths in the lavender scent.

"All that matters is that I love you," he says, "That's what I want you to remember. The only thing I want you to keep from this night."

Aris looks at the small house-like structure that belongs to the Hotel of the Desert. There are others like it in the vicinity. This one is farthest from the others and is located at the end of a quiet and dark path. It sits on four stilts off the uneven, rocky land. They walk up the five stairs to the porch. It is empty.

"We'll have to break in," Metis says.

The wall-sized glass door does not look difficult to force open. In a world where there is no theft, security is minimal. Metis fiddles with the door, and the latch turns. They walk in. The space is dark and silent. Their steps echo—two prowlers in the night. Around them shadowy shapes of furniture crouch low to the ground like animals waiting to pounce. The smell of chlorine lingers.

"Lights on," Metis says.

Nothing changes.

"Your voice command doesn't work. We're not supposed to be here," she says and walks to the bathroom.

In one of the drawers she finds a candle and a lighter. She lights the candle; it emits a small, warm glow. She brings it out and looks around.

The house is one large room. The ample living area with an L-shaped gray sofa is connected to a kitchen of shiny white cabinets. A large pendant light that looks like a cloud hangs above a substantial oak coffee table. Through another glass door at the back of the house, Aris sees a pool. It's long enough to swim laps in. She finds the bedroom hiding behind a floor-to-ceiling bookshelf on the far wall.

"There's food in the refrigerator. Probably stocked for tomorrow's guests. I guess that means we should leave before sunrise," Metis's voice speaks from the kitchen, "I'll make us something to eat."

"Okay. Thank you."

"Do you want to eat now or have a quick shower first?" Metis asks.

She answers by walking back into the bathroom. Its sleek whiteness contrasts with the darkness outside. A glass wall looks out onto the empty unknown.

She sits the candle on the countertop and peels each article of clothing off her body. The heaviness of the day sinks into her pores, making her extremities feel like lead. She tends to harbor stress in her back. The weight of everything and everyone is on it. She needs to wash them off so she can feel like someone resembling herself again.

There is no timer for the shower. No five-minute rule. The hotel is a vacation spot—a place where people don't have to think about time. She turns on the rain showerhead and lets the warm water pour down her hair, her face. The stream travels down her body to her feet. The string that winds her so tightly starts to unravel.

She lathers in shampoo and soap and reminisces of the days when things were simpler. The time when she did not question reality. When she could walk the world knowing where she belonged. But she belongs with Metis, she tells herself.

Only for a month.

Melancholy returns. In a few weeks he will be gone from her memory. He will live only in her dreams, to be reawakened later by whatever triggers her brain is receptive to. If at all.

Maybe she will find Absinthe in the next cycle. But what if he cannot remember her then? Can she stand the pain of looking into the eyes of someone she loves and seeing no recognition? Seraphina said it is more painful than one can imagine. Metis has lived it.

She opens her eyes and sees him leaning against the doorframe.

"How long have you been standing there?" she asks.

"Not long enough."

"I'm almost done."

"Is there room for me?" he asks.

She nods, and he sheds his clothes. In all the times they have been intimate together, she has never seen his naked body from this distance. He is well made—tall with lean muscles and a strong chest wide enough to sleep on. His handsomeness is striking. It is not the conspicuous, peacock-like handsomeness Benja owned. His is born from the stillness of his features and the focused intensity of his eyes. Real. Warm blooded. And very male. She feels her core heating up.

The door to the shower opens, and his skin is on hers at once. His hands run over the topography of her body like a river over land, leaving evidence of its passage. Her skin, slippery from water and soap, abides. She feels the roughness of his stubble raking down her neck.

He continues lower until he is on the floor, kneeling. His hands are holding her by her hips. She feels tremors coming from him. He is crying.

Suddenly her heart expands to accept everything she feels. The love she has for Metis. The loss they will soon face. The death of her friend. The emptiness left by those who killed themselves tonight. The sorrow of those who cannot be with the ones they love.

She kneels next to Metis and wraps her arms around him. She hums the tune she sang Benja to sleep with.

«

Thane waits. He is in a white room with no windows inside the police station in Elara. The artificial light coming from overhead gives it a stark, clinical look. He feels agitated. One of his knees bounces uncontrollably. He doesn't want to be here. Across from him sits a man in a brown fedora who has introduced himself as Officer Scylla. He is why Thane cannot simply leave.

"Is there a reason you still need me here?" Thane asks.

"We just need a few more answers."

"I told you everything I know." His voice is gruff. He did not know the process with the police would take so long. He needs to be out there, finding Aris and Metis.

"You still haven't established the reason you were at Bodie's house on a Thursday night," Officer Scylla says.

"I was lost. I walked from downtown and wanted to see the view. So, I went up the hill. I knocked on the house to ask for directions. When no one opened the door, I looked through the window and saw all the—"

"The house is registered to a Bodie and Seraphina. Did you know either of them?"

"No. I told you that."

"How about anyone else who was at the house?"

"No."

"Where did you say you work?"

"The Natural History Museum."

"The one in Callisto?" Officer Scylla asks.

"The one and only."

"So you don't know anyone in this city at all?"

"No, I don't. Why do you keep asking me that?"

"Because, Thane, I'm confused as to why someone from Callisto would be in Elara this late at night. And that he happened to stumble upon a lot of dead people in a house."

Thane springs up. His chair falls backward and clangs against the floor.

"I have nothing to do with this!"

"I'm not saying you do. But something's not making sense to me," the policeman says.

The voice of an AI speaks. "Officer Scylla, you have a reach."

"I'm in the middle of something. Please send to the databank."

"I cannot. It is from the Interpreter Center."

Officer Scylla scowls.

"I'm sorry, I'll be right back."

As soon as the door closes, Thane begins to feel angry. He is upset with himself for being too honest with Officer Scylla. At the Interpreter Center for giving him this horrible job. At Professor Jacob for recruiting him.

His life would have been much more comfortable if he had never accepted this responsibility. What has it gotten him so far? He lost his friendship with Aris. Benja, the man he reported to the Interpreter Center, killed himself. He just saw a lot of dead bodies.

But there was a reason he accepted this job. He wanted to help the Interpreter Center keep peace. He does not want anyone to destroy the Four Cities and the Planner's ideology. That reason has not changed.

Maybe I can tell him I was drunk. Maybe I was following an ex-girlfriend. Maybe I thought I saw them going into the house together. But I was mistaken. It was no one I knew. Jealousy is a good motivation, right?

The door opens and Officer Scylla walks back in. His face is tense with what appears to be suppressed anger.

"Thane, you are required at the Interpreter Center. If I have any additional questions, I will reach out. Thank you for your time."

Thane feels like the weight of the entire building has been lifted off him. He gets up, shakes the officer's hand, and walks out of the Elara Police Station. As soon as he exits, he runs toward the train station. There are only a few places Metis and Aris can be at this hour.

Aris turns on her side and watches Metis's face as he sleeps. Even at rest, he looks worried. She wants to trace her finger on the line between his eyebrows. But she does not. His eyes flit under his lids. What is he dreaming about?

She wonders if he would let her use the copper helmet on him. He has not offered, and she has not asked. Would she see their old lives together? What would that look like? Would she recognize the person she was?

Does she even want to see herself as someone else—a stranger she shared a body with?

A sigh escapes her. She doesn't know if it is the openness of the sky, the barrenness of the landscape, or the sleeping man next to her that makes her feel so raw and fragile. She is not used to this Aris.

Fresh air. She needs it. She eases out of the bed as quietly as she can. She opens the back door to the pool. The water lights up like the bright blue of the midday sky. She looks up and is dazzled by the real sky—black and blanketed with stars. No matter how many times she sees it, it still takes her breath away.

The city lights in Callisto obscure all but the brightest stars. When she missed the night sky, she used to go to the planetarium, one of her favorite exhibits at the Natural History Museum. There, she shot through Jupiter's atmosphere, witnessed the Big Bang, and watched stars die. But nothing replaces the reality of tilting her head up and seeing the brilliant dots of light that have traveled millions of years to her eyes.

A baritone duet of hoots punctuates the air. Maybe great horned owls. In the old times, owl hoots were considered a bad premonition. An omen of a horrible event to come. But considering the season, the hooting is likely amorous. Most great horned owls mate for life. Each year they will find each other to mate before parting ways. A rare thing in the animal kingdom.

In her world, only animals breed. Humans are artificially conceived in the Center of Discovery and Learning. She read that Old World women had to carry little humans inside them for nine months before birthing them. Aris wonders what it would be like to hold life inside her. She will never know.

Aris finds a spot on the edge of the pool and dips her legs into the water. It's warm. The hairs on her arms stand up, reminding her that the rest of her body is still in the cold air. She wishes she had a swimming suit, but then remembers she is surrounded by the nature preserve—the nearest structure is a long walk away. She pulls her shirt over her head, eases off her panties, and lowers herself in.

The water relaxes her at once. She swims laps until her head clears. She flips over and floats. Her entire field of vision is filled with the starry sky.

In the silence of the water, she begins to dissect her situation, the way the old Aris did with any obstacles that came her way.

There are only a few weeks left before Tabula Rasa. That, she cannot change. Or can she? Is there a way to stop it from taking her and Metis down its destructive path?

The idea is farfetched. If there is a way, it would have already been found. The people of the Four Cities have been around long enough to find out.

Is there another way?

What if I don't go to the hospital? the question Benja asked her months ago resurfaces.

She told Benja there must be a way for the system to find the stragglers. There is no place to hide.

But what if there is?

She and Metis can wait out Tabula Rasa. Instead of an AI as the first voice they hear, they would have each other. The idea sounds almost plausible. But she does not know of a place in the Four Cities they could go that would be safe.

She feels a disturbance in the water. Something touches her leg. She screams.

"I'm sorry," Metis says.

"You scared me!"

"This reminds me of the first time we met this cycle. You screamed after running into me in the rain. Remember?"

"How could I forget? You almost gave me a heart attack."

She kicks water up to the sky. A drop touches her lips. It's salty. Untreated ocean water. It tastes of her dream with Metis.

"What are you thinking about?" he asks, wading toward her.

"Tabula Rasa."

"Ah." Melancholy touches his eyes.

She changes the subject. "And something else. The rings that Seraphina asked me to take to the Gift Market. They're like ours. Where did they come from?"

Metis shakes his head. "One of us must have hidden ours in the chair cushion at home. I don't know how we got them in the past. Maybe at the Gift Market."

"Everyone there had them. Was that why Bodie let us in? He thought we were there to—as well . . ."

"Probably. Maybe that's why Seraphina didn't want him to know that we weren't supposed to be there."

"The design—I wonder if it means something."

Metis shakes his head. "There's so much we don't know that we may have once known but have forgotten."

Aris leans back and lets the starry sky fill her vision once more. She thought their rings were unique—that their story was unique. But there are more couples like them, struggling to stay together through Tabula Rasa. There is no point in trying to figure out the riddle. At least not now. There is so little time left. She just wants to spend the rest of it with Metis.

Just me and you.

"The cottage by the beach. Where was it?" she asks.

He pulls her close. "Do you want to go there?"

She nods. "I want to see it in real life. But I don't think I have enough entertainment points left."

"I still have most of mine."

"You didn't use them?"

"Not enough reasons to use them. I can see any concerts I want at Carnegie Hall for free. I don't like eating out by myself. And I didn't date."

"Do you think that'll be enough?"

"We'll have to see. We'll have to go back to my house and get my watch."

She realizes he never has his watch on.

"Why don't you wear it?"

"Tracking. I didn't want to be caught. None of the Dreamers are supposed to wear them."

"And you're willing to wear it now?"

"I'm not the Sandman anymore."

"Who is?"

"I can't tell you. The secret is not mine to share."

Silence follows.

"Metis?"

"Hmm?"

"Should we talk about what happened tonight?"

She feels his grip tighten around her.

"Are you still upset?" he asks.

"It was the worst thing I have ever seen. But I can kind of understand them. The desire to take back control. To make choices. To make their lives their own. To love who they want. To be with who they want."

"Choice is everything. But control is an illusion."

"Yes. Logically you understand. But some of us are too human to embrace it."

"I suppose."

"And you? Are you still upset?" she asks.

"I was. Then I realized there was nothing I could have done to change it. Now, I'm just happy to be here with you. But I suspect I will be upset about it again. I just don't know when."

"I wish I could be that way."

"I've spent most of my life trying to explain everything in logical terms," Metis says. "But I realized it was just my way of putting things at arm's length. It was getting in the way of really feeling, really living. Being present."

He runs his hands along her sides. "At this moment, the feel of your skin is all I want to focus on."

Be present.

She wants to be. She closes her eyes and centers her attention on the feel of Metis's touch against her skin. The warmth of his hands. The smoothness of his long fingers. The way they send electric currents through her body.

In the present, time has no meaning. There is no past. No future. Only this moment exists in the middle of the universe.

She feels the warmth of him in all the crevices of her body. Slowly she opens like a flower. A sigh escapes her lips. She is experiencing it again, that feeling of falling yet filled to the brim. She lets it consume her in its fire.

CHAPTER TWENTY-TWO

Aris and Metis arrive in Lysithea before dawn. A shroud of fog descends onto its dark streets, painting it gray. Droplets cling to her hair and jacket like a desperate lover.

She feels as if she is sleepwalking. The only thing that seems real is the warmth of Metis's hand on hers. She lets herself get lost in the gray pavement and the repetitive rhythm of their steps.

"We're here," Metis says.

She looks up from her feet and gasps at the view of the twinkling city lights below. They had at some point passed the section covered by the low-lying fog. Now they are standing on a hill where the sky is clear and the fog is but an earthly trouble they have left behind.

"Where are we?" she asks.

He turns her body, and she sees the robin's-egg-blue Victorian house. A smile spreads across her face. The chilly air nips at her ears, and Aris wants more than anything to fall into a warm and peaceful sleep in her lover's arms.

"Can I sleep till tomorrow?" she asks.

"Sure. I just have an errand to run tonight, but I won't wake you."

The door opens, and what both she and Metis see makes them stop cold at the threshold. The large vase at the oak table is empty. The arrangement of green flowers has vanished. One corner of the round Persian rug is kicked up into a bunch.

Metis grabs her arm and directs her behind him, shielding her with his body. The forcefulness of his action alerts her to the severity of the situation. He navigates his house as if it is a battle scene. They walk slowly on the spines of the floorboards to keep the creaking to a minimum. His head whips around like a panther searching for prey. Aris follows him like a shadow. She is afraid to breathe, lest the intruder hear her and attack. Her heart is beating to the rhythm of fear.

They enter the parlor. No other soul is here, but someone was. Pulled-out drawers and scattered books lie on the floor. Metis makes his way to the cabinet. He slides open the hidden door inside it.

"It's gone," he whispers.

"What?"

"Absinthe."

"What! Why would you keep it?"

"It was the last batch I made. I was supposed to deliver it to the new Sandman tonight."

"Who would have taken it?"

The spot between his eyebrows scrunches together. He looks as if he has stopped breathing. The color drains from his face.

"We need to go," he whispers.

He looks at her as if he has realized something.

"Aris, take off your bracelet!"

She hears him, but she does not understand the connection.

Why?

He picks up her wrist.

"I don't know how, but the Interpreter Center found me. We can't be tracked. Take it off and let's go!" Metis says, his voice rising at the end.

"What? But—" She touches her bracelet. Its smooth hardness was the first thing she remembered after waking up from the hospital after Tabula Rasa. It connects her to the system. To Lucy. The first voice she heard after the Waking. The one constant in her life.

"Only you can do it. Please, we don't have time. We must go," Metis pleads.

She stares at the silver bracelet. Then she looks up at Metis. The spot between his eyebrows folds like the ridges of mountains. His jawline is taut with tension. His panic-stricken eyes have a kind of terror Aris has not seen before. Not even after he witnessed the mass suicide at Bodie's house.

"We're in danger. We can't be tracked," he repeats.

She runs her index finger across the watch's face. The silver bangle unbuckles. She takes it off her wrist and places it on the side table. Her wrist feels lighter. An empty feeling fills her stomach.

Bye, Lucy.

Aris will miss her.

She turns to Metis. "Where are we going?"

"The only place we can."

Metis takes her hand and pulls her toward the quiet streets. The city is still asleep.

Thane watches as the Professor's hand rubs along the smooth surface of the glass bottle containing the green liquid—the drug the Interpreter Center has been hunting for. He doesn't know why, but the gesture provokes a feeling of disgust in him. Having recently witnessed mass death leaves him on edge. He feels like drowning himself in drink until the image is rinsed from his brain.

"You did well, Thane," Professor Jacob says. "I'm very proud of you."

Thane wishes he could revel in this compliment from the man he admires. But all he wants to do is go home and sleep for the next three days. After leaving the Elara Police Station, he had debated whether to go home instead of to Metis' house, but he could not stop his responsible brain from nagging him to follow through.

He and the Professor are alone in the Interpreter's office. Apollina is somewhere in the building, doing something she prefers to keep secret from them both. Thane can see the darkness of the world through the large paned window. Shadows of bare trees surrounding the Interpreter Center stand like lines of ink drawings against the vast lawn. He longs for the warmth of spring, when life begins.

He wonders where Aris is. He half expected to see her at Metis's house in Lysithea. When he found it empty of its owner, the Interpreter ordered him to ransack it. His gut feeling unearthed the bottle of green liquid. But it was Apollina who told him to take the flowers.

The Interpreter comes back into the room.

"The analysis is done," she says, "The green liquid matches the compound found in both Bodie and Benja. The flowers have the same chemical make-up as the drug. Metis is the supplier."

What does this make Aris? It's not possible she conspired with him. She must not know all his secrets.

"Our drone captured images of him with a woman. I wonder if she's the same one at the crime scene. Did she look familiar to you, Thane?" Apollina asks.

Aris doesn't need to be a part of this.

"No."

"Well, find them. We need to bring them in," she says. "Please."

Thane hates the way she adds "please" to the end of every order she gives him to make it sound less like a command. A few more weeks and he will be rid of her. The thought brings him comfort.

"What were they doing at the house in Elara?" Professor Jacob asks.

Thane shakes his head. "I only saw them go in. They must have used a different exit. I don't know when they left, so it's hard to say whether they had anything to do with the deaths."

"Did you tell the police about them?" the Interpreter says.

"No. I didn't want to complicate matters."

"Good. What else did you tell the police?" Apollina asks.

"Nothing really. Just that I was lost."

The small A-frame cottage gives off the mysterious air of something wild and abandoned. It is hidden in the middle of the park in Callisto behind multiple No Entrance signs.

It's covered almost entirely by ivy and roses. Underneath the intertwining leaves is wood siding, but Aris can't discern the original color. The paint has peeled in strips to reveal the raw wood underneath.

One side of the front facade is sagging under the burden of climbing bramble. Beneath the eaves are empty birds' nests—deserted for the winter, to be filled again in the impending spring. The glass on the windows is opaque from age and neglect. The house gives the feel of being haunted.

A sign reading "Do not enter, under strict order of the Dwelling Council" hangs on the crooked picket fence. Metis opens the creaky gate and enters. Aris looks over her shoulder. The light of the sun is a sliver on the horizon, and she's glad they still have the cloak of gray dawn. She follows him.

The heavy front door sits tilted on its frame. From the specks of paint around the grooves, it may have once been red. Metis pushes it. It lets out a loud creak in protest but gives in.

The inside of the cottage is in even worse shape. The house has suffered the consequences of being open to the elements. The windows are covered gray by years of accumulated dirt. There are random holes in the roof. Aris treads carefully, feeling the bounciness of the worn wood floors. With each step, the roof quivers as if it might collapse under its own weight. Dust stirs as they make their way to the back of the one-room house.

"The Crone lives here?" Aris asks. "It doesn't look like anyone can live here."

In the back of the house, she sees a ladder leading up toward the ceiling.

"We have to go up the stairs," he says and climbs.

She thinks calling the structure stairs is generous. The rickety ladder is precariously attached to the loft above them.

"Are you coming?" he says from the loft. His head looks as if it is floating in midair.

It's harder than she thought to lift herself up with only the strength of her two arms. A layer of dust coats her hands like frosting on a cake.

She reaches the loft and wipes her dirty hands on her pants. She scans around the room. The tiny space is lined on all sides with shelves filled with books. They smell of mildew and memories.

"The first time I was here I felt like Jack climbing the beanstalk. But instead of the goose and the golden eggs, I found this," Metis says.

In his hand is an old book with a cover so tattered she can barely see the words. *Love in the Time of Cholera* by Gabriel García Márquez.

He opens the book and reads a passage. Suddenly, bright light shines up from the book, bathing the room white, like the inside of a hospital. She staggers backward. Her hip hits the corner of a bookshelf, tilting her off balance.

"Don't be afraid. The Crone will show up soon."

Aris walks to him. He wraps an arm around her shoulders.

"It's okay," he whispers in her ear. "It's a hologram."

She's reminded of the same technology at the Natural History Museum and relaxes.

An ancient woman materializes before them. Her conjured image appears as if veiled by fog. She is a vision in white. Skin as pale as the moon. Hair the color of chalk. Her silvery gown blows behind her as if she is standing in a breeze.

"Hello, Metis," the ethereal voice says. "How many days?"

The Crone sounds to Aris like someone talking in a dream.

"It's February twentieth. Twenty-eight days before Tabula Rasa," Metis says.

She looks at Aris. "Hello."

"This is Aris. My wife," Metis says.

Aris's hand goes to the ring on her finger. The Crone's face softens.

"Metis has been waiting for you a long time."

"Hello," Aris says.

"We're being hunted by the Interpreter Center. They stole Absinthe and hypnos from my house. They know my connection to it," Metis says.

The room brightens. Aris can feel the old lady's anger burning the air, sucking out oxygen. The Crone's aura slowly dims.

"So here we are again," the Crone says.

"You've been in this situation before?" Aris asks.

"The Interpreter Center has been trying to destroy Absinthe since its genesis. It has come close many times. And for as long as it exists, they will continue to search with the intent to get rid of it, just as they do dreams they find harmful to the Four Cities."

"We can't let that happen," Aris says.

"No, child, we can't. But that's what they do. They erase everything they think would threaten the Four Cities. They'll want to erase your memories next. Now that you know of my existence."

Aris shudders at her words. "Can we hide here with you?"

"No more than a day or so. We're still in the middle of a city. Soon, we'll be found. We can't attract attention to this cottage," Metis says.

"There's a place. A cave on the edge of the desert. It's a sanctuary for the Sandmen," the Crone says.

Aris's heart leaps. There, she and Metis can wait out Tabula Rasa.

"You've never told me this before," Metis says. His voice sounds hurt.

"I was hoping I wouldn't have to tell you," the old woman says.

She looks at Aris. "Stay here for the day. Traveling at night will be safer. The Crone walks to the window. "Rest, and I'll keep watch."

Metis places his backpack on the floor and sits down. Aris lowers herself next to him. The silence is palpable. The danger they face weighs heavily on him. She knows he feels responsible.

Aris looks at the Crone and wonders what life for Metis would have been like had he not found her and Absinthe. Would he have eventually remembered her on his own? Would he have moved on to another lover?

Metis looks exhausted. They have not slept for many hours. She reaches over and touches his haggard face.

"Sleep, love," she says.

"I miss you calling me that."

He leans over and kisses her. He takes his jacket off and makes a ball for a pillow. He lays down and closes his eyes. She is glad. He has been through so much. His slow breathing tells her he has fallen asleep at once.

The Crone gazes at him with gentleness. The affection the old woman has for her Sandman is evident. Aris has so many questions for her. She picks one from the pile in her mind.

"Have there been many Sandmen before Metis?" Aris asks.

"Yes. Not every cycle. But many."

"How old are you?"

"I've been around since the beginning of the Four Cities."

"How old are the Four Cities?"

The old woman smiles but does not answer.

Aris picks another question. "What are you?"

"I was once alive like you. I'm what you can call 'consciousness.' I am what I was. Just without a body in the traditional sense. What you see as me is my last memory of my physical self. What I am, what I say, is still me."

"What happened to your body?"

"Gone with the wind. Just like all who have died."

Aris thinks of Benja and the Ceremony of the Dead and feels pain in the middle of her chest. "When did you die?"

"A very long time ago." The Crone pauses. "I see you are curious about time. One thing you must realize is that time is the least relevant aspect of your existence."

Aris's hand goes to her wrist and feels the absence of her watch. For someone accustomed to tracking her life through time, it feels unnatural to deny its importance. But she decides on another question. "How did you come to be in this form?"

"I don't know for sure. When I woke up, I was in this form. It took me a while to realize I was still alive. Well, not alive. My heart no longer beats. My lungs no longer breathe oxygen. Conscious is a more fitting word. Only now my mind lives in a different vessel."

She eyes the book next to Metis. "And in a different delivery method."

The old woman turns her gaze back outside. "But there's only one person who could have made it happen, who was powerful enough, and who would have wanted to."

"The Planner?" Aris says, "But why?"

"Sentimental reasons, I suspect," the Crone says.

Aris detects sadness in her voice.

"You knew him?" she asks.

"Before he was the Planner, he was Eli. My Eli. You know him from living in his vision. The paradise he created because of the Last War."

The Crone lays her wispy fingers on the dirty pane. Her eyes are on a spot outside the window.

"We watched the world burn from above. There's nothing to prepare you for it. The certainty of knowing that your home as you know it is no more. Black clouds enveloped the earth, and land fell into the ocean, changing its face. The people you loved, the ones you could not save, dissipated with the dust."

Aris has the sudden urge to wrap her arms around the old woman, except she is just an image.

The Crone continues, "And what we were also not prepared for was the feeling of gut-wrenching guilt. We had survived, while many good people died. The depression accompanying the loss and the guilt was too much to bear.

"We shuttered the windows. We couldn't stand witnessing the destruction. Eli believed we would be next. So we waited for death to come. For a week we survived on nothing in the nest of our despair.

"But one day I opened the window and saw an image that had a powerful and immediate effect on my heart. The world below was blue and clear, beautiful again, even after the atrocity it had endured. We knew there would be survivors, like us. So, we set out to repair what we could. We saved as many as we could and brought them to the Four Cities."

"Thank you. You saved humanity," Aris says.

"That's like thanking me for breathing. It's something anyone would have done in our shoes. Humans cannot survive without each other. It's not possible," the Crone says.

She continues, "Over time, however, Eli was not content in solely saving. He wanted to make humanity thrive. And become better. He was quite a reader and an appreciator of music. A simple thought came to him. It bred the ideology of Tabula Rasa. He believed if people truly knew, not just in theory but by living the consequences, that life is short, they would be kinder to each other."

"The best way to rid society of the evils of human nature is to periodically wipe each person's mind of the prejudices learned through life experience. With the mind a blank slate, everyone has the freedom to author their own soul." Aris recites a passage from the *Manual of the Four Cities*.

"Eli gave that speech to the Councils before enacting Tabula Rasa," says the Crone. "It was a revolution. It changed everything about how we view our lives in the puzzle of this universe. Attachment is the seat of need and greed. No memory means no attachment."

She sighs. "But he was hesitant to impose such a radical idea until . . ."

"Until what?" Aris asks, leaning forward.

"What's not in the historical record is that it was I who gave him the reason to move forward."

"What happened?"

"I had an affair. It was with someone who meant nothing to me. Eli and I had grown apart over the years and under the pressure of carrying the Four Cities on our shoulders. And I guess I just—It's not an excuse for breaking my marriage vow. There's a truth I didn't know . . . Some things, once broken, cannot be fixed."

Aris looks over at Metis's peaceful face. He told her he had forgiven her for not remembering. For having moved on in life. But has he really forgiven her?

"Eli moved forward with Tabula Rasa as a gift for me," the Crone says. "He thought he had chained me with marriage and his love. Tabula Rasa would allow me to author my own life every four years, so I would be free to take life in at its fullest. No attachment means no jealousy, no betrayal. Each person, if they so choose, can experience falling in love repeatedly with as many people as they want."

"But that's not enough?" Aris says.

The Crone looks at her with her downcast eyes. "Even with the decades I had with Eli, it still wasn't enough."

She still loves him.

"Eli couldn't comprehend what I did as just a mistake." The Crone wipes her eyes. "His gift was a curse. Now I only see him in dreams."

Aris realizes that even as a consciousness with no body, the mind still perceives the physical as it did in flesh. Like a person who can still feel pain in their phantom limb. Like knowing something is missing and living it out in dreams.

"After Tabula Rasa, he left Earth. He moved back to the space station and never returned. He left me here. Alone," the Crone says. "But he always knew where I was, keeping track of me. That's how I woke up as *this*, after what was supposed to be my death. He couldn't just let me be. It's not in his nature to let go. To give up control."

Her aura glows brighter in the darkness of the lonely cottage. "I created Absinthe so he would know that he can't control everything. He will not take my memories. I will always remember. The Dreamers will always remember."

The Last War, the Planner, the Crone, Tabula Rasa, love, pain. Each had pushed the world forward. An ideology born from the beauty of a song and launched by the ugliness of deception is the last sacrifice of a heartbroken man. His gift to humanity. Tabula Rasa. And they all pay the price for it.

"Can it be stopped?" Aris asks.

A light smile dots the corner of the Crone's mouth.

"I've lost count of how many times I've been asked this exact question." The Crone looks out the window. The sky is becoming lighter.

"I will answer it the same way I've answered countless times before," she says and disappears.

CHAPTER TWENTY-THREE

It is that lonely time folklore calls the witching hour. There are few souls wandering the streets of Callisto. This late they are either drunk or tired, or both. No one is paying much attention to the two figures who keep to the shadows.

Aris whispers, "How far?"

They are heading to Carnegie Hall. He told her there is a station below with express trains to and from various cities. It's only busy when there is a concert. They will take a train from there to Elara.

"Not far," he says.

She's glad. It is becoming more difficult with the heavy loads on their backs. She has the pack with the helmet and computer. Metis is carrying the provisions they took from the cottage.

"What do you have in there?" Aris asks.

"Flour, rice, salt, hard cheeses, water, a first aid kit, a flashlight, a water purifier, a knife, and a tool that has multiple tools embedded inside—I can't remember what it's called."

"I'm impressed."

"The Crone told me to put it all together for this possibility. I just never thought it'd happen to me."

"I wonder how many Sandmen she's had to send away."

Metis shakes his head. Aris doubts he even knows how many came before him. He must have a lot of faith in the Crone to do her bidding without question. Or maybe he had asked, but his questions went unanswered.

"How long do you think what we brought will last?" she asks.

"I'm hoping a week. Then we'll have to figure the rest out. Maybe there'll be some things at the cave, but I don't know."

They settle into their own thoughts. The grayness of the streets and buildings deepens in the night. The steady rhythm of their feet against concrete is the only sound Aris hears. She looks at Metis's somber face and wonders what is on his mind. Even though he is next to her, she feels as if he is hundreds of miles away.

"Are you okay?" She asks after she can no longer stand the silence.

He stops and turns to her. His eyes are pools of sadness. "Aris, I'm sorry. You're in this situation because of me. I don't know how, but somehow the Interpreter Center or someone knows I'm associated with Absinthe. I'd understand if you want to leave."

He looks guilt-ridden.

"I don't want to leave. I choose to be here with you," Aris says.

Metis leans down and kisses her. His fingers wind through her hair and trace the length of her neck. Aris wraps her arms around his waist and presses herself closer. He pulls back and clears his throat.

"Usually there are drones at this hour," he says, "Just try to—"

Before he can finish, Aris hears buzzing in the air. She looks up in the direction of the noise. Something dark is moving against the night sky. City lights reflect off clouds, revealing their location. There is a flock of them. They are flying low between the gaps of the buildings.

"Drones!" she whispers and flattens herself against a wall.

As soon as they pass, Metis grabs her hand and they run. They zigzag through the city, turning left and right and right and left block after block, trying to put distance between them and the drones.

Aris feels wind whipping against her face and hair. The names of the streets blur by and she cannot tell where she is. They continue until she can no longer catch her breath.

"Wait," she forces out the word as she clutches her side.

"Just a bit more," Metis says, "We're almost there."

Ahead she sees the familiar brick building. They make their way to the back. Metis opens a door, and they run down the dark corridor toward the stairs.

Out of nowhere, someone appears in front of them. Aris screams. It is a familiar face.

"Thane!"

"Aris! What are you doing here?"

Her heart drops to the ground. Thane sees Metis, and the expression on his face changes from surprise to fury.

"Aris, come with me," Thane says. "He's dangerous."

"No! You don't know what you're talking about," she says.

"You can't be with him. He's wanted by the Interpreter Center. Come with me now, or I won't be able to save you."

Thane stretches a hand to her.

"No, Thane, you have it wrong. It's the Interpreter Center that's dangerous. Dreams are memories. They take away memories and destroy hope. Everyone whose dreams they erased killed themselves. You're on the wrong side."

Disappointment shows on Thane's face. Then resoluteness. He lifts his wrist to speak into his watch. Aris does the only thing that comes to mind. She swings her fisted hand against Thane's face with all her strength. A sharp pain travels through her fingers. Thane falls backward onto the floor.

She turns to Metis. "Run!"

They sprint past Thane and down the stairs. They turn so many corners Aris loses count. They go past storage rooms and metal pipes, following the path of silver ducts and electrical wires. She is glad Metis knows this place like the back of his hand. She would not be able to navigate it on her own.

Footsteps echo from somewhere behind them.

"Thane's coming!" Aris whispers.

Metis yanks open a door labeled Elara. They see a train waiting at the station. Metis pounds at a button and its door opens. They jump through it. Aris hits another button and it snaps shut. They are the only ones in the car.

The train moves forward. Once they pass the platform, Aris takes a seat. She looks at her left hand, the one she punched Thane with. The pain in her fingers increases. She cradles her injured hand.

"Are you okay?" Metis asks.

"I'll be fine," she says. "The ring bruised me, I think."

A loud guffaw escapes her. The situation is so absurd it feels surreal. Metis looks at her as if she has gone insane.

"I'm sorry. I just . . . it's just . . . Oh, never mind," she says, wiping a tear off one eye.

"Who was that man?"

"Thane. I used to work with him at the Natural History Museum. Until I learned he was spying on Benja for the Interpreter Center. He wrote the report that advised the Interpreter to erase Benja's dreams. There were others on his list. I don't know if they're all Dreamers. I didn't see you on it. But Thane was probably the one who found you. He's very smart."

"Why didn't you tell me this earlier?"

"I didn't know you were a Dreamer and the Sandman until recently." She gives him a look that ends his questioning.

Metis gently touches her hand.

"Ow. That hurts," she says.

"I hope you didn't break any bones."

"Even if I did, it was worth it. I've wanted to do that since I found out what he did to Benja."

The brightly lit train travels at top speed through the dark tunnel deep underground. The only sound is the soft whir of the train. Aris stretches out on the seat with her head on Metis's lap. The last few days seem like one long endless day. They were always on a train, coming from or going to somewhere else. Exhaustion weighs heavily on her shoulders, but she cannot sleep.

In the hours when the mind is foggy, Aris feels it is at its most imaginative. To the hazy brain, the subway tunnel could be anything. Outer space. A wormhole. The birth canal. She pictures them traveling through time, only to emerge hundreds of years from now in the future. What would that world be like? Would there still be the Four Cities and Tabula Rasa?

A thought comes to her. "The flowers they stole. They make Absinthe, don't they?"

"They're called hypnos. A hybrid the Crone created from a few species of flowers. They only grow at her cottage."

"How would the Interpreter Center know about it?"

He shakes his head. "They must know more than I thought they did."

"How do you make Absinthe with it?"

"You use the oil extracted from the flower. It's pretty complicated, and each batch takes half a month."

"So who'll make it now?"

"No one. I made the last batch needed for the meeting before Tabula Rasa. But now that it's stolen . . . I suppose the Crone could tell the new Sandman the instructions, but they'd need water from the mountains."

"What?"

"In the spring when the snow melts, the water travels into the creeks at the nature preserves in all the cities. It won't be spring until after Tabula Rasa."

"Why melted snow?"

"The processed water we drink in the Four Cities has too much salt."

She remembers Benja saying the water she gave him after he took Absinthe was salty.

A thought comes to her. She sits up. "I asked the Crone if Tabula Rasa can be stopped, but she didn't tell me."

"She doesn't readily give answers. Not often anyway. It used to really bother me. But I just figure it's her way of telling you to find out on your own."

"Do you think it can be stopped?" she asks.

He turns to look at her. "Do you want to stop it?"

The question is one she cannot easily answer. Tabula Rasa has robbed her of memories of Metis and everyone she knew. It took away every bit of knowledge she had of herself. She had to discover who she is and rebuild a new life around the new person she's become. Even so, Aris still believes it does more good than harm.

"I don't know. It controls my fate. Starting me at zero every four years.

But it brought peace to our world. I don't think I can be the one to make that decision. It would affect more than just me. And I don't think I should make it for someone else. How about you?"

Metis sighs. "We're taught that attachment is bad. And sometimes I feel selfish for wanting you by my side for the rest of my life. It's desire and greed. It's everything we're told is the bane of humanity. And there's truth in that. Because I can honestly say at this moment that if someone were to make me choose, I would sacrifice everyone in the Four Cities to save you from harm."

"That's horrible," she says.

"I know," he whispers.

"If someone were to make you choose, I would really prefer you spare the Four Cities," she says. "I don't think I could survive the guilt."

"That's your logical side thinking. I have that ability too. To weigh the pros and cons. To understand and see the value of each life being equal. To know that trading many lives for one is not a fair exchange. But in practice, my heart would win out every time. I'm not capable of choosing others over you, no matter how many," he says and pulls her tight against him.

"That's a scary thing, isn't it?" she asks, leaning her head on his shoulder.

"Let's hope no one will ever make me do the choosing," he says.

Silence shrouds the train car. Questions pile on top of one another like dead leaves in her mind. Aris stares out at the gray tunnel wall and pretends she is floating on a raft along a river. It calms her.

The train slows down. A feeling of déjà vu hits her. They were here just a week ago to say goodbye to Benja. Now they are back for a reason just as grim. They are hiding. From the Interpreter Center and the world.

She sees a flash of red on the tunnel wall. A web with no beginning and no end. A flower. A mandala. A microcosm of the universe. She lifts her hand and looks at her ring—a reminder of a promise she made. A bread crumb from the past. The overhead light casts a soft shine on its silver metal. A green bruise is forming on her ring finger.

"Aris," Metis's voice speaks. His voice sounds far away.

She looks up. Beyond her palm are blurry figures standing on the train platform. She drops her hand. The figures become clearer.

The thin form of Apollina, the Interpreter is there. Her pale face and blond hair blend into the white surroundings. Around her is a group of men. They are all wearing brown fedora hats. Officer Scylla. They are all Officer Scyllas!

Clones?

Aris's heart thumps uncontrollably. The sound of blood pumping through her veins fills her ear canals. She has read of cloning. Throughout history, scientists had done it with animals and plants. But at one point, every country agreed to enact a law to prevent its use on humans.

Suddenly her arm feels as if it's being ripped apart. Metis is yanking her. His mouth is moving, but she cannot hear him.

"What?" she asks.

"Aris! We need to go! Now!" Metis yells.

Her feet begin to move, and they sprint toward the back of the train. It is long and empty. The bright light overhead hurts her eyes. Her head throbs.

They reach the last train car. In the back is a door. Metis opens it as quietly as he can. They lower themselves to the ground, and their feet touched gravel.

"Where are we going?" she whispers.

"The red graffiti on the wall. Someone had put it there. There must be access into—and out of—that spot."

The underground tunnel is faintly lit by overhead lamps placed sparingly at equal intervals. They are walking from darkness into the light, then darkness again. Their eyes, so used to the abundance of light, struggle to adjust.

They keep to the left of the tunnel. Their feet amble forward as they feel their way with their hands like antennae. The surface of the wall is cool to the touch. Aris's fingers feel the roughness of the concrete. With each step, crunching sounds echo off the walls of the cavernous passage. They could be walking on gravel or skeletons. Aris does not look down.

"Do you remember where you saw the red mark?" Metis asks.

"It was right before I saw the platform. But the train was going really fast."

Her fingers begin to tremble. It's the wall. The wall is vibrating.

"A train is coming!" Metis yells.

They run. The kicked-up pebbles bounce against the wall and across the path. Ahead, a light as bright as the sun is moving toward them. An image of them becoming red splatter on the tunnel wall flashes across Aris's mind.

"There!" Metis says, pointing to a spot ahead.

They run faster. Acid pumps through her veins; pain stabs her sides. The light is coming closer.

A door. Metis pushes against it.

"It won't open."

"The train is coming!" she yells. She pounds on the door. Her arm hurts.

"Stand aside," Metis says and kicks. It rattles against its frame. He kicks it again. A gap forms.

The light is shooting toward them like a meteor.

"Metis! Hurry!"

He kicks and kicks, widening the gap.

The light is as big as the moon and grows exponentially with each passing second.

"Hurry!"

The door gives, and they hurl themselves through. Aris watches as the train flashes by. A wave of goosebumps runs across her entire body.

"We need to keep going," Metis says.

"How do we get out of here?"

He points up. Above them is a system of pipes that looks as complicated as neurotransmitters inside the brain. Lights blink at each juncture. Green. Red. Green. Red.

"Let's walk," Metis says.

They come to a T-junction after what feels like an hour. Without her watch, she has lost her sense of time.

"Right or left?" she asks.

"Left."

"Do you know where you're going?"

"Not really. But if we're lucky, we'll end up at a station on the edge of Elara."

"And if we're not?"

"We're heading back toward Callisto."

They come to a ladder. It seems to go up forever. They are deep underground.

"Let me go first," Metis says.

They climb until Aris's arms hurt. She looks down and sees a black pit. Fear creeps up, trying to grab hold, raising goosebumps over her skin.

She hears Metis speak. "There's a door."

He opens it and pushes himself out.

"What's out there?" Aris asks.

There is no answer. She sees his hand reaching down. She takes it and feels her body being pulled up.

Darkness. The fresh smell of the desert touches her nose. They are outside. Free.

The path is dark with only the crescent moon to light the way. Aris and Metis follow the North Star, keeping the silhouette of the mountains on their right. The scent of sage is in the air. It's almost spring, but the desert night is freezing. Aris welcomes it. The weight of her backpack feels heavier the longer she walks.

What's today? Aris automatically looks at her wrist. It's bare. She thinks back. Yesterday was the twentieth, so today is the twenty-first. Unless it's past midnight, in which case it would be the twenty-second. She wonders how she will keep time without Lucy. Then she remembers what the Crone said about time being the least relevant thing in their life.

Their path ends at the foot of a hill. Aris looks up at the sky. The North Star shines bright above it.

"It lines up," she says. It's just as the Crone had told them.

"It'll take us a while to climb up without light. Do you want to rest first?" asks Metis with a concerned voice.

She looks over her shoulders. No drones. No Officer Scyllas. No Interpreter. Yet she feels the need to keep going. She shakes her head. They are on flat ground. Exposed. The only thing cloaking them is the night. They need to get there before daybreak.

"Let's just go," she says and grabs the straps of her backpack. Her eyes focus on the dark spot ahead.

"What do you think is in the cave?" she asks.

Metis shrugs. "As long as it's big enough to lay down in, I'm good."

Aris raises her eyebrows.

"What?" Metis asks.

"I wasn't expecting to hear that from someone used to living in a grand home in Lysithea."

"Well, nothing is truly ours, is it?"

The side of the hill is covered in boulders that look like pieces of a toy a giant forgot to put away. The higher they go, the harder it is to stay upright. They use their hands for balance and grip.

Despite the cold weather, a bead of sweat drips from the nape of Aris's neck down the groove of her back. As she scales, she feels like an ant climbing over crumbs. Her hands hurt from the sharp edges of the rocks. They are slippery. She periodically wipes them on her pants so she would not lose her grip and slide down to death below.

She can only hope they are close to their destination. It's too late now to turn back. Behind them is their old life and the Four Cities. But they have each other. She looks at Metis. His body is like a cat in the night. Graceful limbs extending and retracting. Reaching toward the sky.

Aris feels a shiver coming. She fights it. She concentrates on the hardness of the ring digging against the bones of her fingers. She must keep climbing.

"We're almost there. I can see the opening," Metis says.

Aris pulls herself up on the last rock and finds herself standing on a ledge. In front of her is the cave. It's made of boulders coming together to form a chamber. Her heavy breathing is constant in her ears. Her hands sting. Blisters are forming.

She feels the warm tips of Metis's fingers on her hand.

"Look," he says and gently turns her.

She is stunned by the sight. A sliver of moon is high against an expanse of stars. In the distance is the twinkling city of Elara. Beyond it are clusters of brightness that are the other cities.

"It's beautiful," she whispers. She can see a light smile on the corner of his lips. It is the first smile on him since they began their journey.

Metis leads her into the cave. He pulls a flashlight from his backpack and shines it around, being careful to keep it away from the entrance. The Interpreter, the Officer Scyllas, and their drones may still be out there.

The walls are rocks of various shapes and sizes. The ground is compacted earth. Inside the cave is empty but for a ring of stones with the charred remains of an old fire in one corner. Metis sticks a foot into the ring, kicking the black logs around. The ashes clump together from accumulated moisture. No one has been here for a long time.

This is the place the Crone wanted us to come to? Aris wonders. It looks like an ordinary cave—the size of an average room. There is no bed, no food, no water. Nothing here indicates this place is a sanctuary. How are they going to survive?

We don't even know how to grow a head of lettuce.

Metis lets go of her hand and walks to the far end of the cave. She lowers herself to the ground. Her entire body aches from the long walk and climb. Her mind is exhausted from being suspended in fear and uncertainty. She shrugs the backpack off and feels the beginning of tears in her eyes. This is the first moment she allows herself to feel sorry about her fate. At least this place gives her that.

"It keeps going," Metis's voice yells, "There's an opening. Not that big. But it looks like a tunnel."

She gets up and follows him. They squeeze through a small passageway barely wide enough to walk single file. Aris feels suffocated. She is pressed from both sides.

"I see light from the other side! It just came on," he says.

"Is someone in there?" Aris asks.

Metis stops. "I haven't seen any signs of people. Do you want to turn around?"

Aris ponders the probability of someone being there against the idea of having to leave this place. "No. Let's just keep going."

They squeeze out of the tunnel and arrive inside a rectangular room with white walls. The room is bigger than the one they came from and looks nothing like it. It is built into the cave by expert hands. There's no one here.

In the middle sits a lab-grade chemical distillation kit on a large wooden table. Aris approaches the table with curiosity. She examines the kit, bringing her face close to the glass bottles and tubes. A trace of green stains the bottom of the receiving flask.

"It's for Absinthe," Metis says. "Someone was making it here."

Aris looks around. In one corner is a bed. It looks to be a tight fit for both her and Metis. There is a side table with a lamp, and next to it is an overstuffed bookcase. Stacks of books that could not fit into the shelf line one wall. It looks like a small library was transported to this place.

"How is this here?" she asks.

Metis shakes his head. He grabs her hand and walks over to the bed. He pulls her down onto it. She complies. They kick off their shoes and curl up together on their sides.

"Tomorrow," he says and wraps his arms around her. "I can't think anymore."

Her eyes wander to the bookcase. She closes them and soon drifts off to sleep.

"Would you care to explain yourself?" Apollina asks.

Thane shifts in his chair. They are alone in her office. Behind her is the vast expanse of the park. The charcoal sky and dark leafless trees add to her intimidation.

The Interpreter stares at him with resentment in her eyes. She has always treated him like a necessary nuisance. He knows she wishes she had never needed him in the first place. He is a liability.

She says, "You told me you didn't know the woman with Metis. Come to find out, you worked with her in the past. You've jeopardized our entire operation!"

Thane feels his own anger rising. He has spent nights in the freezing cold stalking suspects and has sacrificed friendship for the Interpreter Center. He has given up more than he should.

"How did I jeopardize it?" he says. "I found Metis. I got you the green drug. You didn't have either one before."

"Had you not withheld, we could have taken them both in without the police getting involved."

"How? It's just me, you, and Professor Jacob. How were we going to capture two people?"

"I have my ways."

Thane does not doubt it. That was another reason he decided to contact the police. He does not trust her.

Apollina huffs. "Now they're gone. Hiding somewhere in the desert of Elara."

"The Officer Scyllas will find them."

"Tabula Rasa is quickly approaching."

"Where's Professor Jacob?" he asks.

"Cleaning up your mess. The police need an explanation for your presence at the house in Elara. You lied to them, then you changed your story. You're lucky you have him and his reputation to back you up."

Thane has a feeling that if it were just Apollina, he would have been discarded once his purpose had been served.

Aris blinks her eyes open. Metis's back is to her. Next to him are stacks of books. The image elicits a sense of déjà vu.

"Good morning," she says.

He turns around, and she sees a small smile on his face.

"Good morning. Are you thirsty?" he asks.

"Yeah."

He hands her a silver can labeled "water." There is a tab on the top with a hole. She pries it open, and the entire top comes off. Clear liquid is inside. She tips the can into her mouth, letting the cool water rinse out the sleep from her throat. There's no taste to it. *Strange.*

"There's food also." He gestures to a metal locker sitting on another end. She goes over and opens it. In it are shelves filled with silver cans labeled "water" and "food." She doesn't know who put them here or how long they've been around.

"At least we won't starve," she says.

Aris has never had food from a can before. She wonders what it would taste like. Everything she has ever eaten in her life has been freshly harvested.

She looks over her shoulder. "What are you reading?"

"A journal."

She closes the locker and goes back to him.

"Who wrote it?" She hands him the water. He drinks from it and gives it back.

"I don't know. There's no name," he says, "There're more on the shelf and the floor."

Aris looks around and sees several black bound notebooks with no titles. She picks one up from a pile, sits with her back against a wall, and begins to read.

They are daily accounts of life in the cave. Mostly things she already knows. How cold the desert nights are. How hard it is to go up and down the mountain. The flora and fauna of the desert. She flips through the pages, scanning for more significant clues. She comes across a passage.

"Hey, listen to this," she says and begins to read out loud so Metis can hear.

"'The Resistance sent word that they will use Elara as its headquarters. It's the farthest from Callisto and the prying eyes of the system. It makes me immensely happy. I thought I'd have to learn to hunt the rodents and birds of the desert. Not having to worry about food and water will save a lot of time. Time I can use to work.'"

The idea of having to eat animals make Aris cringe with disgust. She, like all the citizens of the Four Cities, has been subsisting only on vegetables and vegetable-based foods. She is just as happy as the writer of this journal for not having to hunt down food.

She flips through the journal and sees another entry.

"'A scout found a water source nearby. It's a little spring seeping between rocks inside another cave. I may be able to get there easily enough to refill the cans.'"

Aris looks up. "We should try to find that cave. We can do the same thing."

She goes back to the journal and scans through more pages.

"'Almost got spotted by a drone today. I was careless. I should have known Eli would be looking for me. I'll have to limit being outside to only at night from now on.'"

An idea forms. Aris searches the pages more urgently for evidence.

"Listen!" she says. "'It took more than four men to bring up the table and distillation set. A beaker and a flask broke in the process. Someone will have to go to Callisto to get more of those. They won't be easy to replace.'"

Aris raises her head from the journal. "I think the Crone wrote this."

Metis flips through the journal in his hands and reads a page.

"'The experiment has been slow going, but I still feel strongly that I'm on the right track. Tabula Rasa destroys nerve cells. At the same time, it increases the level of enzymes that break down the neurotransmitters for memory. I'm close to a formula that would counter the effects of Tabula Rasa. If I'm successful, it will inhibit the enzymes from breaking down the neurotransmitters and help rebuild the severed connections.'"

He looks at Aris.

"She was working on Absinthe's formula here. Aris, this is from the beginning of the Four Cities. When she was human."

He goes through more pages and stops.

His clear voice fills the cave. "'Word from Callisto says Eli is planning on making a fail-safe for Tabula Rasa. He believes that for his plan to work, everyone in the Four Cities must have their memories wiped at once. The Resistance has been recruiting people. More planned to refuse Tabula Rasa. The network inside Elara is working on hiding places so that people will not be collected and forced to take the treatments. I fear what Eli will do. He's too smart and cunning—no one will be safe. He will find a way.'"

"A fail-safe?" Aris asks, "What does that mean?"

"It means that if the Planner was successful, Tabula Rasa cannot be stopped."

"Is there anything in there to confirm whether or not he was successful?" she asks.

Metis looks through the rest of the journal and shakes this head. He pulls out another from the shelf and scans through it.

"I found something!" Metis says.

She gets up from the floor and walks to him. His hand holds a page open. On it is a design similar to that on their rings. A mandala of interwoven lines. Underneath it is a word. *Resistance.*

Aris feels like her head is spinning. Thoughts fight each other for attention. But she is too exhausted to think. She puts the journal in her hand down on the side table and picks up the backpack by Metis's feet. She walks back to the locker and begins emptying the bag. The task of putting supplies into the locker calms her.

Metis comes to stand next to her. "Are you all right?"

"I'm fine."

He reaches for her hand. She pulls back. She did not mean to do it, but it is too late. A flash of sadness touches his eyes.

"I'm sorry," she says.

Silence follows.

"You know I saw Benja the week before he died. It was at his apartment," Metis says.

She pauses, wondering what he is getting at.

"Why were you there?" she asks.

"To find out what happened to him," he says.

"And what did you find?"

"The effects of the Dreamcatcher. He didn't remember me. I looked familiar to him, but he couldn't place where he had met me. That's what the Dreamcatcher does to a person."

"It didn't just take his memories," Aris says, "it drained him of hope."

"He was in the middle of making you the origami cranes. Pieces of blue paper were everywhere. It reminded me of my own house when I had to make all those cranes for the Dreamers."

"You were the one who folded the cranes for each meeting?"

"Every single one."

"You know the first crane Benja got wasn't given to him," she says.

"Oh?"

"Someone had left it for me. Except I didn't know what it meant. Benja did. I didn't believe that dreams were portals to the past. He did."

"It was lucky we met at all," Metis says.

"Did you know that Benja wouldn't see me the last week before he killed himself?" she asks.

"He didn't want to hurt you. He thought he wasn't good for you."

Aris feels tears streaming down her face. Too much has happened the past few days, it's hard to believe the Ceremony of the Dead was just last week. She has not fully healed from her friend's death.

She wipes her tears. "Why did he think that?"

"He knew that, for you, attachment would only bring pain. He said you feel and care too much for your own good," Metis says.

Aris feels suffocated. She needs fresh air.

Metis takes her hand in his. "Like Benja, I don't think I'm good for you. For that, I'm sorry. It's my fault we ended up here. You were content in your life, and I dragged you back into the past."

"I think your memory fails you. It was I who told you about my dream on the beach. You chose the present."

"I chose you. Wherever you decide to be."

She looks at him. "Let's just stay here and wait out Tabula Rasa. There's food and water. We can learn to forage."

"We can't know what will happen after Tabula Rasa. We could wake up with no memories the day after. We won't have our AI to guide us this time." he says.

Aris revisits the thought she had while swimming in the pool at the Hotel of the Desert.

"We have the helmet," she says, "I still have the vial of Absinthe Benja gave me. Maybe you can figure out how to distill more if we can find hypnos. We can write instructions for when we wake up next cycle. A whole map for our future selves to follow. We have almost a month to figure it all out."

The more she talks, the more she feels excited about the possibilities of preserving their memories of each other. From a look, she knows Metis feels the same. She scans around for her backpack, the one with the helmet and the computer. She realizes she left it at the front of the cave.

"I'll be right back," she says and walks off.

She squeezes through the passageway, away from the brightly lit room and toward the darkness of the cave entrance. The rough wall scratches her elbows, but she does not mind. For the first time, she feels like she has a semblance of ownership over her memory.

Each day inside the cave moves slowly, like dripping liquid amber. The only way Aris tracks the movement of time is through the waxing of the moon. It's nearly full. When they first arrived, the moon was but a sliver. It must be March, though she is not certain of the exact date. The Crone was right—time isn't the most relevant aspect of their existence. Being in the moment is.

Aris and Metis spend their hours making love, talking, and reading. The Crone's journals paint for them a life in the early days of the Four Cities. They learn of the struggles between the Resistance and the system—one side refusing to subject themselves to memory wipe, the other dedicated to preserving peace through Tabula Rasa.

They discover that the Crone rarely ventured outside the cave. The majority of her time was spent making and testing batch after batch of the memory potion. Her journals were filled with chemical and mathematical formulas. Results were written with meticulousness and insight. Each failure propelled her to work harder and longer. Aris wishes she could have experienced the Crone and the Planner together. She imagines it a magnificent partnership. After all, they had created the Four Cities.

One day, after a short walk below the cave, Aris and Metis decide they are ready to test the helmet.

"When I wore it while awake, it only showed what I was seeing," Aris says as she fits the helmet on Metis's head.

The image on the computer is of herself staring back. She smiles.

"Okay, now close your eyes," she says.

Metis does. The image turns black. Then globs of lights and shadows float around the screen.

"Nothing," she says.

"Well, I'm not really dreaming." He opens his eyes.

"You want to try?"

"Let's go to the bed."

Aris narrows her eyes. As much as she loves Metis, her body needs rest.

Metis chuckles. "I'll be good. Promise."

"Should we use Absinthe?" she asks.

"No, let's stick to the plan."

They had agreed that Metis would be the one to take the vial of Absinthe after Tabula Rasa if they wake up with no memories. His mind contains more images of their past together. They think the fortress inside his brain may be stronger because of music.

Aris places the helmet on Metis's head. It is a little more difficult with him lying down.

"Are you comfortable?" she asks.

"Umm-hmm. I'd be more so if you were lying next to me," he says.

"But no one would be looking at the computer."

"Maybe we can do it another time," he says.

"No, no, no. That's what you said yesterday. You can't slither out of this again. Just close your eyes and try to think calm thoughts."

"Not sure if I can at the moment." He grabs her hand and brings it toward his leg.

She takes her hand back. "Well, you're just going to have to try harder. You promised."

"All right, all right."

After a long while, Metis's breathing becomes slower and steadier. His chest rises and falls to the rhythm of his breath. He is slowly sinking into the arms of sleep.

The image on the computer changes. At first it looks hazy, as if she is gazing through thick fog. Then she sees green. The color separates into different shades, slowly revealing an image of leaves on a tree. A leaf falls and lands on a path. A park. She sees a hand. The long fingers of Metis. The hand is holding another. Aris sees a glimpse of silver. A ring. She raises her left hand and sees that it matches the one on the screen.

The image changes. She sees herself in a garden through a window. It is the garden in the back of Metis's Victorian house. *Has he always been there?* She thought the Dwelling Council assigns housing randomly. Maybe that is not the case for some. It would be a difficult task to move a grand piano from one place to another every cycle.

The image on the computer increases in luminosity until the only thing Aris sees is bright white. Then slowly it takes shape. A room with white walls. White bedding. She sees her own sleeping face, her long hair spraying on a pillow. She is Metis watching herself sleep. They are at the beach cottage. The image from Metis's perspective is clearer than hers. She looks over at him. She feels like the creator of the universe, watching everything across different times through different eyes.

The helmet works.

It is their salvation—a way for them to get back their memories so they can spend the next cycle living without pain.

She hears a sound. A low hum. A buzzing in the air.

What is it?

She has heard this sound before. Dread clutches at her stomach.

Drones!

She shakes Metis. He opens his eyes and confusion crosses his face. He sees her and springs up. His face is drained of blood.

Aris pulls the helmet from his head and grabs the computer. She stuffs them into her backpack and shoves the bag under the bed.

"Look for an exit!" Metis yells.

They feel along the walls for anything resembling a door. Aris pushes at spots she thinks may reveal a secret door. *Nothing.*

Then Aris hears bodies forcing themselves through the passageway. The suffocating feeling returns. A man in a brown fedora appears. Then another. And another. And . . .

CHAPTER TWENTY-FOUR

Aris opens her eyes. The light is bright and piercing. She blinks to adjust, and the room slowly reveals itself. The whiteness is blinding. The walls and floor glow as if lit from within. Flowing through her is a calmness that feels eerily foreign, as if she does not have a worry in the world. There is no fear in her, and that makes her wonder if she should be afraid. Could she be dead?

But if she is dead, why is there a feeling of tightness on her arms? She looks down and expects to see two strong hands on them. Instead, there are silver bracelets around the smallest part of her thin wrists. She saw one like this on Benja the morning she picked him up from the police station. She wonders why they are on her, but beyond that, she does not care.

"Hello?" she says. Her voice is lost in her parched throat.

She tries to pull up her arms, more out of curiosity than anything. They are immovable. The bracelets anchor her to the chair she is sitting on. They are not uncomfortable, so she focuses her attention instead on moving her legs. They, too, are rooted in place. She is trapped in the chair. But she is in no hurry, she tells herself. She will sit here awhile.

The door opens. Officer Scylla enters.

"Hello, Aris. It's nice to see you again."

"Where are the rest of you?" Words fall out of her brain like a river without a dam to filter and block its flow. You're being quite rude, Aris, she thinks.

He smiles.

She wonders if the many Officer Scyllas were from a dream. Maybe they were a figment of her imagination. Maybe this moment is a dream.

"Are you real?" she asks.

"Yes, I am. My brothers are back at their police stations."

"Brothers?"

"Well, that's what we call each other. But to be scientifically accurate, we're clones."

Her mind shrugs it off. There is a constant throb in the back of her head. The pain increases when she thinks. She hears a buzzing in the lights above and cranes her neck to look up.

"Where am I?" she asks, squinting at the lights.

"The Interpreter Center."

Her neck begins to hurt. She looks back down. Officer Scylla. He is blurry. She blinks a few times. She knows the reason she is here, but why is he here?

"Why are you here?" she asks.

"I'm here, Aris, because you're a suspect in a crime. I have a few questions for you."

"Crime?"

"Don't you remember what happened at Bodie's house in Elara?"

Is suicide considered a crime? They didn't hurt anyone but themselves.

"I do," she says.

"Can you please tell me why you were there?"

I don't want to.

"Metis and I went to help Bodie get his dreams back." She looks around. "Where's Metis?"

"Don't worry about him for now. Let's go back to the reason you were at Bodie's house."

"I have a Dreamcatcher. Well, not really. I only have the helmet. It projects dreams into images. It doesn't erase anything. Bodie had his dreams erased here, did you know that?"

"Yes, I do. He came here for a treatment."

She laughs. Her laugh sounds dry in her ears. She is thirsty.

"Oh no, you're wrong. He didn't want it. Neither did Benja. They steal dreams here."

"They do?"

"Benja killed himself because of it," she whispers. "Now he's with the blue birds of happiness."

He leans forward. "One thing at a time okay? Let's get back to Bodie's house."

"Sure. It's a nice house. The walls are happy."

"I mean, can you tell me what happened there?"

I shouldn't.

"Seraphina and Bodie's wedding."

"How do you know them?"

"Metis knew them. Seraphina was so pretty. I didn't like her. Not at first."

"Why not?"

"I thought she and Metis were lovers. But she only loved Bodie."

"Did you know that Seraphina worked for the Center of Disease Control?" he asks.

"Did she?"

Aris begins to lose interest in her conversation with Officer Scylla. He asks too many questions, and none of them pertain to her. And it bothers her, though only in passing, that she told him things she didn't want to. A spot on the wall attracts her attention. It's a tiny black spot that vibrates. She stares at it, trying to figure out what it is.

"Her job was to synthesize plants for medicine," Officer Scylla says.

"Well, that makes sense."

"Aris, who made the poison?"

"You just told me."

"Did I?"

"Yes, silly. You forgot already? Seraphina."

"So, she killed all those people?"

"No. Well, yes. But not really." The black spot on the wall moves. Aris squints, trying to focus. Her vision seems foggier than usual.

"You're not making any sense," Officer Scylla says.

"I think that's a fly," says Aris of the thing on the wall.

"What?"

She tries to pull up her arm to point at it, but they are stuck. She had forgotten about the bracelets.

"Officer Scylla, I have to say, this is the most useless conversation I've ever had," she says. She is not angry but merely expressing her opinion.

"I'm sorry about that. I assure you, the feeling is not mutual. Can we get back to Seraphina?"

"If you want. I didn't know her very well. We only met there the one time."

"Did Seraphina kill the people?"

"She only made the poison. But she didn't kill them."

"Then who did?"

"They did. They all wanted to die."

"They all killed themselves?"

Aris nods.

"But why?" he asks, his voice perplexed.

The affable policeman's face goes through multiple emotions. Confusion. Grief. Sadness. Despair. Seeing it makes Aris feel as if she is watching blue sky being swallowed by storm clouds. For a moment she wants to give him a hug. But she cannot. She is stuck here in this chair.

"Because they didn't want to be without the ones they loved," she says. "Now can you please tell me where Metis is?"

Metis stares at the shiny copper contraption above him. It is the size of the entire ceiling. No matter where he looks, he cannot escape it.

He thinks of Benja. Toward the end of his life, his sunken eyes had no trace of hope in them. A man without his dreams.

What will a dreamless life be like for him? A life with no memories of Aris or of their past together. He focuses his mind on the spot on her palm, the one he used to lie awake at night remembering. It's etched in his brain like music. What if they take away his memory of music with it?

An existence without Aris or music. He wonders how he will end it. Benja used poison and went in peace. Quick and painless. At least he hopes it was.

He and Aris were within grasp of a way out of Tabula Rasa—a way to remember each other in the next cycle. Now that hope is gone. Without his dreams, there would be no point to the helmet. All the Absinthe in the world would be useless to him.

On one wall is a large window that reflects the room back to him. He cannot see beyond it, but he knows the Interpreter is there.

Where's Aris?

He begged the Interpreter to not erase her dreams. He told her Aris is just the woman he loves. Not a Dreamer. Not a threat to the Four Cities. Apollina did not care. So he did the only thing he could. He bargained.

Shame slithers over his skin like a snake. He is disgusted with himself, ashamed of his weakness. But he did not have a choice. He never did. He loves Aris too much. He once told her he would trade everyone's lives to keep her from harm. And he has. He has sacrificed everything.

Attachment . . .

Thane enters the dilapidated cottage with trepidation. The only lights are the threads of the sun's rays shooting through the random holes in the roof. He walks slowly, hoping not to fall through the decaying floor.

Metis gave up the source of the drug—the reason for its reappearance every cycle. He did it so Aris could keep her dreams.

He loves her.

This is the weakness Tabula Rasa was created to erase. Thane asks himself if he would have sacrificed the peace of the Four Cities for Aris. It is a big price for one person. He knows his answer.

He reaches the back of the small house. He sees the rickety ladder. He yanks at it, testing its strength. It remains intact. He climbs.

At the top he finds the saddest-looking library he has ever seen. The shelves lean like drunks. A crust of dirt and dust covers everything. He fears breathing mold spores into his lungs.

He brings one arm up and covers his mouth with the fabric of his jacket. He looks around at the disgraceful state of the books. They are so ancient the titles on the spines have faded. The smell of mildew permeates everything. How is he going to find *Love in the Time of Cholera* in these shambles?

Why that book? he wonders. He read it a long time ago but found it pointless. What is the purpose of being in love with someone who does not return affection? It is a waste of a life.

He pulls out a book. No. Another. No. Discarded books slowly rise next to him like a tower.

Thane goes through the entire bookcase. He moves on to the next and the next until piles of books stack like high-rises on a city block. He wipes his dust-painted hands on his pants.

Metis lied. There is no book.

But why would he? A delay tactic to buy time? But what would he do once Apollina finds out? She would never forgive him. There is not a compassionate bone in her body. She is like Dr. Juvenal Urbino from the book—a rational figure who values order and science. Thane feels a pinprick in his chest. What will happen to Aris?

He touches his cheek—the spot where she hit him. The pain is still there, though the bruise is long gone. She really meant to hurt him. He is no longer angry. He had been. He acted on his anger and led the Interpreter Center and the police to them. That, he cannot take back.

At least he is glad he had contacted Officer Scylla. If he had not, and with Apollina the only one in charge, Aris and Metis would have been erased long ago. No questioning. No due process.

He places the books back on the shelves, being careful with each. At the end, he wishes there were more for him to put away so he would not have to go back to the Interpreter Center. To Aris. He does not know whether he can stand seeing her in misery.

«

Aris gazes at Metis on the table. He is motionless—as still as a corpse. Her head hurts. There are no bracelets around her wrists anymore, but their latent effects are still in her veins.

She asked the Interpreter to move her to be with him. She wants to see with her own eyes the moment Apollina excises her lover's dreams. She wants the memory of it to be ingrained in her mind. She needs to remember the hatred she has for the Dreamcatcher and the Interpreter Center for all the cycles to come.

She thinks of the helmet and the vial of Absinthe she hid in the cave. She wants to remember those too so she can go back. Metis told her Absinthe would be useless without dreams to be reawakened. But maybe there is a chance he is wrong. Maybe there is a lockbox inside her brain no one else can get to. Hope is a dangerous thing. But it's all she has left.

She is aware she is being studied like an organism under a microscope by whoever is on the other side of the dark mirror. She had been on that side before, watching the Dreamcatcher destroy Benja's dreams.

She looks at Metis. She wonders what he is thinking about. Maybe he is dreaming. Can one dream with eyes wide open? Which dreams will the Dreamcatcher take from him? Will he still be the same Metis? She imagines him like Benja—drained and demented. She knows what will follow.

She shifts her eyes to the copper cloud above. It is empty of images. But soon the images of their lives together will appear. Then the Interpreter will erase them with a push of a button. His memories of her will be irretrievable. It will be as if they had never met. Hers will be next. She begins to implore all the Old World gods she had read about for a miracle.

"Why is Aris in that room?" Thane asks. "Didn't Officer Scylla say he's coming back for her?"

"She wants to be there. Makes it easier, since she'll be next."

Thane feels his heart sinking to his stomach. "You're going to erase her too?"

"Metis lied to us," Apollina says.

"Then punish him. What did she do? It's unfair that she be punished for his crime."

The Interpreter looks at Professor Jacob. "He doesn't understand."

The Professor steps forward and places his hand on Thane's shoulder.

"It must be done, Thane. She's a danger. She knows too much. We need to protect the Four Cities."

Aris? Dangerous?

This is the same girl he has known for almost a whole cycle. The one who needed to hide from the world after every time she had to show the children from the CDL the horror of the Last War. Thane steps back, letting the professor's hand fall in front of him.

"What if she's just caught up in this mess without knowing? I know her. She believes in Tabula Rasa. She doesn't want to destroy the Four Cities."

"They ran. If they were innocent, why run?" Professor Jacob says. "Let's not argue this. All that matters is that we have them now, and they won't be able to harm anyone else anymore."

Thane looks at Aris. She appears more fragile than he remembers. She is absentmindedly playing with her hair just as she usually does when in deep thought. She is inside her grief. Her sunniness and warmth cast aside. He finds himself affected by her sadness.

Officer Scylla told him the dead people Thane found inside the house in Elara killed themselves. They were not murdered. He said they did it because they did not want to be taken away from their loved ones. Thane thinks of the girl with desert flowers in her brown hair. Officer Scylla said it was her wedding day. Thane cannot help but wonder whether Aris will make the same decision. He does not want to find out.

Apollina looks at her watch and says, "The drugs should be in full effect soon. Then we can begin the procedure."

She pushes a button and speaks. "Date: Monday, March ninth, one thirty p.m. Subject: Metis of Lysithea. Procedure: Dreamcatcher."

Thane cannot stand being there any longer and walks out of the room. He needs to find Officer Scylla—any one of them—before the Interpreter can put her claws on Aris. He brings his watch up. Before he can speak, he sees the man in the brown fedora walking toward him.

"Hello, Thane. I need to speak with you."

"Officer Scylla, I need your help. The Interpreter is going to use the Dreamcatcher on Aris, and she didn't do anything to warrant it. You have to stop it."

"That's why I'm here."

Thane notices a book in Officer Scylla's hand. The cover is faded. Thane can barely read the title.

Love in the Time—

Thane's breath catches in his throat. He thought the book did not exist. He thought Metis lied.

The officer holds it up. "You were looking for this, weren't you?"

Thane does not answer. He takes a step back and wonders what is happening. He feels as if he were in a weird dream.

The man in the brown fedora says, "One of the responsibilities my brothers and I were entrusted with is to protect this book at all cost. This old book existed long before I was born. And it will exist long after I'm dead. Do you know why?"

Thane shakes his head.

"Because he can't live without her," Officer Scylla says.

Thane cannot understand him. Does he mean Metis? But it does not make sense. Nothing makes sense.

"I'm afraid we both may have strayed too far from our intentions," Officer Scylla says. "We all want to keep peace in the Four Cities, but the Interpreter Center has been erasing people's dreams without their consent. That's not sanctioned by the Planner. The problem is, everyone whose dreams were erased is dead. I have no proof."

Officer Scylla is right, Thane thinks. He is far from his intention. When he first accepted Professor Jacob's request for help, all he wanted to do was keep peace and the Four Cities safe. He did not know the path he took would lead to Benja being dead and Aris hating him. He needs to make amends, even if Aris could never forgive him.

"If I help you, will you make sure Aris will be unharmed?" Thane asks.

"I'll do everything in my power."

"Then you have me. I know everything."

The Officer smiles. "Now let's go fix this."

The first image appears on the copper-colored cloud. It is of her and Metis sitting side by side at a piano. They are in Metis's Victorian home. It's dark except for the flickering candles that make shadows play on the walls. There is no sound, but Aris knows what song is being played.

Aris is determined not to cry. She does not want the pain to leak out of her. She needs it inside to cement this moment in her memories.

The door opens. She looks over her shoulder and sees Officer Scylla. Next to him is Thane, the man she once considered a friend. Loathing bubbles beneath her skin. She turns away to look back at the copper cloud.

"What do you want?" she asks, her voice hard.

"You need to come with us," Thane says.

She ignores him.

"Please, Aris," Thane says. "I know you hate me, but this is for your own safety. You need to come with Officer Scylla if you don't want your dreams erased."

"No. I'm not going anywhere. I can't leave Metis here alone," she says.

"I know you don't believe me, but dreams are portals to the past." She points to the cloud. "You know, I don't remember that memory, but it happened. And now Metis won't have it either. I'm going to lose him like I did Benja, and I will never let myself forget how much I hate you."

Suddenly the image on the cloud cuts to black. Aris wonders if it is all over. Has the Interpreter erased all of Metis's dreams?

The Interpreter enters the room. Her usually emotionless face is filled with rage. The skin pulls taut on her face, making her look as if she is being suffocated by a thin plastic mask. Professor Jacob appears next to her. He is staring at Thane with disappointment in his eyes. Aris regards the old professor in his fake glasses and wonders how she ever thought he was brilliant.

"What are you doing with my patients?" the Interpreter asks. She looks at Thane as if she wants to tear him to pieces.

"They're not your patients," Thane says. "They don't belong here."

Officer Scylla says, "You've been erasing dreams without consent. That's not legal."

Apollina squares her shoulders. "All my patients agreed to undergo the Dreamcatcher procedure. What proof do you have?"

"He has my words," Thane says. "I told him everything I did for you and this place. The spying. The lying. The stealing."

"How dare you use those foul words to describe what we've entrusted you to do in the name of peace!" Apollina screams. "Our responsibility is to the Four Cities. To the vision of the Planner."

Officer Scylla pulls out a silver bracelet and advances toward the Interpreter. "You should not use the Planner's name to advance your illegal activities. Your actions led to, whether you meant them to or not, the deaths of several citizens of the Four Cities. I'm not going to ask again. Stop the procedure on Metis and release him and Aris to me."

The Interpreter steps back. "Under whose authority?"

"The highest."

CHAPTER TWENTY-FIVE

On a screen that spans the dimensions of the wall is a face ravaged by time. The Planner, the world creator, presides over the large white room like a Titan from Greek mythology. The wrinkles on his skeletal face fold in on each other like stained parchment. Veins rise on his temples, resembling the gnarled limbs of an ancient oak tree. His hair and beard are as white as the mountain of salt on the edge of the Four Cities.

His eyes are the only things that appear untouched by age. They stare at the wispy image of the Crone as if she were the only being that exists in the room. In the world.

They have been here countless times before. It is a game of cat and mouse that ends with each cycle, only to begin again in the next.

"Must you keep them here until Tabula Rasa?" the Crone asks.

"It's for their own good while the Officer Scyllas straighten out all the mess they were a part of."

"What will happen to them?"

Metis's face is smooth and expressionless. Aris is next to him, silent in forced slumber. Their bodies are in reset mode. They will not wake again until the Planner allows them to. It is his way.

The Crone wonders what is going on inside their heads. There is no conclusive data on what happens to the human mind while it is resetting.

But there are parts of the brain Tabula Rasa cannot touch. She knows. It is what she has been devoting her life to protect.

"In six days, they will be brought to the hospitals—he in Lysithea and she in Callisto. As it has always been. They'll wake up to new lives," the Planner says.

The ancient woman looks up at the owner of the voice. Emotions dance inside his clear deep-brown eyes like fireflies on a warm night. She fears she will not be able to contain her own feelings, so she shifts her gaze to the bed where Metis and Aris lie unconscious.

"They should stay together. It's the right thing to do," she says.

"You know that's not protocol."

"What the Interpreter Center did was not protocol," the Crone says. "Your Interpreter took some of Metis's dreams. I think we should even out the score a little and make it fair. All you have to do is assign the couple to the same city, the same hospital room. The rest will be up to them."

"They mean a lot to you?" the Planner asks.

She turns toward her husband on the screen. "They mean nothing to you. What are two people to the Four Cities?"

"You should know better than most what two people can do."

They hold each other's gaze for a long while. His penetrating stare makes her feel vulnerable. Once upon a time, it made her feel loved. The thought saddens her. She turns her back to him and sighs.

"Without their memories, they're not a threat. It was their separation that started all this."

"Just as Absinthe is not a threat?" he asks.

"It's only a tool to help remember. Like Tabula Rasa is a tool to make people forget."

"The mind needs to be wiped," he says, "Like a room full of clutter. Tabula Rasa cleans it of prejudices and hate. With the mind a blank slate, everyone can be free from the burden of their past and move forward unchained."

The glow around the Crone intensifies, brightening the white room with the power of a hundred stars.

"Spare me your propaganda. It's a concoction of your belief. What you think people should be. It's not who we are. We need our memories. They're a part of us."

"We're still humans—just the best parts distilled in four-year incre-ments. Our ideal selves," the Planner says.

"Our ideal selves," repeats the Crone in disbelief, "A people without the ability to learn from mistakes, without the love of another to smooth out our edges. A civilization of sleepwalkers."

"We've had hundreds of years of peace. Isn't that proof enough?"

"A hollow peace. This is your vision of paradise. Not mine. You've made this place into a prison with death the only way out."

A pained expression crosses the Planner's face. How can his wife not see it? He is the wall that stands between the Four Cities and its demise. The Last War destroyed the Old World—a fearful world. A civilization of people so afraid of losing what they had that they saw one another as enemies. A world where people had their whole life to accumulate prej-udices and harbor hatreds. A lifetime to develop a taste for power and build empires.

He fears that side of human nature. He created Tabula Rasa so another atrocity would never happen. No memories. No attachment. No posses-sion. No one needs to fight, because no one owns anything or remembers owning them. A utopia of amnesiacs. One of life's greatest paradoxes. But it is his to protect.

The Crone looks at her husband from the corner of her eye. She loves him still. For his idealism. For his faults. He is still her Eli. The guardian of those precious few who are left. But the only way he knows how to love something is to control it.

She wants to tell him control is an illusion. Even in the precisely designed perfection the Four Cities created, based on an ideology so beautiful it was a song, it will all come tumbling down. Maybe not soon, but one day.

It has happened throughout history—ancient Egypt, ancient Greece, ancient Rome; the Mongol Empire, the Ottoman Empire; Russia, the United States, China. Powerful kingdoms, dynasties that spanned millen-nia, wealthy countries with military might—they all collapsed under the weight of time and at the destructive hands of humans. She knows this, but she lets him dream. With luck, they both will be gone long before the walls of the Four Cities collapse.

She looks at the two lovers. There is something in Aris and Metis that inspires hope in her. They did not want to light the world on fire with change. They simply wanted each other. If each human chooses one another, humanity may endure.

They remind her of herself and Eli when they were younger. It is too late for her and him to be together. But not for them.

"It was being apart that led them here," she says. "That led us here. Haven't we been doing this long enough?"

The lines between Eli's eyes fold like a curtain. When he decided to leave Earth and his wife, he severed a part of himself. A part that was weak and possessive. And he is better for it. He can see the true meaning of life. There is no life in death. To live is to survive. And he will live.

He is no longer hindered by a physical body. Without it, he is free. Just as she is. Both are digital essences of themselves because he could not bear the thought of life without her. Though he knows she may never forgive him for it.

Now they are on opposing sides. He as the enforcer of order. She as the catalyst for change. She speaks of the "right thing to do." For him, that has always been to protect the Four Cities at all costs. Except one. He can never hurt her. Even if she will be his undoing.

"Are you tired of this life?" he asks, his voice gentle.

"Just as you have your vision, I have mine."

"It's futile. Tabula Rasa can never be stopped. It's life. Like breathing, eating, making love. It will continue to happen until the world perishes."

There is no escaping Tabula Rasa. She knows. A long time ago Eli won. She and the Resistance watched helplessly as he succeeded in genetically engineering the next generation of humans to forget. The stealer of memories is embedded inside every citizen of the Four Cities. It is his fail-safe against the wicked side of humanity. But they can still dream.

CHAPTER TWENTY-SIX

The sound of birds chirping comes from somewhere outside the warmth of the Victorian house on the hill. Spring is here. Through the windows, a woman sees tiny green buds peeking out from the tips of the otherwise barren branches, readying to unfurl from their long restful hibernation. Right on time. Just as the Planner intended.

She runs her finger absentmindedly on the engraved lines of her silver ring. The feel of it calms her. She leans her head back against her lover's chest. On his warm lap is her favorite place to be when they are in quiet repose. He does not mind the constant weight of her body on him. He prefers it. Her presence is as familiar to him as his own.

He is reading. In his hand is an old book with a cover ragged from age and use. On the table next to them is a stack of tattered tomes of all sizes. Some appear as if they might disintegrate if handled without care. He loves the smell of them, these containers of memories—earthy and nostalgic. They found them here in the house.

His eyebrows are knotted in deep thought. He has been reading, searching, for a way out. He wants to believe there is an answer hidden in the wisdom of books. He wants to keep what they have forever. But she knows there is no such thing.

They have four years before they hit the reset button and start anew. Everyone knows this. Everyone is taught it. In four years, the past will cease to exist. She will no longer remember him. Her mind will shed itself of her name, her life, and even this moment. He cannot bear the thought. So she lets him read.

A question comes to her.

If a tree falls in a forest with no witness, not even itself, would it remember?

Yes, she answers.

There would be a physical consequence of its fall. A gouge on its bark. Or a broken branch. An invisible trace. She does not know how she knows. But she does.

She studies the contours of his face. His serious face carries the weight of the world. She reaches out and massages the spot between his eyebrows—the deep line that appears as if someone had tried to cut out his third eye. He looks at her and smiles. She knows. Her heart, too, bears a mark of a fall.

Love endures.

Dear reader,

Thank you from the bottom of my heart for reading *Reset*. I began it after a very frustrating night of writing. I decided to erase what I spent months writing and started over with a blank slate. Tabula Rasa. As I was staring at the white page, I thought, what if humans could reset our lives every so often? What life would we have? What kind of world would we live in?

The world of *Reset* was inspired by John and Yoko's "Imagine." A song that's more than a song, it's a call to action—to imagine a world of peace, a society rid of greed, a place where everyone lives in unity. For the characters in this world, the price for this utopia is memories. For Aris and Metis, it means they'll lose and find each other cycle after cycle.

Is it necessary for memories to be erased in order for people to coexist in harmony? The answer would depend on whether one has faith in humanity. The Planner didn't. I do. We all are a byproduct of our history, but we are also capable of redesigning our future. The brain can be rewired. It can adapt and change as a result of experience. We can reassign new meanings to old labels. We can embrace positive ideals with action. We can choose love over fear as our guide. All without having to erase our memories.

Just as "Imagine" asks us to take a journey of imagination toward a better world, it is my hope that *Reset* asks the same of you.

> With optimism,
> Sarina Dahlan
> June 30, 2020

ACKNOWLEDGMENTS

Reset would not be what it is without those I'm grateful to:

My husband, who read the many versions of this story, including the terrible early drafts. Thank you for giving me the time and space to explore this new path and for believing that I'm a good writer. You're a constant in a world of chaos.

My children, for inspiring me to write stories that I hope will contribute to a kinder, more empathetic world. You are the light of my life.

Naomi Gibson, Simeen Mirza, Sarah King, and Natalie Grann, my beta readers. Though from different corners of the world, your common appreciation of *Reset* made me believe that others will like it too.

Bobby Videña, for letting me force this story on you on our road trip. You were a good captive audience and are an even better friend.

Lenis Choi, for helping me hone my query pitches and author's note. Thank goodness for your English degree.

Julie Gwinn, my agent, for hearting my #DVpit pitch and being the first to request a full manuscript. More importantly, for finding *Reset* a home at Blackstone Publishing. You're the right mix of optimism and honesty.

Peggy Hageman, my editor, for reading *Reset* in a day and a half and for your profound insight. Thank you for asking all the right questions. Through your eyes, I saw the story for all its potential. Your kind encouragement meant more than I can ever express. Rest well.

Michael Krohn, for polishing my sentences with an eye toward improving the reading experience. Thank you for your thoughtful suggestions and exceptional attention to detail.

Kurt Jones, cover designer extraordinaire, and the design team. As soon as I saw the first mock-up, I was in love. Thank you for including me in the process and for making the best cover I could have ever hoped for.

Rick Bleiweiss, for acquiring *Reset* for Blackstone Publishing and for believing in this book. Your decision kept me on this path at a time when I wasn't sure if I should continue. I'll always be grateful.

Megan Wahrenbrock, Mandy Earles, Josie Woodbridge, Jeffrey Yamaguchi, Lauren Maturo, and everyone at Blackstone Publishing, for your help in bringing *Reset* to the readers.

Classical pianist Jeeyoon Kim for her album, *Ten More Minutes*, which played on constant rotation while I wrote many of the scenes in this book.

John Lennon and Yoko Ono for having written "Imagine," the song that inspired the utopia of the Four Cities. You asked us to imagine, so I did.

Friends who are family and family who are friends. Jane, Carmel, Dawis. Your optimism knows no bound. There are so many of you in my life. Thank you for cheering me on.

Yvette, Laurie, Grace. Food, travels, and laughter. Always.

My happy hour ladies: Carrie, Erika, Kefey, Nicole, Shannon. So many good conversations. You have kept me sane during the pandemic.

Finally, to those who have made an indelible impression on me. I always look for you in the stars.